THE DEAD HAND OF HISTORY

Recent Titles by Sally Spencer from Severn House

THE BUTCHER BEYOND
DANGEROUS GAMES
THE DARK LADY
THE DEAD HAND OF HISTORY
DEAD ON CUE
DEATH OF A CAVE DWELLER
DEATH OF AN INNOCENT
A DEATH LEFT HANGING
DEATH WATCH
DYING IN THE DARK
A DYING FALL
THE ENEMY WITHIN
FATAL QUEST
GOLDEN MILE TO MURDER
A LONG TIME DEAD
MURDER AT SWANN'S LAKE
THE PARADISE JOB
THE RED HERRING
THE SALTON KILLINGS
SINS OF THE FATHERS
STONE KILLER
THE WITCH MAKER

THE DEAD HAND OF HISTORY

A DCI Monika Paniatowski Mystery

Sally Spencer

This first world edition published 2009
in Great Britain and in the USA by
SEVERN HOUSE PUBLISHERS LTD of
9–15 High Street, Sutton, Surrey, England, SM1 1DF.
Trade paperback edition published
in Great Britain and the USA 2010 by
SEVERN HOUSE PUBLISHERS LTD

British Library Cataloguing in Publication Data

Spencer, Sally.
  The Dead Hand of History.
  1. Woodend, Charlie (Fictitious character) – Fiction.
  2. Police – England – Fiction. 3. Polish people – England –
  Fiction. 4. Detective and mystery stories.
  I. Title
  823.9'14-dc22

ISBN-13: 978-0-7278-6805-3   (cased)
ISBN-13: 978-1-84751-170-6   (trade paper)

For Lanna

Typeset by Palimpsest Book Production Ltd.,
Grangemouth, Stirlingshire, Scotland.
Printed digitally in the USA.

PROLOGUE

She was in a dark, dark place.

She suspected that she was inside, rather than out, because the air was still and musty. But if she *was* inside, in some kind of room, she had no idea how large or small that room might be.

'Concentrate!' she ordered her fuzzy brain.

The first thing to consider, she decided, was not *where* she was, but *how* she had got there.

She had been at home.

She was sure of that.

It had been the evening, and she had been at home.

Was it *still* evening?

That didn't matter! What had happened next?

She'd had a fight with her husband! It had been a God-awful one, and he'd been angrier – and *braver* – than she'd ever seen him before.

And then?

And then – nothing!

She didn't know how the fight had ended, or what had happened after it.

Focus on the present, then.

She was in this room – which might be as small as a cupboard or as large as an auditorium – and she was standing up.

But she couldn't move! *Why* couldn't she move?

She couldn't move because she was tied to something.

A workbench, perhaps?

Could be.

At any rate, whoever had tied her up had made a good job of it. Her ankles were bound together, and fastened to the leg of the bench – if that's what it was – and there were more bonds mooring her waist to the flat top.

But it was what had been done to her *hands* which was the real mystery. They had been bound in such a way that her arms were spread to their maximum, and so that the hands themselves were palm-down on a cold metal surface.

She should be more frightened, she told herself.

And perhaps, when the fuzziness had cleared from her head, she would be.

But for the moment, the important thing was to work out exactly what was going on.

Somewhere in the middle distance a door opened, allowing a chink of light to leak into the room – just enough for her to realize where she was.

But knowing where she was only raised more questions, didn't it?

She still had no idea *why* she was there, or who had brought her there.

The door closed again. The only thing she could now see was the blinding light of a powerful torch, the only thing she could hear was the soft footfalls as her captor approached her.

It was the steadiness of the light – the sure nature of the footfalls – which finally brought on the fear.

'Who are you?' she heard herself croak. 'What do you want?'

The light drew ever closer, and though she closed her eyes she could still feel the dazzle burning into her retinas.

'Is it money you're after?' she asked, as a rising panic threatened to drown her. 'Is it? Because if it is, I've got plenty.'

There was no response, though the footsteps kept on coming.

'You'll never get away with it, you know,' she said, changing tack. 'I've got influence in this town. I'll have you tracked down wherever you try to hide.'

Her kidnapper had walked past her, and was standing at the edge of the bench.

No, not bench – she knew *exactly* what it was now.

'Why don't you say something?' she sobbed. 'Why don't you tell me why I'm here?'

'You already *know* why you're here,' said a voice.

And it wasn't just *any* voice! It was a voice she recognized – a voice she knew very well.

Oh God, no! she thought. It isn't . . . it *can't* be . . .!

She was sure the torch was still shining directly in her eyes, and that when she opened them it would hurt.

But she *had to* open them.

Because how could she make her appeal for mercy with them closed?

She forced herself to do it. At first all she could see was the blinding glare, but then, by moving her head to one side, she regained a little of her peripheral vision.

And that was when she saw the meat cleaver, raised high in the air.

'Please, no!' she screamed.

And she was still screaming when the cleaver reached its target – slicing through flesh, crushing and splintering bone.

ONE

The River Darne was too shallow for any but the smallest craft to navigate, and too narrow to require one of those mighty arched stone bridges which spanned more substantial rivers. But that said, it was pleasant enough, in its own quiet way. Swans glided majestically along its course, and bulrushes grew in abundance along its banks. Weeping willows overhung – and were reflected in – its water, and on warm summer days the path that ran alongside it was popular with both strollers and picnickers. But there were no strollers or picnickers on the river bank that early June morning in 1973. Instead, it had been invaded – and then occupied – by a dozen men with an official purpose.

Ten of the men were uniformed, had established themselves in fixed positions and now stood scanning the near distance for any sign of the sensation-seekers who always appeared – almost by magic – whenever a grisly incident like this one occurred. The men in plain clothes, on the other hand, strode back and forth along the path, as if by this action alone they were achieving something of significance.

'Not that we can do much of anything until *she* gets here,' Detective Sergeant Walker complained. 'After all, we don't want to go treading on her toes on her first day in her shiny new job, now do we?'

'You sound a bit pissed off to me, Sarge,' DC Crane said.

'Do I, indeed?' Walker said reflectively. 'Now I wonder why that could possibly be?'

'Don't know, Sarge.'

'How old would you say I am, Jack?'

DC Crane examined the other man. Walker was square-bodied. His hair was just starting to show signs of greying at the temples, and while the bags under his eyes were not yet quite coal sacks, they were certainly noticeable.

'I'd guess you were thirty-five,' the detective constable said, deciding his wisest course would be to err on the flattering side.

'I'm thirty-bloody-nine,' the sergeant growled. 'Which – if you can do the sums – makes me around the same age as our new bloody boss. So there you have it – born a few months apart, but already separated by two steps in rank. Of course, there's a perfectly understandable reason for that, isn't there?'

'Is there? And what is it?'

'*I* haven't got tits, have I?'

I should have known, Crane thought. I shouldn't have even bothered to ask.

But he was only three years out of university – where everyone was terribly earnest and terribly enlightened – and he was still finding it hard to adjust to the fact that beyond the cosy confines of the campus lurked a tribe of snarling Neanderthals.

'Got a good record, though, hasn't she?' he said, knowing he shouldn't, but somehow unable to stop himself.

'A good record?' Walker repeated incredulously. 'Whatever gave you that idea?'

'Well, I know I've not been around here long . . .'

'You can say that again, young Crane. As far as I'm concerned, you're still wet behind the ears.'

'. . . but I did hear that when the DCI was working with Mr Woodend, the two of them were a really excellent—'

'Not working *with* Mr Woodend, working *for* Mr Woodend,' DS Walker corrected him. 'In fact, if the rumours I've heard are true – and I've no reason to doubt them – she was working *under* him.'

Crane didn't believe that for a minute. As an officer low down in the pecking order, he'd only known Charlie Woodend from a distance, but even so, the chief inspector hadn't looked like a man who'd cheat on his wife, especially with a member of his own team.

'Yes, working *under* him,' Walker repeated, with some relish. 'And in my opinion, that's a woman's proper place – under a man, with her legs spread so far apart they're hanging over the sides of the bed.'

Neanderthal wasn't in it, Crane thought. There must once have been primitive slime, still crawling out of the swamp, with more developed sensibilities than Detective Sergeant Walker had now.

The sound of an engine being driven at high revs made

Crane turn. Raising his head, he let his eyes climb the sharp grassy incline to the minor road at the top of it, which had once been a donkey track. It was then that he saw the car, a bright red MGA, pulling up.

'She's here!' he said.

'So she is,' Walker agreed. 'Well, I suppose all we have to do now is stand back admiringly, as we watch a brilliant mind at work.'

The paved steps down the river bank were some distance away, but Monika Paniatowski showed no interest in taking them. Instead, she chose to descend the grassy slope at an angle.

'It'd really make my day if she lost her footing, and went arse over tit,' Walker said.

Yes, it probably would, Crane thought, but it looked as if the sergeant was due for a big disappointment, because despite the fact that the grass was still slippery with the morning dew, the new chief inspector certainly seemed to be sure-footed enough.

Crane followed Paniatowski's progress with interest, though with entirely different motives to those of his sergeant. Her blonde hair was just lovely, he decided. And though her nose was on the large side for Lancashire taste – that would be the Polish influence, wouldn't it? – *that* was quite nice, too. But it was her figure that really got his approval. *It* certainly didn't look thirty-nine – and though Paniatowski was an old woman by Crane's standards, he had to admit, somewhat guiltily, that he really quite fancied her.

As the DCI drew almost level with them, Crane was surprised to note that, despite his earlier derogatory comments about her, Walker snapped smartly to attention. And not wishing to be left out, the young detective constable decided he'd better do the same.

'It's certainly a privilege to be working with you, ma'am,' Walker said.

'Thank you, Sergeant,' Paniatowski replied.

'It's bad luck to be landed with a case like this on your first day in the job, but then there's nothing like a baptism by fire for showing what you're really made of, is there?' Walker continued.

'Probably not,' Paniatowski said, with less conviction than she might have wished.

'And there's no doubt in my mind that with your brilliant track record, you'll have a result in no time,' Walker said.

Professional pleasantries were all very well in their place, Paniatowski thought, but really, enough was enough.

'*We'll* get a result, Sergeant,' she corrected her new bagman. 'As a *team*. Because that's what good policing is – teamwork.'

'You're quite right there, ma'am,' Walker agreed.

'So what can you tell me about the investigation so far?' Paniatowski asked crisply.

'The object in question was discovered by a man called Edgar Harper, about an hour ago,' Walker said, in his best policeman-in-the-witness-box voice. 'Mr Harper was out walking his dog when—'

'Strictly speaking, ma'am, it was the dog which did the finding,' Crane interrupted.

Walker gave him a look which could have frozen blood and then continued, '. . . when the dog disappeared into those bushes over there, and reappeared again with the plastic bag in its mouth.'

The bushes were not tall, but they were quite thick, Paniatowski noted, and if the dog hadn't found it, the plastic bag could have lain hidden there for days.

So what had been the point of putting it there at all?

'Where's this bag now?' she asked.

Walker took his cigarettes out of his pocket, lit one up and blew smoke down his nose.

'I had it sent over to the mortuary, so that that Paki doc . . . so that Dr Shastri could have a look at it.'

Paniatowski's eyes hardened, and for a moment it looked as if she was about to deliver some kind of rebuke. Then she nodded again and said, 'Good, that was the right thing to do. And what *else* have you done?'

'Nothing, ma'am.'

'Nothing?'

'Every boss that I've ever worked for has his own particular way of doing things, ma'am,' Walker said. 'And until we'd found out what the *right* way was for you, we thought it best not to go barging around doing the *wrong* thing. Isn't that right, DC Crane?'

'Er . . . yes,' Crane said.

What the sergeant had just said made good sense,

Paniatowski thought. A wise bobby always modified his own style – to a *certain* extent – to fit his boss's. That was one of the many lessons she'd learned from working with Charlie Woodend.

'I want the river bank searched for half a mile in either direction,' she said. '*Carefully* searched.'

'I'll see to it right away, ma'am,' Walker promised.

Paniatowski turned to face the grassy slope she'd so recently descended. Its incline meant she could not see much beyond it. But she didn't need to, because this was her old stamping ground – the backcloth of an unhappy childhood – and she was only too aware that on the other side of the road lay a patch of waste ground, and beyond that the edge of a housing estate – red brick, featureless and laid out on a strict grid pattern.

'I also want a door-to-door inquiry conducted,' she continued. 'It should take in *any* houses with easy access to the river along a two-mile stretch, but I'd like you to *start* with the Pinchbeck Estate.'

'The Pinchbeck Estate?' Walker repeated, sounding slightly surprised. 'You do *know* it's a council estate, don't you, ma'am?'

'Yes?'

'Which means, as I'm sure you'll appreciate, that the people who live on it are the scum of the earth. Skivers and layabouts to a man. Or to a woman, for that matter.'

Paniatowski hesitated for the briefest of moments, then she said, 'And apart from those obvious virtues you've just so clearly described, are they also all *blind*, as well?'

Walker seemed puzzled by the comment. 'A few of them may be – or at least *claim* to be, so they can scrounge even more disability benefits off the government – but, as far as I know—'

'Then if they've got eyes,' Paniatowski interrupted, 'they might – just possibly – have *seen* something.'

'With respect, ma'am, you're missing the point.'

'Am I?'

'Yes, I rather think you are. The people who live on that estate are such idle bastards that they don't *get out of bed* until the pubs open. Which means, in my humble opinion, that conducting an inquiry on the Pinchbeck Estate would be a complete waste of police resources.'

Paniatowski forced a smile to her lips. 'Every boss has their own way of doing things, Sergeant, as you've just pointed out yourself,' she said. 'And my way, in this particular instance, is to conduct a door-to-door on the estate, whatever you might think.'

'I stand corrected, ma'am,' Walker said, as he too commanded a reluctant smile to appear on his face.

'Right, that's it,' Paniatowski said. 'If you've got something to report before twelve-thirty, you'll find me in my office.'

'And after twelve-thirty?'

'The chances are that I'll be found in the public bar of the Drum and Monkey.'

'Ah,' Walker said, as if enlightenment had suddenly dawned. '*Mr Woodend*'s old haunt.'

'That's right,' Paniatowski agreed evenly. 'And not just Mr Woodend's – *my* old haunt, as well.'

She turned and began to climb the bank again. Walker and Crane watched her until she reached the top.

Only when she had finally disappeared from view did Walker allow himself to chuckle.

'See the look on her face when I said the scum of the earth live on the Pinchbeck Estate?' he asked Crane.

'Yes, she did look a bit taken aback,' Crane admitted. 'But I thought she rallied very well.'

'She was gutted!' Walker said firmly. 'Because *she* knows I'm right, and she knows that *I* know that *she*'s one of them.'

'One of them?'

'What is it they say – you can take the woman out of the council estate, but you can never take the council estate out of the woman? So don't let that smooth exterior fool you, Jack, because deep inside herself she's still wearing plastic curlers in her hair and robbing the electricity meter.'

'If you feel like that about her, why don't you put in for a transfer?' Crane wondered.

'Because *I* won't let her get away with things – and the feller who replaced me just *might*.'

'I'm not sure I follow you,' Crane said.

'Then you must be thicker than you look,' Walker told him. 'So let me explain it to you another way. I didn't much like being at school, and I could hardly wait till I turned fifteen and could leave. And if you look through the records of any *good* bobby, you'll find pretty much the same story.'

He paused, as if waiting for Crane to challenge the statement.

'I couldn't wait to leave either,' Crane replied.

Walker nodded approvingly. 'Good for you. Anyway, as I was saying, most of my teachers were shit, and they'd tell you any old rubbish as long as they got paid at the end of the month. But there was one thing I *did* like – a poem about a Roman feller called Horatius.'

'Oh, I remember that myself, Sarge,' Crane said. 'He was a Roman warrior, and when the Etruscans tried to invade Rome—'

'I'm telling this story, lad,' Walker said harshly.

'Sorry, Sarge.'

'Anyway, these other wops were attacking Rome, you see, and the Romans weren't ready for them. But in order to get into the city, the invaders had to cross this bridge. And that's where Horatius comes in. It's a narrow bridge they have to cross, and Horatius stands in the middle of it – on his own – fighting off these other wops one at a time.'

You're forgetting Lartius and Herminius, who were standing beside him, Crane thought – but it obviously suited Walker's purpose to ignore them, and he knew better than to interrupt again.

'And while he's killing these other wops, his mates behind him are demolishing the bridge,' Walker continued. 'In the end, the bridge collapses, Rome is saved and Horatius is a hero. Get the point *now*?'

'I'm not sure that I do,' Crane admitted.

'There's an army marching on this Police Force, intent on destroying it. It's being led by DCI Paniatowski, but there's a barrowful of other bloody women behind her. And not just women! There's Pakis and nignogs as well. And if she breaks through, how long do you think it will be before we have an Asian DCI?'

'I don't know,' Crane admitted. 'I've never really thought about it.'

'Well, I have,' Walker told him. 'That's why I've planted myself squarely in the middle of the bridge – to make sure she *doesn't* get through.'

TWO

The bakers had been hard at work since five o'clock, the van drivers had reported for duty at half-past six. By seven o'clock, the first consignments of Brunskill's Prize-Winning Bread were already sitting on the shelves of dozens of small shops in the Whitebridge area, ready to be picked up by shift men on their way home from work. And once that basic need had been met – once it was certain there would be fried bread for breakfast, and sliced bread for the kids' dinner-time sandwiches – the bakery turned its focus onto its secondary business, the production of Brunskill's Famous Meat Pies and Cornish Pasties.

The office block was single-storey and was located at the far end of the bakery. It had two entrances, one for the clerical staff at the left-hand side, and one for the management at the right – and it was through the right-hand door that Elaine Dunston walked at just after a quarter-past eight.

Once inside, she gazed around with the kind of masochistic expression on her face which said that she was hoping everything had miraculously changed overnight – but was virtually certain that it hadn't.

I'm right, she told herself, with grim satisfaction. Everything is still the bloody same!

There was her own hateful desk – right in the foyer, where she was clearly on show for anyone who happened to walk in through the door.

There was the office which Jenny Brunskill shared with her brother-in-law Stan, and which, because it had no access to outside light, had glass panels running from waist height to the ceiling.

And there was her sister Linda's office – the big chief's office – with its imposing oak door.

Jenny Brunskill was already at her desk, Elaine noted, but that was hardly surprising, either. She was always the first of the management team to arrive, and the last to leave. She just loved being a martyr to her work, and probably told herself that while Linda was undoubtedly the powerhouse who was driving the business on to bigger and better things, she was the one who did the spadework which ensured that these grand ideas actually worked out. Well, she could tell herself whatever she liked – but as far as Elaine was concerned, that didn't make her commendable, it just made her a mug.

Elaine sat down at her desk. She'd been a secretary before her marriage, but she'd hated it, and had got out of it as quickly as she could. She'd conned Eric Dunston into marrying her by telling him just one tiny little white lie about being pregnant, and once they were married she'd looked forward to never having to work again. But things had never been the same after she told Eric she'd lost the baby that she'd never actually been carrying. In the end, the bastard had run off with her hairdresser – which, since she'd been a *good* hairdresser, had been a double blow – and Elaine had found herself reluctantly back on the job market.

The loud roaring sound in the car park announced the arrival of Jenny's brother-in-law, Stan Szymborska, on his Honda CB 750. The bike was a continuing source of friction between Stan and his wife, and Linda's harangues on the subject were a continuing source of pleasure for Elaine, whenever she was lucky enough to overhear them.

'What do you think you're doing, still riding that big bike around?' Linda would demand. 'That's the sort of thing you'd expect a kid to do. But you're a company director, and you're nearly fifty. Don't you think it's about time you started acting your age?'

Stan would say nothing in reply, and though he was normally putty in his wife's hands, on this one matter he refused to bend.

Jenny, on the other hand, would speak volumes on the subject when Stan wasn't there.

'Stan was the youngest pilot in the Polish Air Force,' she'd remind her older sister.

'The war was over a long time ago,' her sister would reply.

'It might be for you and me, but I don't think it seems *that* long ago to Stan,' Jenny would counter. 'And isn't it only natural that he still gets a thrill out of speed?'

Elaine lifted herself slightly from her seat, so that she could see into the glass-walled office.

Jenny Brunskill was lighting a cigarette. She'd only started smoking recently – probably because she'd decided it would make her look older and more sophisticated – and she still wasn't very good at it. Elaine waited until Jenny had inhaled and started to cough, then sank back down into her chair chuckling, just as the door opened and Stan Szymborska walked in.

'Good morning, Mr Szymborska,' Elaine said, with the cultivated brightness she used to mask the toad-like venom flowing through her veins. 'And how are you today?'

'Fine,' Stan Szymborska grunted.

Well, he didn't look fine, Elaine thought, not without a certain degree of enjoyment. He looked as rough as anything, which meant he'd probably been at the Polish vodka again.

She waited until Szymborska had entered his office, then reached out and clicked down the switch on the intercom.

'*Good morning, Stan,*' said a crackling voice through the speaker. '*Gosh, you do look a little under the weather today.*'

'*I've got a headache,*' Szymborska replied.

And serves you right, too, thought Elaine, who, while she sometimes got a little squiffy herself, considered *other people* getting drunk to be extremely reprehensible.

'*Will Linda be arriving soon?*' Jenny asked.

'*Why do you want to know?*' Stan demanded.

Elaine chuckled again. Normally, they were so very polite to each other, but with Stan acting like a bear with a sore head, today might turn out to be a little more interesting.

'*I asked why you wanted to know,*' Stan said.

'*There's . . . there's just something I need to talk over with her.*'

'*What sort of thing?*' Stan asked, and even through the crackling speaker the suspicion in his voice came over loud and clear. '*Something she's been doing that I'm not supposed to know about?*'

Jenny laughed. '*Now what could Linda possibly have been doing that you're not supposed to know about?*'

But there was no return laugh from Stan. Instead his voice grew gruffer, and he said, '*So if it's not that, what* is *the problem?*'

'*Sales are down,*' Jenny said.

Elaine groaned. She'd been hoping for something dramatic

– a nice juicy scandal – and all that bloody Jenny Brunskill was worried about was that sales were down!

'*So sales are down and you want to go running straight to your big sister with the bad news?*' Stan asked, almost contemptuously.

'*Yes, I do*,' Jenny agreed. '*Sales matter.*' She laughed again, to signal that a joke was on the way. '*Making bread is how we make our bread and butter, you know.*'

Pathetic, Elaine thought. Really pathetic!

'*Well*, should *we be expecting Linda soon?*' Jenny asked.

'*I don't know.*'

A sigh from Jenny. '*I suppose what I've really been asking, in a roundabout sort of way, is if she was about ready to leave home when you set off yourself?*'

'*I'm not sure.*'

'*But she must know we've got an appointment with the catering manager of the Royal Victoria in just over an hour. Landing their business could be very good for us. I'd better give her a ring, in case she's still at home.*'

'*Don't disturb her*,' Stan said.

'*I beg your pardon?*'

'*She's . . . er . . . not feeling very well. She said she might stay at home and try to sleep it off.*'

'*But this meeting we've arranged . . .*'

'*You can handle it.*'

'*I wouldn't want to . . .*'

'*You're better at business than you think you are.*'

Elaine lifted herself from her seat again.

One day they would catch her watching them, and demand to know what she was doing, she thought.

But when they did, she could always fob them off with some story about standing up because the doctor had told her that she had high blood pressure and needed to do gentle exercises while she was at work. Yes, they would swallow that, easily enough. They would probably even be concerned about the state of her health, because *those kinds of people* always were.

Caution counselled only a quick glance, but when she sat down again, she had seen all she needed to.

Stan no longer looked merely rough, he seemed quite worried.

Jenny, on the other hand, was looking much happier. And why? Because Stan had said she was better at business than she thought she was, and now she sat there basking in the rosy glow of his approval.

'Pathetic,' Elaine Dunston said, for the second time that morning. 'Really pathetic.'

Whitebridge town mortuary was a squat square building, constructed of large concrete slabs which had started to discolour almost as soon as they'd been slotted into place. It gave all the appearance of having been commissioned by someone with no taste, and built by someone with no pride. But the truth was, Paniatowski thought, as she pulled into the car park, that neither lack of taste nor lack of pride had had anything to do with it. Rather, the mortuary stood as a silent monument – and rebuke – to the blackmail and municipal corruption which had only ended when she and Charlie Woodend had arrested the builder and several town councillors.

Dr Shastri was already waiting for her in the doorway of the mortuary, and was, as usual, wearing a colourful sari.

Her saris had drawn a great deal of comment when, in the wake of her predecessor being sent to prison for – among other things – tampering with evidence, she'd first become the official police surgeon.

'If you like that sort of thing – and it certainly wouldn't do for me – then I suppose it's comfortable enough in the heat of summer,' people had muttered. 'But just wait till proper winter comes,' they'd added, with dark satisfaction. 'Wait till the icy winds start blowin' in off the high moorlands. Then – you mark my words – you'll soon see a change in her. Then you'll see her start to dress more sensibly – more Lancashire!'

But people had been wrong – as folk who understand no one's attitude but their own so often are. When the weather *did* turn cold, Shastri stuck to her sari, but added a heavy sheepskin coat to shield her from the worst of it.

The saris definitely suited her, Paniatowski thought. But then Dr Shastri would have looked good in an old flour sack, because she was undoubtedly a beautiful woman – slim and delicate, with a skin that was a soft coffee colour and shining eyes as black as coal. Looking at her perfect little hands, it was impossible not to imagine them gently tinkling small bells at a Hindu wedding, but put a scalpel in them and they became precision surgical instruments themselves.

'What a pleasure it is to see you, as always, my dear chief inspector,' the doctor called out, as the new arrival drew closer.

Paniatowski fought the urge to look over her shoulder to see if there was a *real* chief inspector standing behind her.

'And what an honour it is for me that you have come to visit me on your first morning in your new post, Monika,' Shastri continued, with just a hint of mischief in her voice.

'It's not an entirely social visit, Doc,' Paniatowski said. Then she grinned, and added, 'But you already knew that, didn't you?'

'Of course I knew that,' Shastri agreed. 'And how is your charming daughter?'

'Louisa's fine. You must come round and have tea with us sometime,' Paniatowski said. She paused, but only for a single beat. 'So what have you got for me, Doc?'

Shastri's smiled widened. 'You are becoming just like your dear Mr Woodend, Monika – immediately down to business, with absolutely no time at all for polite chit-chat.'

'Sorry to sound so abrupt,' Paniatowski said awkwardly. 'But I'm under real pressure with this case.'

'Of course you are,' Shastri replied, with mock gravity. 'In fact, though I have worked in this dismal cave of a place for over eight years, I cannot recall a single instance in which the police were *not* under real pressure with whatever case they happened to be handling at the time.'

'Thank you,' Paniatowski said humbly.

'For what?'

'For reminding me of the need to keep a sense of proportion.'

Shastri shrugged. 'Is that what I have done? Being a simple Indian doctor, I know nothing of such things, but if I have assisted you in some way, then I am, of course, delighted. Shall we go and discuss my findings now?'

'Yes, that would be good idea,' Paniatowski agreed.

The freezer bag was lying on Dr Shastri's dissecting table. It was pale blue, and decorated along the top with darker-coloured blue fish and pork chops, as if the manufacturer believed that his customers would be too stupid, without this information being presented to them graphically, to realize that the bag was intended for food.

At the bottom of the bag were two tears, about three inches apart.

'I am told it was discovered by a clever doggy,' Dr Shastri said.

'It was.'

'Though the dear little doggy was plainly not clever enough to avoid damaging it.'

'Can I see what was inside?' Paniatowski asked.

'Of course,' Shastri agreed, opening a refrigerated drawer and taking out a human hand which had been severed at the wrist.

'How old was she?' Paniatowski asked.

'*Was*?' Shastri countered. 'I am not entirely convinced there is any *was* about it.'

'What do you mean?'

'My examination has revealed that when she lost the hand, she was still very much alive.'

Paniatowski shivered. 'But she *could be* dead by now?'

'Certainly. If she had a weak heart, the shock might have killed her. And if she was not given medical attention after the amputation, she would quickly have bled to death.'

'How was it done?'

'With more enthusiasm than skill, I would say.'

'And the weapon?'

'The instrument used could have been *any* sharp, broad instrument, but a meat cleaver is a strong possibility.'

'And what does the hand tell you about the woman herself?'

'That she is a Caucasian. That she was – or still is – somewhere between thirty and forty years old. And that while she has obviously not been involved in heavy domestic work for any length of time, she has not been particularly protective of her hands, either.'

'In other words, you're saying that she was neither a washerwoman nor a fashion model?'

'Well put.'

Paniatowski took her cigarettes out of her handbag, and offered the packet to Shastri.

The doctor shook her head. 'I am trying to put a rein on

the vices into which you have led me, Monika,' she said. 'And I have to report, in all modesty, that I am being quite successful at it.'

Paniatowski nodded, lit up a cigarette herself, then said, 'So what else can you tell me?'

'I am ashamed to admit that that is the full extent of my knowledge at this moment.'

Paniatowski looked at the palm of the hand, then turned it over and examined the back. It was, she decided, totally unremarkable.

'Where are the clues?' she demanded.

'What clues?'

'The kind you always seem to get in detective novels. The unusually mounted ring which some intelligent jeweller remembers having sold to a certain Mrs X. The expensive manicure which the detective knows immediately is only available in one exclusive salon.'

Shastri smiled again. 'Or the unusual scar which has undoubtedly been caused by a special kind of hook, and would lead you to search for a woman with an interest in deep-sea fishing?' she suggested.

'Bloody right!' Paniatowski agreed.

'I regret there is nothing of that nature. But were you to bring me *another* hand, I would be able to tell you almost immediately whether it came from the same woman.'

Paniatowski shivered again. 'Now there's a cheerful thought,' she said.

THREE

The car park, which was for the exclusive use of those people having business in the Mid-Lancs Police Headquarters, was located at the back of the building. It was roughly oblong, and it was covered with the sort of tarmac which has a tendency to melt a little in warm weather. It served its mundane function perfectly, and though it was not normally a place in which strong feelings were evoked, there was a definite excitement buzzing through the air of the car park on that morning.

The feeling was being generated by a group of five men and three women who all worked for either one of the local nightly newspapers or for the BBC local radio station.

When asked by friends, or members of the general public, about their work, these journalists would invariably say that they gained more real satisfaction from doing their current jobs than they could ever hope to achieve from reporting the news at a national level. They would say it – and some of them would even manage to smile and sound sincere – but they were lying through their teeth.

The truth was that when they read the bylines of reporters working in London, they found the taste of bile welling up in their mouths. And that when they were forced to cover yet another wedding, christening or Women's Institute cake-making competition, they yearned to scream out that none of this mattered – that there were *real* stories out there waiting to be covered.

And so it was that when one of these real stories actually broke close to home they felt their pulses quicken – because this story just might be *the* story which would lift them out of the provincial furrow which they had been so painstakingly and grudgingly ploughing for so long, and finally elevate them to the position they rightly deserved.

All of which explained why, when they spotted the bright red MGA approaching, a collective quiver ran through them.

'Where do you think she's going to end up parking that

flashy motor of hers?' asked Mike Traynor, who worked for the Lancashire *Evening Chronicle*, as he surveyed the still-available spaces.

'Now she's seen us all standing here, she might decide it might be wisest not to stop at all,' replied Lydia Jenkins, the rising star at BBC Radio Whitebridge. 'She might just drive out again.'

Traynor dismissed the idea with a shake of his head. 'If you think that, Lydia, then you don't really know our Monika,' he said.

Without any noticeable decrease in speed, the MGA swung in a wide and easy arc around the hacks, then, finally slowing down, slid effortlessly into a narrow space some distance from them.

The reporters, who had all been bunched together until this point, broke ranks and ran – with various degrees of efficiency, speed and grace – towards the newly parked car.

Monika Paniatowski watched the pack of baying news hounds approach her with an assumed look of mild interest on her face – and a totally unplanned feeling of mild disquiet beginning to simmer in her stomach.

Though she'd hoped that the press would be kept in blissful ignorance for just a little while longer, it was now plain that they already knew *something* had happened.

It was, she supposed, almost inevitable that they *would* have got a whiff of the fact that something was afoot, given the number of bobbies who'd been involved in the operation on the river bank. But even allowing for that, she was determined that she wouldn't go into the details of what that something actually *was* until she was good and ready.

The reporters finally drew level with her.

'Tell us about the hand!' Lydia Jenkins screamed as she waved her microphone vaguely in the right direction. 'Do you know who it belongs to yet, Chief Inspector?'

The mild disquiet in Paniatowski's stomach rapidly transformed itself into a bubbling broth.

'The hand?' she repeated. 'What hand?'

The reporters looked first at each other, and then back at her. 'You're surely not denying that a hand was found down by the river, are you?' Mike Traynor asked, incredulously.

'I'm neither denying nor confirming *anything*,' Paniatowski

said. 'When I want to issue a statement, you'll be called to
the press room, just as you always were in the past.'

But she was thinking, God, I sound so stiff – so formal and
ill-at-ease. I'm sure Charlie would have handled it better.

'Is it a *woman*'s hand?' one of the reporters called out.

'What happened to the *rest* of her?' another shrieked.

'As I said, I'll be issuing a statement later,' Paniatowski
said, trying – and failing – to sound a little more natural.

'Will you be calling on DCI Woodend for help, Chief
Inspector?' a third reporter wondered.

Great! Monika thought. Bloody great! Will I be calling on
Charlie for help? That's *just* what I wanted to hear!

The middle managers were gathered around the large table in
Warren Tompkins' office, and sat in silence – almost holding
their collective breath – while Tompkins himself took a leisurely
gaze out of the window at the bread-delivery vans parked below.

Tompkins turned to face the team. He was a heavily built
man, but one who knew how to use his excess weight to its
best advantage. With his customers – especially the important ones – he was a jovial fat man, a friendly uncle figure
who charmed them, and left them with the feeling that he was
much more concerned about their interests than he was about
his own. With his employees, however, the flab became a
mountain of malice which threatened – if they displeased him
in any way – to roll over on them and bury their careers.

'Five years ago, I was a sergeant-cook in the army,' he
announced. 'A sergeant-cook, for Christ's sake!'

The middle managers nodded, in a way which they hoped
their boss would view as both serious and interested. But it
wasn't an easy trick to pull off, because they had heard this
same story countless times before, and they could pretty much
have delivered the rest of it themselves.

'And look at me now,' Tompkins continued. 'I own this
bakery, lock, stock and barrel. It's a big business by a lot of
people's standards – and a lot of people would say that the
sergeant-cook had done very well for himself. But I don't see
it that way at all. For me, it's only the start.'

He paused, and the managers all nodded again.

'And how did I build up this big business of mine?' Tompkins
asked.

The other managers turned towards the dispatches supervisor – whose turn it was to respond – and right on cue, his raised his hand.

'Yes?' Tompkins said.

'By playing by no rules but your own, sir,' the dispatches supervisor said dutifully.

'By playing by no rules but my own,' Tompkins repeated. 'And that's how I want *you* to play it.'

(Once, a year earlier, the assistant personnel officer had said, 'You mean that you want us to play it by *our* own rules, sir?' He had intended it as no more than a joke, but when he received his dismissal notice at the end of the week, it had no longer seemed the least bit funny. Since then, *everybody* had stuck to the script that Tompkins had dictated.)

'I'm not saying you should do anything that might be described as dodgy,' Tompkins told them. 'In fact, if I find you cutting corners, you're for the chop. But I *am* saying that if you play it right along the straight and narrow, you'll never meet your quotas – and if that happens, you're out as well. Have I made myself clear?'

The managers nodded again.

'Right, you can go,' Tompkins said curtly.

The managers rose to their feet, and as they walked towards the door they tried to convey the impression that their eagerness to leave was more related to a desire to return to the work they loved than to an urge to quickly put the maximum distance between themselves and their boss.

One man, however, remained seated, and seemed perfectly happy to do so. His name was Dick Cutler, and he was in his mid-thirties. He had a bullet-shaped head, and a jagged scar running along his left cheek which was a souvenir of his thuggish youth. His official title within the Tompkins Organization was Assistant Maintenance Manager, but he knew very little about maintenance and a great deal about intimidation. He was, in fact, the company's attack dog – its hatchet man. He had been with Tompkins from the start, and the organization's success was due, in no small part, to his efforts.

Once the rest of the managers had left – the last one closing the door firmly behind him – Tompkins turned his attention to Cutler.

'I wanted to ask you, in general terms, about that thing we were discussing the other day,' he said.

'You mean the—' Cutler began.

'I mean the *thing*,' Tompkins interrupted.

'Right,' said Cutler, who did not count either quick-thinking or subtlety among his talents. 'The *thing*.'

'Well?' Tompkins demanded. 'When's it going to start?'

Cutler grinned, and the scar on his cheek puckered. 'It's already started,' he said.

Though Charlie Woodend had been both her hero and her mentor, Monika Paniatowski had always considered his habit of pacing up and down the office to be slightly over-dramatic. Now, filling his shoes for the first time, she not only understood why he'd done it, but found herself doing exactly the same thing. But what she still *didn't* understand was how he'd appeared to have all the space in the world for his agitated perambulations, while she herself seemed to be constantly running the risk of banging into the furniture.

She tried to clear her mind for more important matters, but all that did was to shift her attention from the desks and filing cabinets and focus it instead on an irritating scratching noise which had been coming from beyond her office door for some time.

No, not from *beyond* it, from the actual door itself – about halfway up.

What *was* the bloody noise?

She stopped pacing, and looked out of the window. She had hoped the reporters would already have left the scene, but they were still there, bunched around her car.

'Who tipped them off about the hand, Colin?' she demanded. 'Was it the man who found it – the one who was walking the dog?'

DI Colin Beresford shook his head. 'He swears he hasn't talked to *anybody* – and I believe him.'

So it had to be somebody on the Force, Paniatowski thought. Somebody, perhaps, who resented her for getting her promotion.

Well, that certainly narrowed it down!

The scratching at the door continued.

'There's not a dog *out there*, is there?' Paniatowski asked.

Colin Beresford grinned. 'Shouldn't think so, boss. Not unless it's a very *big* dog.'

Paniatowski lit a cigarette.

She was smoking too much, she told herself – but there were good reasons for it.

'Why?' she wondered.

'What do you mean – why?' Beresford asked. 'Why did a case like this have to land on your desk on your first day?'

Paniatowski shook her head. 'No, not that. Although, now you mention it, God knows I'd have preferred a nice little armed robbery or a cosy domestic murder over a crime which is so sensational – so bloody *gothic* – that the press have already started watching every move I make.'

'Then what *did* you mean?'

'Why did the killer – if he *has* actually killed her – cut the woman's hand off? And even if he had a good reason for doing it – at least, good enough to satisfy the workings of his own twisted mind – why did he then put it in a plastic bag and leave it down by the river?'

'Beats me,' Beresford admitted. And then he looked a little shamefaced, and added, 'Sorry, that doesn't help very much, does it?'

'He could have buried the hand on the moors,' Paniatowski continued. 'Or lit a bonfire and burnt it. Or since he was already *by* the river, he could have simply thrown it into the water. But he didn't do any of those things, did he? And I'm wondering why.'

'Maybe it was because he wanted the hand to be found?' Colin Beresford suggested.

'But that just leads us to yet another *why*,' Paniatowski said. '*Why* did he want it found?'

Maybe because he's playing some sick kind of game with the police, she thought. Or worse – maybe because he's playing some sick kind of game with *me*, personally!

'How's work going with setting up the operations centre?' she asked her inspector.

'The phones are being installed, we've put in requests for detective constables to be drafted in from other areas in the division and the whole thing should be operational within an hour.'

Paniatowski nodded. 'Good. And once it *is* operational, I'd like you to run it yourself, Colin.'

'If you don't mind, I'd much rather work with you, Mon
. . . ma'am,' Beresford said.

There was something in both the words themselves, and in
their tone, that seemed to strike a raw nerve with Paniatowski.

'Oh, for God's sake!' she said.

'I beg your pardon, ma'am?'

'I'm not an inspector any more – and you're not a sergeant.
In case you haven't noticed, we've joined the grown-up world
now – so we have to start acting like we're grown-ups
ourselves.'

'Yes, ma'am,' Beresford muttered, looking down at the
floor.

'I'm sorry, Colin, I shouldn't have put it like that,'
Paniatowski said, as a wave of guilt washed over her. 'What
I *meant* to say was that I need someone I can really trust in
the operations centre – and that means you.'

'Thank you, ma'am,' Beresford said.

'We've been through a lot together, you and me,' Paniatowski
said. 'Cases we thought we'd never solve. Cases where we've
put our own jobs on the line, so we *could* solve them.'

'That's true, ma'am.'

'So when we're alone together like this, there's no need to
keep calling me "ma'am" as if you were a trained parrot.'

'Yes, there is – when you think about it,' Beresford replied
firmly. 'As you just pointed out yourself, we've joined the
grown-ups' world now.'

Paniatowski was on the verge of saying that didn't matter
– that they were still Colin and Monika in the privacy of the
office – when she realized that Beresford was right, and it
actually *did* matter.

'We need to run a complete check on any person – on any
woman – who's gone missing in the last few days within a
thirty-mile radius of Whitebridge,' she said crisply.

'It's already under way, boss,' Beresford assured her.

'And it'd probably be a smart idea for me to set up a meeting
with the chief constable.'

'Agreed.'

'What about a press conference, Colin? How soon do you
think I need to hold one?'

'It seems to me that the sooner you do it the better. The
pack have already smelled blood and they're not going to be

easy to handle even if you *do* throw them a few bones – but they'll be a bloody sight worse if you *don't*.'

'All right, set it up for me,' Paniatowski agreed. 'But *before* I address them as a group, I think I need to have a few quiet words with just one of them.'

'Which one?'

'I've been wondering about that myself. What I'm looking for is a reporter who'd cheerfully cut his own granny's throat if he thought it would get him a good story.'

'Then pick one at random,' Beresford suggested.

'But, at the same time, I'm also looking for one who isn't quite the fearless news hound that he fondly imagines himself to be. Which of them would you recommend?'

'I'd go for Mike Traynor of the *Evening Chronicle*,' Beresford said, without much hesitation.

Paniatowski nodded. 'He's the one I would probably have picked out myself,' she said. 'Ask Mr Traynor to come up and see me – but don't let any of the others *see you* asking.'

'Now that sounds a bit of a challenge, boss. How am I supposed to manage it?'

Paniatowski grinned. 'You're a bright lad – you'll think of something,' she said.

'Yes,' Beresford agreed, with a slight sigh. 'Because I'm a bright lad, I probably will.'

The scratching outside the door continued.

'And on your way down, do you think you could find out what's causing that bloody irritating noise?' Paniatowski asked exasperatedly.

'*Another* challenge!' Beresford said. 'You really do work me, Chief Inspector, don't you?'

But what he was really saying, Paniatowski thought, was, 'It's all right, Monika, we may just have had a few bumpy minutes, but I want you to know that I'm still on your side.'

'Of course I work you,' she said. 'In this life, you're either use or ornament – and you'd make a bloody awful ornament.'

But that wasn't true, either, she thought – Beresford was a good-looking lad, and still almost as fresh-faced as when he'd first joined the team as a detective constable.

As Beresford headed for the door, Paniatowski walked over to the window, and saw, with dismay, that the reporters in the car park had now been joined by a camera crew.

'That's one problem solved, anyway,' she heard Beresford say from the doorway.

She turned, and saw that the inspector was holding a long plastic strip in his hands.

'This was what was causing the trouble,' Beresford said. 'It's been stuck on the door so bloody long that the maintenance department had a devil of a job getting it off.'

Paniatowski didn't bother to read what was written on it. She didn't need to, because she'd seen it almost every day for over a decade.

This had been Charlie Woodend's office, and the name on the strip was his. She wondered whether her own name on the door would ever look quite so convincing.

FOUR

'I'm pleased to see you're starting out on the right foot, Chief Inspector,' Mike Traynor said.

It was his smile that Paniatowski found the most annoying, though there was certainly much else in the man to be annoyed with. She didn't, for instance, like his air of superiority, especially since he seemed to have so little to feel superior about. Nor did she like the fact that – though far too old to be a callow youth, and far too young to be a dirty old man – he seemed unable to resist the temptation of continually glancing at her cleavage.

And his dandruff didn't exactly impress her, either.

'Starting out on the right foot?' she repeated. 'What exactly does that mean, Mr Traynor?'

'Well, for openers, I couldn't help noticing as I walked in that you've already had the name on the door changed – which announces to the world that you've well and truly arrived.'

'That had nothing to do with me,' Paniatowski said. 'If anyone was announcing I'd arrived, it was the maintenance department.'

'Of course it was,' Traynor agreed, favouring her with a heavy wink. 'But more important than getting your name on the door, there's the fact that you decided to see me.'

'That's important, is it?'

'More like *significant*, if you know what I mean.'

Paniatowski frowned. 'No, I don't think I do know what you mean,' she said.

'The very fact that I'm here shows that you know which way the wind's blowing.'

'Really?' Paniatowski asked.

'Really,' Traynor confirmed. 'You see, Chief Inspector, a lesser woman than you might well have decided to give her first interview to local radio, but you realize that's all that it is – *local*.'

'And isn't your newspaper *local*, too?'

'You're quite right – that's exactly what it is. But you're forgetting that I also work for the *Daily Globe*.'

'But only as a stringer, surely?'

'Stringer?' Traynor repeated, as if he'd never heard the word before. 'What's a stringer?'

'He's a reporter who doesn't actually work for a newspaper in any formal sense of the word, but has been given the right to submit any stories that he thinks might be of interest to it,' Paniatowski said. 'I would have thought that, being in the trade, you'd have known that yourself.'

And of course he had known – he just hadn't known that *she* knew!

'In that sense, I suppose you could call me a stringer,' Traynor told her, looking hurt. 'But in this life, it doesn't matter what title you're given,' he continued, rallying. 'What's important is whether or not you have influence. And I do, because I have the *Daily Globe* editor's ear.'

'Is that right? And do you carry it around in your pocket, or do you leave it on the mantelpiece at home?' Paniatowski asked, thinking, even as she spoke, that that sounded like a very Woodendesque remark.

'Pardon?' Traynor said.

'You seem to be labouring under the misapprehension that this is an interview,' Paniatowski said.

'And isn't it?'

'No. I'm not talking to you as a reporter – I'm talking to you as someone who's become a material witness in my investigation.'

'Material witness? Me?'

'How did you know about the hand?' Paniatowski demanded, with a sudden hard edge to her voice.

'I'm a reporter,' Traynor countered.

'And what is that meant to imply, exactly?'

'It's meant to imply that I have my ways and means.'

'Ways and means,' Paniatowski repeated, rolling the words around in her mouth thoughtfully. 'In other words, what you're saying is that you got a phone call. Was it anonymous?'

Traynor lifted his arm and rubbed the back of his head. A waterfall of dandruff cascaded down on to his collar.

'At this juncture I am simply not prepared to reveal my confidential sources,' he said.

'Confidential sources?' Paniatowski repeated. 'How many reporters were in the car park when I arrived, do you think?'

'Dunno. Seven or eight?'

'It's good to see that you have all the facts at your finger-tips. There were *nine*! And why were they all there? Was it because you, yourself, had *told* them to be there?'

'Of course not. Do I look like a complete fool?'

Not like a *complete* one, no, Paniatowski thought.

'So when you talk about your *confidential* source,' she said aloud, 'what you really mean is that whoever decided to ring *them* up, also decided to give *you* a buzz as well.'

'I suppose so,' Traynor said sulkily.

'Well, that *is* a valuable source, and well worth guarding,' Paniatowski said. 'I can quite understand why you're not prepared to talk about it to me.'

'I never said I wouldn't talk about it,' Traynor protested.

' "At this juncture I am simply not prepared to reveal my confidential sources",' Paniatowski quoted back him.

'Well, maybe I said it,' Traynor admitted. 'But I didn't *mean* it. It was what I call a negotiating tactic.'

'Along the lines of "You scratch my back and I'll scratch yours"?' Paniatowski suggested.

'Well, exactly.'

'But I don't *need* to scratch your back, Mr Traynor. If you don't want to help me – and you're perfectly entitled to refuse – then I'm sure Lydia Jenkins will be more than willing to . . .'

'It was a man who called me,' Traynor admitted, in a rush.

'Does he have a name?'

'*Everybody* has a name.'

'Well, then?'

'I just don't know what his is.'

'Which means you didn't recognize the voice?'

'Correct.'

'But the accent was local?'

'Yes,' Traynor said, uncertainly.

'Why the hesitation?'

'Well, the accent *was* local, but it wasn't perfect. It was if the feller had come from somewhere else and sort of picked it up.'

'How old was he?'

Traynor made a great show of giving the matter his deepest concentration. 'Hard to know for sure. The voice was a bit muffled, like he was talking through a handkerchief.'

'What did he say?'

'He said that if I went down to the river bank, I'd find a severed hand in a plastic freezer bag, hidden in the bushes.'

'*When* did he call you?'

'Half-past seven.'

'You're sure about that?'

'Positive. I was listening to a news programme on the wireless, and they'd just given a time check.'

Paniatowski glanced down at her notes. The call from the dog-walker had been logged at seven thirty-six, so the one to Traynor had been made *before* the police had been notified – which, in turn, meant that whoever had tipped off the media, it hadn't been someone on the Force.

So who *had* tipped them off?

There were only two possibilities.

The first was that the dog-walker had done it.

The second was that the caller had known where the hand was because he'd put it there himself!

'What did you do when he'd rung off?' she asked.

'I finished my breakfast,' Traynor said, as if the answer was obvious.

'That must have taken real self-discipline.'

'You what?'

'I'm just putting myself in your shoes, Mr Traynor. You're given a red-hot tip, but instead of chasing it up immediately, you force yourself to finish your breakfast. As I said, that shows tremendous self-restraint.'

'Well, you see, Chief Inspector, I wasn't sure whether or not to take it seriously,' Traynor said.

'And you thought that finishing mopping up your egg yolk might help you decide?'

'I *thought* it was probably a crank call, if I'm being entirely honest with you, Chief Inspector. After all, this is *Whitebridge*, isn't it? That kind of thing simply doesn't happen here.'

Except that it apparently does – and on my first day on the job, Paniatowski thought.

'So if you considered it unlikely there was a story in it, what were you doing in the car park?' she asked.

'Ah, that was because of the second call,' Traynor explained.

'The second call?'

'About twenty minutes later, the feller rang me again. And this time he said that since I hadn't gone down to the river bank already, there was no point in going now – because the bobbies had arrived, and they'd never let me through. Then he went on to say that probably the best place to get a lead on the story would be police headquarters.'

'How did he know you hadn't *already* gone down to the river?' Paniatowski wondered.

Traynor smirked. 'I should have thought that was obvious. If I'd gone down to the river, I couldn't have answered the phone the second time he called.'

Paniatowski sighed. 'All right,' she said. 'What made him *suspect* that you hadn't gone, as he probably imagined any reporter who was worth his salt would have done?'

'The bastard was watching my house!' Traynor said angrily. 'He was watching my *bloody* house!'

I take back what I said about you not being a complete fool, Paniatowski thought.

'And was he watching the houses of all the other reporters as well?' she asked.

'How do you mean?'

'*None* of the hacks went down to the river. All of them came *here*, just like you did.'

'He wasn't watching my house at all – he was watching the river bank!' Traynor said, finally catching on.

'He was watching the river bank,' Paniatowski agreed.

And it took some nerve to do that, she thought – not just dump the hand, but stay around to see what happened next.

But *why* had he stayed around? Come to that, why had he left the hand there in the first place, and why had he phoned the reporters?

Was it simply that he got a kick out of moving people around, like pieces on a chessboard?

Or was it that he wanted to make sure the discovery of the hand made as big a splash as possible?

Traynor was looking as if he was about to be sick.

'Is something the matter?' Paniatowski asked.

'If . . . if I'd gone there when he told me to, I might have seen him,' the reporter said.

'You might well,' Paniatowski agreed. 'Still, look on the bright side.'

'What bright side?'

'At least you had a good breakfast.'

The street that ran along the eastern end of the Pinchbeck Estate was called River View Road, which proved that while the planners who'd named it might have lacked originality, they had at least prided themselves on their accuracy.

Positioning herself next to the red telephone box, halfway along the street, Paniatowski looked down at the river. While she could see the far bank clearly enough, her view of the near one was marred by the sharp slope – so that when the uniformed constables who were engaged in searching the bank bent down, they became completely invisible to her, and even when they were standing, she could only see them from the waist up.

So it wasn't a perfect view, by any means, she thought, but – as far as the killer was concerned – it had certainly been good enough for his purposes.

She realized that it was the first time she had consciously used the word 'killer' to describe the man she was looking for.

But why *wouldn't* she think of him as a killer? Because what were the chances that the man who had cut the woman's hand off would let her live to tell the tale?

'Are there any other phone boxes in the immediate vicinity?' she asked DS Walker, who she'd already briefed on her conversation with the obnoxious Mike Traynor.

Walker thought about it. 'None that you'd call really close, ma'am,' he said finally. 'The nearest is outside a pub four or five streets further into the estate. It's called the . . . the . . .'

'The Black Bull,' Paniatowski supplied.

'Oh, so you know the place yourself, do you, ma'am?' Walker asked slyly.

'Yes, I know it,' Paniatowski replied.

Know it *all too well*, she thought.

It was in the Black Bull that her stepfather had regularly got drunk, before coming home and doing those unspeakable things to her which still gave her nightmares.

'Do you think this is the phone box the killer made his calls from?' Paniatowski asked.

'Undoubtedly, ma'am,' Walker said, without hesitation.

'He couldn't have just dumped the hand and gone somewhere else to place the calls?'

'No, ma'am.'

'How can you be so sure?'

'Because there were *two* rounds of calls.'

'Go on,' Paniatowski encouraged.

'If there'd only been one round of calls to the press, he could have made them from anywhere. But it's the second round – the ones he made twenty minutes later, just after our lads arrived – which give him away. Because if he'd been making the calls from somewhere else, he wouldn't have *known* the police had arrived, would he?' Walker paused, and smiled. 'You'd already worked all that out yourself, hadn't you, ma'am?'

'Yes, I had,' Paniatowski agreed.

'So why ask me?'

'I wanted to see if our minds ran along the same lines – and it seems as if they do.'

'So he leaves the hand in the bushes, phones the press and then just waits,' Walker said. 'That takes a lot of balls, don't you think?' He paused, as if he'd suddenly realized that he'd said the wrong thing. 'Sorry, ma'am, didn't mean to use bad language.'

'I'm a working bobby,' Paniatowski told him. 'I'm *used to* bad language. And you're right – it *did* take a lot of balls.'

'And even when the police arrive – which he can't have been expecting – he doesn't panic,' Walker continued. 'Instead, he uses the same phone box he's used previously, to call the press again. And it *must* have been the same box, because he simply wouldn't have had time to reach another one.'

'It must also have been the box that Mr Harper used to make *his* call, once his dog had discovered the hand,' Paniatowski mused. 'Did Harper report seeing anyone else hanging around?'

'Sorry, ma'am, I didn't ask him about that,' Walker said. 'Well,' he added apologetically, 'it never actually occurred to me the killer *would* hang around once he'd got rid of the hand.'

'No, in all fairness, I don't suppose it would have occurred to me, either,' Paniatowski conceded. 'But I still want him questioned again – more thoroughly, this time.'

'I'll get right on to it,' Walker told her. He paused again, as if weighing his words very carefully. 'I think that we're looking for a man with military training, ma'am.'

'And just what's made you reach that conclusion, Sergeant?' Paniatowski wondered.

'It's hard to pin it down exactly,' Walker admitted. 'But there's something about the precision behind the planning – and the fact he knew how to improvise when that plan of his unexpectedly went wrong – which definitely suggests a military man to me.'

'I'm not convinced,' Paniatowski said.

'With the greatest respect, ma'am, that's because you're a woman,' Walker countered.

Of course it was, Paniatowski thought. What did women know about anything? What right had they to even be in the man's world that was the Police Force? And worst of all, how dare they presume to lead a serious investigation?

'How would my being a man make me any more convinced?' she asked, keeping her temper reined in – but only just.

'If you'd been a man, you'd have done national service,' Walker explained. 'And if you'd done your national service when *I* did, the chances are you'd have been sent to Korea, to deal with the commies.'

'Oh, *you're* the one who was sent off to fight the Red menace, were you?' Paniatowski asked. 'I always wondered who it was.'

'Sorry if I gave the wrong impression, ma'am,' Walker said. 'I was only an acting corporal – a minor cog in the wheel.'

Well done, Monika, Paniatowski told herself. *Really* well done! You've only been in the job for a couple of hours, and you're already bullying and belittling your subordinates.

'I'm sorry, too,' she said. 'Go on with your theory.'

'We were given basic training under combat conditions before we ever went out there, so we thought we knew what to expect,' Walker said. 'But we were dead wrong, because there's a big difference between having blanks shot over your head and being exposed to real bullets. The first time we came under fire, I panicked, and if it hadn't been for my sergeant, who'd experienced it all before, and kept me in line, I swear I'd have done a runner. The second time was easier, and by the third I'd learned how to handle the situation.'

'So you're saying it's not just that the killer *kept* his nerve, but that, in your opinion, he'd been *trained* to keep his nerve?'

'Something like that, ma'am,' Walker agreed. 'Of course, he doesn't have to have been battle-hardened by being in the services, it could simply be that this isn't his first murder. But if he had done this kind of thing before, we'd have heard about it, don't you think?'

'Yes, we'd certainly have heard,' Paniatowski agreed.

FIVE

Back in the old days, the basement of Whitebridge police headquarters had been a repository for all kinds of junk that no one knew what else to do with, and only when there was a major crime was the junk cleared out and the space used as an incident room. All that had changed towards the end of the sixties. Police headquarters was to be extensively remodelled, the town council had proclaimed loudly. It would be turned into a thoroughly modern building which would meet the needs of a thoroughly modern Police Force.

An incident room – a *dedicated* incident room – had been central to the planning. And if that meant there was less space for other activities – if the canteen was a little smaller, and the office space more cramped – the council was sure the officers wouldn't mind, since they would understand that the changes would lead to more effective policing.

The incident room had been opened with a great fanfare – 'A show put on by *paid* officials who know nothin' about policin', for the benefit of *elected* officials, who know even less,' Charlie Woodend had said sourly at the time – and the ceremony had received extensive coverage in the local press.

And then the officials and the press all went away, and the incident room was used for major incidents when there were any – and as a repository for junk that no one knew what else to do with when there weren't.

The appearance of the plastic-bagged hand on the river bank had ensured that, that morning, the incident room was fulfilling the function the councillors fondly imagined it *always* fulfilled. Telephones had been reconnected, desks had been set up in a horseshoe pattern and the junk had been scattered – temporarily – throughout other parts of the building.

Colin Beresford was standing in the doorway, preparing himself to address the young detective constables gathered there, many of whom would probably be bubbling over with excitement at the very thought of being allowed to work on their first major case.

So this was it, he told himself. This was the moment at which he would cease to be a merely theoretical detective inspector – one who so far only existed in official records. A minute or two from now, he would be briefing his men – a minute or two from now he would become a *real* inspector.

He was just about to step inside the room and take command when WPC Brenda Clegg appeared.

'There's a phone call for you, Inspector,' she said.

'Whoever it is, tell them that I'll ring them back when I can,' Beresford replied, irritated.

'All right, if that's what you want,' Clegg agreed, hesitantly. 'But she did say that it was important.'

'*Who* said it was important?'

'The woman from the Greenside Residential Home.'

'Oh, my God!' Beresford groaned.

'Is something wrong?' Clegg asked, concerned. 'You've suddenly gone quite pale.'

As well I might, Beresford thought.

'Mr Beresford?' the receptionist at the Greenside Residential Home asked down the phone.

'*Inspector* Beresford,' he corrected her.

'That's right,' the woman agreed. 'Would you mind holding the line for a moment, Mr Beresford? The warden would like to talk to you.'

Beresford said nothing. There would have been no point, since what had been phrased as a request was clearly an order – and anyway, the receptionist had already put down the phone.

'How could I have forgotten?' he asked himself. 'How could I have bloody well forgotten? Jesus Christ, I'm getting to be as bad as my mother.'

And then – almost immediately – he started to feel guilty.

His widowed mother had shown the first signs of Alzheimer's disease just after her sixty-first birthday.

'And it can only get worse,' the doctor had cautioned him. 'I'm afraid you must prepare yourself for that, Colin.'

'Only get worse?' Beresford had repeated. 'How is that possible?'

It had certainly seemed terrible *enough* at the time – *she* had seemed terrible enough – but looking back on it, he understood exactly what the doctor had meant, because now those early stages of the disease seemed like almost a golden age.

At least, back then, he could occasionally have what might pass as an intelligent conversation with her.

At least, back then, she sometimes appeared to be aware of who he was, and how they were related.

Now, all that had gone. She lived in a fuzzy world which was ordered by a fuzzy logic, and though she might sometimes fervently believe herself to be the girl she'd once been, she was no longer capable of thinking of herself as the woman she had become.

He had tried (God, how he had tried!) to hold it all together – to balance his position in the Police Force with his role as a dutiful son.

When he wasn't at work, he was with his mother, but as the job had become ever more demanding, he'd been forced to rely more and more on the efforts of kindly neighbours.

Then, when even those neighbours' kindliness had been stretched beyond endurance, he had had to supplement their efforts by resorting to paid help – so that now his savings were gone and he lived from hand to mouth.

So, finally, he'd agreed to do what his mother's social worker had been urging him to do for years – had accepted that he could no longer look after her himself, and that she needed full-time residential care.

It hadn't been an easy decision to make – because although he continually told himself that she was so unaware of her surroundings it wouldn't matter where she was, he still felt as if he was betraying her. But he had gone ahead and made the arrangements anyway.

'Mr Beresford?' asked a new voice on the line – a firm authoritative voice that he recognized as belonging to the warden.

'Yes, I'm here.'

'It's almost ten o'clock. We were expecting you to have brought your mother in by now.'

'I know, but . . .'

'If you leave it much later, it will make it *very* difficult for us to get her properly settled down by lunch time.'

'I'm afraid I won't be able to bring her in at all this morning,' Beresford told the warden.

'I beg your pardon?'

'I said I'm afraid . . .'

'I *heard* what you said – I just found it rather difficult to *believe* that you'd said it. You do appreciate, don't you, that it is most unusual – not to say highly irregular and extremely inconvenient – to have the arrangements cancelled at the last moment?'

'I know,' Beresford said miserably. 'But something has come up at work, and I'm afraid that I can't get out of it.'

'And do you *also* realize that you're not the only one who has a job?' the warden demanded crossly.

'Yes, I . . .'

'And that the children of our other residents *also* have careers, but *still* find time to do what's right by their beloved parents?'

'Couldn't I . . . couldn't I bring her in tomorrow morning, instead?' Beresford asked.

'No, I'm not sure that you can,' the warden said.

Which means, 'No, you sodding well can't,' Beresford thought.

'When you choose to cancel established arrangements to suit your own convenience, you must accept that any new arrangements will be made to suit ours,' the warden told him.

'But you can admit her *some time* this week?'

'That's possible, I suppose.'

'Thank you.'

'But it's equally possible – in fact, *more than* possible – that you'll have to wait until *next* week.'

'Could you ring me when . . .?'

'No, I most certainly will *not* ring you, Mr Beresford. I shall expect *you* to ring *me*.'

'Fair enough,' Beresford agreed. 'I'm sorry for all the trouble.'

'And so you should be,' the warden said.

What a bloody mess, Beresford thought, as he hung up. He'd made an enemy of the warden who would be entrusted with caring for his mother before that caring had even begun.

But what choice had he had? He couldn't simply desert his old friend Monika.

Not on her first day.

Not with a case like *this* one.

*   *   *

When Jenny Brunskill entered the office which she shared with her brother-in-law, she found Stan bent over his desk, looking down at the same pile of documents that he'd been looking down at when she left it.

And 'looking down' at them was exactly the right way to describe what he was doing, she thought. Not *reading* them – the pile was as thick as it had ever been – but just gazing at them *blankly*.

'You don't happen to have seen Tom Whittington this morning, do you?' she asked.

'What?' Stan replied.

And from the *way* he said it – rather confused and perhaps a little nervous – it was clear that it was the mere sound of Jenny's voice, rather than the question she'd asked, which had brought him back to life.

'Tom Whittington,' Jenny repeated. 'I've been round the entire bakery twice, and I couldn't find a single person who'd admit to having so much as caught sight of him this morning.'

Stan shrugged. 'So what?'

'So what? So he's our head baker – that's what.'

'I was aware of that.'

'And it's his job to see that things are running smoothly.'

A slight, thin smile played on Stan's lips. 'I thought you considered that *your* job,' he said.

'It's *my* job to see the paperwork keeps moving along,' Jenny said seriously. 'It's *my* job to make sure the figures add up – although they haven't been recently, and that's something I want to talk to Linda about – but I don't know anything about the technical side of things.'

'Linda knows about it,' Stan said, perhaps a little sourly. 'Linda knows about everything. She's a superwoman.'

'But Linda isn't here, either,' Jenny pointed out. 'So the only two people who can be relied on to make sure our products get on the right shelves at the right time have gone missing.'

'So what?' Stan said, for a second time.

'I thought I'd just explained . . .'

'You worry about the little things too much,' Szymborska told his sister-in-law. 'Relax, Jenny. Enjoy yourself, for a change.'

'The little things?' Jenny said hotly. 'The *little* things! Our father started out with nothing. He built up this bakery from *nothing*. And it's our responsibility to see that his legacy is maintained.'

'Your father . . .' Stan began, and then tailed off.

'What about him?'

'Nothing.'

Your father was a narrow-minded little man who never liked me, he thought. Your father never *really* built this business up at all. It was dying when you and Linda took over. Why can't you see that for yourself?

'Say what's on your mind!' Jenny demanded.

'I was wondering why you don't find yourself a boyfriend,' Stan said, in an attempt to change the subject. 'You're a good-looking woman – a *very* good-looking woman. There'd be no shortage of candidates.'

'Oh, you're impossible, Stan!' Jenny said exasperatedly. 'Here I am, trying to discuss important matters with you, and you treat the whole thing as if it was no more than a joke.'

'Your *life* isn't a joke,' Stan told her, seriously. 'You could have a beautiful life, if you'd only put your mind to it.'

'I'm going to look for Tom again,' Jenny said. 'Maybe he'll have turned up by now.'

She swept out of the office, and Szymborska returned his attention – or rather, his *lack* of attention – to the papers on his desk.

He'd been lying to Jenny when he'd said that what he'd been thinking about was *her* life.

The truth was, he'd been thinking about his *own* life: about the horrific things he'd seen when he'd returned to Poland after the war – the hunger, the devastation and the imprint that the communist jackboot was already leaving on the people; about his heartbreaking decision to leave his beloved home-land for ever and settle in England; about his decision to marry Linda . . .

But most of all, he was thinking about the last few terrible hours of the previous day, and the first few terrible hours of the present one.

When Chief Constable George Baxter held briefing sessions with any of his senior officers, he did not do it from behind the protective cover of a large imposing desk, as his prede-cessor had done. That was simply not his style. Instead, he led them across to the corner of his office, where two easy chairs – but not *that* easy – faced each other over a plain coffee table.

It was in one of these chairs that Paniatowski was sitting at that moment, looking across the table at the solid man with red hair and a bushy red moustache, who was unquestionably a very *masculine* man, but who, nevertheless, had always reminded her of a big ginger teddy bear.

'This isn't exactly the ideal case for you to kick off your new career with, is it, Monika?' Baxter asked.

'No, sir,' Paniatowski agreed awkwardly.

She *always* felt awkward in Baxter's presence.

When she'd first heard that the Yorkshireman had been appointed chief constable of mid-Lancashire her stomach had turned over, because though coming in from the outside, he was a stranger to everyone else in the division, he was certainly no stranger to her.

Those feelings of awkwardness had never gone away, even though Baxter had now been his post for five years. If anything, they'd got worse recently, because at least when Charlie Woodend had been there, she'd been able to avoid seeing much of the chief constable. But now Charlie was *not* there – and meetings such as this one would inevitably become a regular occurrence.

'Just what exactly is the killer's game, do you think?' Baxter asked.

'I really don't know, sir,' Paniatowski admitted. 'It's too early in the investigation to even make a guess at it. But whatever it is, he wants what he's doing to be noticed.'

Baxter nodded. 'But you think you can handle it?'

'Yes, sir, I believe I can,' Paniatowski said with more conviction than she actually felt. 'But I'd like to make a few changes in my team.'

Baxter raised a sandy eyebrow. 'Isn't it rather early to be thinking of making changes?'

'Perhaps it is,' Paniatowski agreed. 'But given the nature of the case, I need a team I can rely on absolutely.'

'And who *can't* you rely on?'

'Sergeant Walker.'

'I'm surprised to hear you say that,' Baxter told her. 'He has a reputation for being a very competent officer.'

Yes, and the reputation is probably well founded, Paniatowski thought. He'd certainly been able to work out for himself why the killer had to have used the telephone box at the top of the slope, and no other. And while she didn't quite buy into the theory that the killer must have had some military training, she couldn't entirely dismiss it, either.

And yet . . .

And yet, she still didn't trust him. For all that he'd expressed his enthusiasm for working as part of her team, she was far from convinced that enthusiasm was genuine. In fact, she was inclined to believe that he had no respect for women in general – and for her in particular.

She hadn't liked him calling Dr Shastri a Paki, either. Nor had she appreciated him lumping together all the inhabitants of the Pinchbeck Estate – the estate on which she'd grown up – as the scum of the earth.

'I'm sure that Detective Sergeant Walker would make a really excellent bagman for some other DCI, but I'm not convinced that it will work out with me,' she said.

'Make it work,' Baxter said firmly.

'But, sir . . .'

'I can't afford to be seen to be doing you any favours, Monika. Not with our history.'

'Our history!' Paniatowski repeated silently – and bitterly.

They had met when she'd been investigating a case which had links to his patch in Yorkshire, and they had – unthinkingly and almost carelessly – become lovers. But though she had liked him – and even admired him – she had never managed to transfer the passion he raised in her in bed to a passion for him as a man out of it.

It was he who had broken off the relationship, and she hadn't blamed him. The blame was entirely hers. She was convinced of that. She should have tried harder to love him – should have brushed aside thoughts of Bob Rutter, her first and only true love, and accepted George for what he was.

'When all's said and done, sir, our history's just that, sir – history,' she told Baxter.

'I take it from what you've just said that you are unaware that there are a number of people in this building – perhaps even a *large* number – who know all about our previous relationship.'

'Yes, sir, you're right, I *am* unaware of that. In fact, I'm not sure there's any truth in it. How *could* they know? Our courtship—'

'Is that what it was, Monika?' Baxter asked, with a small, ironic smile playing on his lips. 'Our *courtship*?'

'Our affair, then,' Paniatowski said, feeling an anger beginning to build up inside her. 'Or our bit of mindless casual sex on the side, if that's how you'd prefer to think of it.'

'I think, on the whole, that I'd prefer to think of it as our affair,' Baxter said quietly.

'Fine. Our *affair* was carried out entirely in Yorkshire. By the time you came to Whitebridge, we'd broken up. So how *can* anybody know?'

'They know. Word gets around. Don't ask me *how* it gets around, because I couldn't tell you. But it does! Of course, what we once were to each other didn't matter as long as you were Charlie Woodend's protégé, but the moment there was a possibility you might be promoted to DCI, the rumours started to fly. There are plenty of people who believe that I only pushed your promotion through because of what happened between us.'

'And did you?'

'Of course not. I honestly thought you were the best qualified person for the job. But we have to be careful, Monika. If somebody is seen to cross you, and the next day he's out on his ear, tongues will start wagging.'

'In other words, sir, if this request had been made by any other DCI, you'd have granted it without a second's thought?'

'Not without a *second*'s thought, no,' Baxter said, choosing his words carefully.

'But you *would* probably have granted the request.'

'We're dealing with a hypothetical situation here, so it's impossible to say anything for certain. But yes, I think I probably would have agreed to let the chief inspector have his way.'

'But because it's *me*, you don't think you can?'

'Essentially, yes.'

'So my ability to investigate this case is to be undermined by office politics?' Paniatowski asked bitterly.

Baxter made an expansive gesture with his big ginger hands.

'That's the way of the world, Monika,' he said. 'We not only have to *be* squeaky clean, we have to be *seen* to be

squeaky clean. Learn to work with Walker. Try to find a way
to make him *want* to nail his colours to your mast. And once
this particular case is over, we'll reassess the whole situation,
and perhaps I'll be able to give you what you want.'

'Providing that I get a successful result?'

'Providing that, of course.'

'Which you're expecting me to achieve with one hand tied
behind my back?'

Baxter smiled. It was not exactly an amused smile, though
there were elements of amusement in it. And it was far from
being a cruel smile – though Baxter would not have been human
if he hadn't felt just a *little* satisfaction at seeing the woman
who had turned his life completely inside out in an uncomfortable situation for once. Overall, it could perhaps have been said
to be a reassuring smile – but with a warning attached.

'Welcome to the higher echelons, Detective Chief Inspector
Paniatowski,' he said.

The phone rang on Baxter's desk.

'Excuse me for a moment, Chief Inspector,' he said, standing
up and crossing the room.

He was always polite, Paniatowski thought. He was always
the perfect gentleman.

Why *couldn't* she have learned to love him as he so *deserved*
to be loved?

Baxter picked up the phone. 'Yes,' he said. 'Yes, I see.'

His voice was growing heavier with every word, Paniatowski
thought.

Why was it growing heavier?

The chief constable put the phone down.

'Things didn't start out very well this morning, but they've
just turned even nastier,' he said gravely.

'A second body part's turned up?' Paniatowski guessed –
because what else could it be?

'That's right,' Baxter agreed. 'Another hand.'

'Poor bloody woman,' Paniatowski said with feeling. 'We
simply have to assume she's dead now, don't we?'

'I'm afraid it wasn't a woman's hand this time,' Baxter told
her. 'It was a *man's*.'

SIX

Mike Traynor had been on the phone to the London *Daily Globe* for almost half an hour.

The first five minutes of that half-hour had been highly unsatisfactory. When he'd asked to speak to the editor, he'd been told – by a very bored-sounding minion – that Mr Stevens was not available. When he'd pointed out that he was *the* Mike Traynor, the *Globe*'s northern correspondent, the same minion had been completely unimpressed, and it was only when Traynor reluctantly pushed *himself* into the background, and the *story* to the forefront, that things started to happen.

The lackey he'd been talking to had quickly been jerked away from the phone, and returned to whatever cupboard he lived in when he wasn't required for fobbing off provincial reporters. He had been replaced by a man who announced himself as the *assistant* editor, and while it would have been better to talk to the *deputy* editor, Traynor decided to settle for what he'd got.

As he told his story, he sensed that the assistant editor's interest was quickening.

'Have you still *got* the hand in your possession?' the other man asked.

'Well, of course I haven't still got it,' Traynor told him. 'Apart from it *being* a severed hand – which is not exactly something you want to keep around the place – it's evidence of a crime, isn't it?'

'So what did you do with it?'

'I phoned the police, and they came round to the office and took it away with them.'

'Ah,' the assistant editor said.

'But I've got a *photograph* of the hand, which is all you'd need,' Traynor pointed out.

'And the note that accompanied it?'

'I've got a copy of the note, too. They *could* both be on the next train to London.'

The assistant editor paused, as he considered the implications of the 'could both be'.

'I suppose we just might be able to use this little story of yours,' he said finally, and in an airy manner. 'It all depends, you see.'

'On what?'

'On how slow the rest of the news is today. If there's an earthquake in China, for example—'

'You'll put that on page three, like you always do with stories about foreigners,' Traynor interrupted him. 'And why? Because we both know that your readers don't give a toss about what's happening on the other side of the world. But they *will* care about the story that I'm offering you. It's front-page material – and we both know that, too.'

'Perhaps it might be front-page material in . . . where was it? . . . you said you were calling from Lancashire, didn't you?'

'Yes,' Traynor agreed. 'Lancashire.'

'But the *Globe* is a national newspaper, and . . .'

'Perhaps you're right,' said Traynor, who was starting to enjoy himself. 'Perhaps the story isn't much use to you. I'll tell you what – I'll send it to the *Gazette* instead.'

'Let's not be too hasty,' the assistant editor cautioned. 'I'm willing to pay you fifty pounds for the story, whether we use it or not.'

'I want a *hundred* pounds,' Traynor told him. 'And I want the story appearing under my byline.'

There was another pause, then the assistant editor said, 'I think we can agree to that.'

Of course they could, Traynor thought, wishing he'd asked for *two* hundred pounds.

Traynor had only just put the phone down again when the office boy appeared at his door.

'Chief Inspector Paniatowski just rang up and asked if you were here,' the boy said.

'And what did you tell her?'

'That you were. Did I do right?'

'Of course you did. We should always cooperate with the police. Did she say anything else?'

'She said she was on her way over, and she'd be grateful if you didn't go out before she got here. Only . . .'

'Only what?'

'Only, the way she said it, it seemed like she was really saying that if you weren't in, there'd be hell to pay.'

'Yes, and I'm sure that's just exactly how she *intended* it to sound,' Traynor said.

And he was thinking, What a difference a few hours can make. Earlier this morning she was summoning me to see her, and now – even if she does do her best to make it seem as if she's still in charge – *she's* coming to see *me*.

'Is there anything else I can do for you while I'm here, Mr Traynor?' the office boy asked.

'No,' Traynor said, but as the boy was heading towards the door, he changed his mind and called out, 'Actually, there is.'

Traynor reached into his drawer and took out a large buff envelope. Then he placed the envelope on the desk top, and hurriedly scribbled an address on it.

'Take this down to the parcel office at the railway station,' he told the boy. 'Find out what the quickest way of sending it is, and send it that way. It doesn't matter what it costs. Got that?'

'Got it,' the office boy said.

When DCI Paniatowski entered Traynor's office she did not look in the best of humours. But then, the reporter told himself, it would have been a bloody miracle if she had.

'Chief Inspector Paniatowski,' he said jovially. 'How nice to see you again – and so soon after our last meeting as well. Do take a seat.'

Paniatowski remained standing. 'I want to hear about the second hand,' she said.

'Certainly,' Traynor agreed, still on a high at the thought of a byline *and* a hundred pounds. 'But since I've already given the details to your Sergeant Walker, it's pretty much *second-hand news*, don't you think?'

Paniatowski glared at him. 'Two people may already be dead, and more could follow,' she said.

'I know that, but even so, Chief Inspector, if you can't have a sense of humour about things . . .'

'And if you don't stop pissing me about, *Mr Traynor*, you could be one of them!'

She didn't mean it, of course, Traynor thought. It was just

one of those things people said, like, 'I'll knock your teeth down your throat.' Nevertheless, he found the words were having a sobering effect on him.

'The note was delivered by hand,' he said. 'No joke intended,' he added hastily. 'That's just the way it came.'

'Delivered?' Paniatowski repeated, questioningly.

'It was slipped under the door.'

'Which door? The front door, that opens out on to the High Street?'

'No, the back door. The one that's in the alley.'

'Show it to me,' Paniatowski said, holding out her hand.

'The note?'

'Yes.'

'I'm afraid I can't do that, because I've already handed it over to your sergeant.'

'Then you'll just have to show me the copy you made, won't you?' Paniatowski said.

'But I didn't *make* any—'

'Now!'

With a sigh, Traynor opened his drawer, took out the copy and laid it on the desk.

The letter had been pasted together with words cut out of magazines . . .

IF you want a real SCOOP, here's one,
Mr Traynor
Go and take a **look** at the **dustbin**
behind YOUR office. **There's** a
human hand IN IT

'You have to admit that whoever he is, he's short and to the point,' Traynor commented.

Paniatowski picked up the note, folded it neatly and slipped it into her jacket pocket.

'Here, hang on . . .' Traynor protested.

'Is this the *only* copy? Paniatowski asked.

'It is,' Traynor replied.

'Apart from the one that the office boy's taking down to the railway station, even as we speak,' he added mentally.

'I don't want you discussing the contents of this note with anybody,' Paniatowski said. 'Is that understood?'

Traynor nodded. 'It's understood.'

'Good. And now we've got that out of the way, I'd like to see where you found the hand.'

Traynor stood up. 'Follow me,' he said.

The alley was wide enough to accommodate any delivery vans which might need access and a row of battered dustbins.

Paniatowski looked up and down the alley. The killer had chosen his spot wisely, she thought. It was true that, in addition to the *Chronicle* offices, it was overlooked by half a dozen shops on either side, but those with a window looking out on to the alley had put up blinds – since no business wants the retail spell it is trying to weave spoiled by the bedazzled customer spotting the dustbins.

She lit up a cigarette. Yes, the killer had been very clever, she thought, because though things can always go wrong *however* carefully they're planned, he could have been reasonably confident that no one would see him when he made the drop.

A uniformed constable was standing, somewhat languidly, at the end of the alley, but the moment he noticed Paniatowski walking towards him, he stiffened up and saluted.

Paniatowski smiled at him. 'Did you know that I can read your mind?' she asked.

The constable looked confused. 'Can you, ma'am?'

'I think so. You were just telling yourself that you didn't join the Force to stand guard over dustbins. Am I right?'

The constable's confusion grew. 'Well, actually, ma'am . . .'

'But even a seemingly menial job like this one can play a vital part in an investigation – which is why I hope you've been doing it properly.'

'I have, ma'am,' the constable assured her. 'I've not let anybody get near them bins.'

Paniatowski nodded. 'Good,' she said. 'We all have to climb the promotion ladder step by step, you know.'

'I *do* know, ma'am.'

'And if you're not careful and conscientious, you'll falter on the first one, and then you'll *never* get any higher. That's happened to more officers than you'd ever imagine.'

'It won't happen to me,' the young constable said firmly.

Paniatowski smiled again. 'I'm sure it won't.'

'Thank you for your time, ma'am,' the constable said – and sounded as though he meant it.

'My pleasure,' Paniatowski told him.

She turned and walked back to the dustbins, where Traynor was waiting for her.

The journalist sniggered. 'What was that I just witnessed?' he asked. 'A pep talk to one of the poor bloody infantry?'

'You're smarter than you look,' Paniatowski told him. 'But then, you'd have to be, wouldn't you?'

'And what's that supposed to mean?' Traynor demanded.

'Which one of these bins was the hand in?' Paniatowski asked, ignoring the question.

'This one,' Traynor said, tapping the one on the end of the row with his knuckles. 'Did you notice that?'

'Did I notice *what*?'

'That I only touched it with my knuckles. I did it that way to make your job easier for you. No fingerprints, you see.'

'So when you opened it the last time, you were wearing gloves, were you?' Paniatowski asked.

'Ah, I see what you mean,' the journalist exclaimed. 'It would have been better if I *had* been wearing gloves, wouldn't it?'

Paniatowski sighed. 'You could say that,' she agreed. 'So tell me exactly what you did?'

'Well, I took the lid off, and rummaged about inside.'

'And where was the hand?'

'Just below the surface.'

Yes, it would have been. The killer wouldn't have wanted to spend too long at the bin, in case he was spotted.

'Was it wrapped in anything?' she asked.

'It was in a blue plastic freezer bag. I could see immediately that it wasn't like the other one – because it was far too big to be a woman's hand.'

'You should be a detective,' Paniatowski said drily.

And it was not until Traynor said, 'So the other hand *was* a woman's,' that she realized she'd made a mistake.

'I'll send one of my lads round with a van to pick up this bin,' Paniatowski told him.

'I said, so the first one – the one on the river bank – *was* a woman's hand,' Traynor repeated.

'He should be here to collect it within the half-hour,' Paniatowski replied, stonily.

'If you're taking the bin away, I'll need a receipt,' Traynor said, giving up on the confirmation, and shifting to a different tack.

'A receipt?' Paniatowski repeated.

'Yes.'

'For a *dustbin*?'

'Well, when all's said and done, it *is* Lancashire *Evening Chronicle* property,' Traynor said.

'It's Whitebridge Council property,' Paniatowski countered. 'And if you think I'm going to give you a receipt so that you can publish it on the front page under the headline, "The *Chronicle* finds the hand of horror", then you've got another think coming.'

'Hand of horror,' Traynor mused. 'Do you know, Chief Inspector, that's really not bad at all. Maybe, just as I should have been a detective, *you* should have been a journalist.'

'No receipt,' Paniatowski said firmly.

'Fair enough,' agreed Traynor, who'd already got more out of this meeting than he'd ever expected to.

The lounge bar of the Drum and Monkey was populated in roughly even numbers by a small group of travelling salesmen drinking gin and tonics and a few office workers who restricted themselves to halves of bitter – but would still manfully suck their way through several strong peppermints before they returned to their places of business.

The public bar, in complete contrast, was doing a roaring trade. Irish navvies knocked back pints of draught Guinness like there was no tomorrow. Bookies' runners exchanged notes and smoked small cigars, while waiting for their punters to make up their minds on whether or not to place one more bet. And old men in cloth caps clacked both their false teeth and their dominoes, as a furious game of fives and threes was fought out.

In the corner of the public bar, there was the *special* table. Locals knew better than to sit at it, and visitors were advised by the landlord that even though it was unheard of to reserve tables in a pub, reserved was definitely what it was. It was the table Charlie Woodend had used for brainstorming with his team for the ten or more years he had held the post of DCI – and Monika Paniatowski, on her first day in the job, saw no reason to go anywhere else.

Paniatowski took a sip of her vodka, then turned to DS Walker, one of the two men at the table.

'Anything to report?' she asked.

Walker shook his head. 'If you were hoping for any clues from along the river bank, you're out of luck, ma'am,' he said. 'And as for the feller who phoned us – Harper – he saw nobody when he was making his call.' He grinned. 'Just to make sure, I put his dog through the third degree, but he wouldn't admit to having seen anything, either.'

'How about the door-to-door inquiries?'

'Nothing, ma'am.' Walker hesitated for a second, then continued, 'But I did warn you that would be the case, didn't I?'

'It's far too early in the investigation to give up on that particular line of approach,' Paniatowski told him.

And Walker smiled, and replied, 'If you say so, ma'am.'

'How are things going back at headquarters, Colin?' Paniatowski asked Beresford.

'The team's in place, and raring to go,' the inspector said, 'but until you throw it something it can really get its teeth sunk into, there's not much for it to do.'

But I haven't *got* anything to throw it yet, Paniatowski thought. I've not even got much to chew on *myself*.

'What I don't understand is why the killer changed his modus operandi when it came to disposing of the second hand,' she said aloud.

'Why decide to dump it in the centre of town, instead of leaving it in the countryside?' Beresford asked. 'It can't have been that he thought that we'd have all likely sites in the countryside under observation – because even someone who knew virtually nothing about the Force would surely have realized that we don't have *that much* manpower available to us.'

'I'm not talking about *where* he dumped it,' Paniatowski said. 'What's important is how he chose to *announce* the fact that he'd done it. He left the woman's hand by the river bank, and then called up every local reporter he could think of. But when it came to the man's hand, he sent an anonymous note to just *one* reporter – the revolting Traynor.'

'He could have suddenly decided that by using the telephone he was running the risk of someone recognizing his voice,' Walker suggested.

'There was nothing *sudden* about it,' Paniatowski told him. She took the note Traynor had given her out of her pocket, and laid it flat on the table. 'Read that, Sergeant.'

'I've *already* read it.'

'Then read it again.'

'If you want a real scoop, here's one, Mr Traynor,' Walker read. 'Go and take a look at the dustbin behind your office. There's a human hand in it.' He nodded. 'Nice touch, using Traynor's name like that. Makes it sound more authentic, somehow.'

'And makes it all the more difficult to put the note together,' Paniatowski said. 'That's why I said there was nothing *sudden* about it. I think this note was pasted together sometime yesterday – and that's at the *latest*.'

'Sorry, ma'am, I don't think I'm quite following you,' Sergeant Walker admitted.

'Searching for the right words, even for a relatively simple note, can take time,' Paniatowski explained. 'If, on the other hand, you decide to make life more complicated by using a word like "scoop" – and that's just what the killer *did* want to do, because he knew that was *just* the word to get Traynor excited – you have to allow more time to find it. And if you want to use somebody's actual name – and the killer wanted to do that, too – you have to be prepared to trawl your way through a fair number of magazines.'

'So what you're saying is the killer *always* planned to tip us off about the second hand with a note?' Walker asked.

'No, I'm saying he always planned to tip *Traynor* off,' Paniatowski corrected him.

She was right, Walker thought. Bang on the button.

And while he told himself he could probably have worked all that out for himself – given time – the simple fact was that DCI Paniatowski had *already* worked it out.

'What I still don't know is what he wants *us* to do,' Paniatowski continued. 'But whatever it is, he's using the press as a way of making sure that we do it.'

'So if he'd already decided to use an anonymous note to reveal the location of the second hand, why didn't he do the same thing for the first?' Beresford asked. 'What's the point of changing horses midstream?'

Paniatowski gave him a thin smile. 'If you remember, Colin,' she said, 'that's the question *I* asked *you*.'

SEVEN

Mike Traynor read through his article in the first edition of the *Evening Chronicle* with no small degree of satisfaction.

Human hand discovered on river bank!
Police this morning discovered a severed hand hidden in the bushes on the river bank close to the Pinchbeck Estate. The hand was in a blue plastic freezer bag.

He was guessing about the freezer bag, but it was a pretty good guess, because the second hand had been in such a bag, and so there was no reason why the first one shouldn't have been.

Though no general statement about the hand has been issued, a well-placed and reliable source in Whitebridge Police Headquarters has confirmed – exclusively to this reporter – that the hand is a woman's.

And that was no lie, Traynor thought – it *had* been confirmed, though it was certainly true that DCI Paniatowski had never *intended* to give him any such confirmation.

There were further – even more bizarre – developments later in the morning, but for the moment, and at the specific request of the police authorities, I have decided not to report on them.

Well, that should definitely put the cat right among the pigeons, Traynor told himself.

Of all the reporters covering the case, only *he* was in a position to state that the hand was definitely a woman's – and only *he* had any basis for hinting that more was to follow.

He had been tempted to tell his readers that they could find the 'more' that he had alluded to in the following morning's *Daily Globe*. But he had quickly decided that his editor – who (totally unreasonably) cared more about the *Chronicle*'s success than he did about his reporters getting on in the world – would never have stood for that.

He wondered how his editor would react when he *did* read the *Globe*. Probably go ballistic, he thought. He'd probably claim that since the *Chronicle* was paying his salary, the *Chronicle* should have the first bite at any stories he'd uncovered.

Well, sod that! This story was too *big* for a provincial rag. This story was *national*.

The administrative area in Whitebridge Police Headquarters was the part of the building which was least likely to be visited by street-level bobbies. It occupied much of the second floor, and consisted of a warren of small offices, linked by a long corridor which was painted battleship grey and had a lovely view of the car park. It was here that overtime payments were calculated, maintenance work was approved and officers' leave time was registered. But it was also here that the Criminal Records Department had its slightly fusty home, and it was that particular office that Sergeant Walker had been very eager to visit.

Standing in the corridor outside the CRD, DC Crane at first kept himself occupied by counting the cars parked below, but that task was soon completed, and he found himself at a loose end.

What was Walker doing in there, he wondered.

And wonder was all he *could* do – because, despite the fact that the sergeant was clearly excited, he'd shown no signs of wishing to share the source of that excitement with his partner.

The door swung open, and Walker stepped jubilantly into the corridor, clutching a piece of paper in his hand.

'We've got a lead,' he said. 'And not just any old lead, but a bloody *good* one.'

'What kind of lead, Sarge?' Crane asked.

'Nothing you should worry your little head about,' Walker replied, clearly enjoying himself. 'Only the name of the second victim!'

'That's great!' Crane exclaimed. 'We'd better find the boss right away, and tell her.'

Walker scowled. 'Tell *her*?' he said. 'Why should we want to go and do something like that?'

'Well, you know, she is supposed to be the one in charge of the investigation,' Crane pointed out.

'And so we have to go running to her with every little thing that we find, do we?'

'No, not *every* little thing,' Crane conceded. 'But as you said yourself, Sarge, this is a major lead.'

'And it's also something we're perfectly capable of handling by ourselves,' Walker said.

He marched off down the corridor, and had covered half the distance to the fire door when he realized Crane wasn't with him. He stopped, spun round and saw that the detective constable was loitering uncertainly by the Criminal Records Department.

'What's the matter with you?' Walker demanded. 'Got a bone in your leg or something?'

A couple of years earlier, when he was new to the area, Crane would not have known what the sergeant was talking about, but now he understood well enough.

'Got a bone in your leg or something' was 'deep Lancashire' for 'Why the hell are you still standing there when there's work to be done?'

Even so, the DC hesitated. This wasn't right, he told himself. The boss should be informed immediately of any new developments, and it was up to her to decide what to do next.

'Come on, lad, shape yourself!' Walker called out. 'There's not a minute to lose.'

Still, Walker *was* the sergeant, while he himself was only the constable, Crane argued. So it wasn't really up to him to judge what was appropriate and what wasn't.

'Coming, Sarge,' he said, striding quickly – though still reluctantly – to where Walker was waiting for him.

There was a lift down to the car-park level, but Walker didn't have the patience to wait for it to arrive, and so they took the stairs instead.

'Now you'll get to see the sharp end of policing for yourself,' Walker promised Crane, as the two men almost raced across the car park to Walker's Ford Escort.

'Yes, now you'll see how it's done,' Walker continued, once they were in the car and he had fired the engine.

'Can I ask you a question, Sarge?' Crane asked, as the sergeant set off at what was almost a racing start.

'Ask away,' Walker told him.

'Just as a matter of interest, Sarge, what's the *real* reason we aren't telling the boss what we're doing?'

Walker sighed. 'We're not telling her because I don't think she's got the stomach to do what needs to be done,' he said. 'We're not telling her because I'm worried she'll take the best lead we're likely to get on this case, and make a complete balls-up of it. All right?'

'All right,' Crane said, though he didn't sound convinced.

And despite having given the reasons himself, Walker wasn't convinced either.

The truth – the *real* truth – which he was still fighting off acknowledging as best he could, was not so much that he believed Paniatowski would make a balls-up of it, as that he was frightened that she *wouldn't*.

Brunskill's Bakery claimed in its advertisements that all its products were freshly baked every day, and despite the fact that it *was* in the advertisements, the claim was actually true.

By three o'clock in the afternoon, the drivers had completed their scheduled deliveries and gone home. In the bakery itself, the ovens had been shut down, and the master bakers sat around – smoking and chatting – while their apprentices un-enthusiastically cleared up. Even in the offices – though it was still two hours to clocking-off time – there was a feeling that the day's work had been done.

Jenny Brunskill did not share in this general lethargy. She had still not been able to isolate the reason for the recent decline in sales, but she was determined that she would do so before she went home.

She was going over the figures yet again when Elaine Dunston appeared with the evening paper, opened in the middle.

'Thought you'd like to see this as soon as it arrived, Miss Brunskill,' the secretary said.

'You're quite right, I do,' Jenny agreed. She scanned the two pages, as Elaine was leaving the office, then said, 'Gosh, it looks even better than I'd thought it would.'

She looked across at Stan, as if expecting some reaction, but her brother-in-law said nothing.

'It's our new advertisement!' Jenny enthused. 'A double-page spread!'

Still, Stan was silent.

'Of course, as you'd expect, it cost us an absolute arm and a leg,' Jenny continued, 'but if even only one in twenty of the readers decides to buy our pies as a result of it, it will have been well worth the outlay, don't you think?'

'Hmm,' Stan said.

'What's the matter with you today?' Jenny asked, slightly crossly. 'Are you coming down with the same bug as Linda did?'

'Life is never what you think it will be, is it?' Stan asked mournfully. 'It simply never turns out as you hoped.'

'Oh, I don't know about that,' Jenny said. 'I'm very happy with the way *my* life's turned out.'

'Are you?'

'Yes, I am.'

'Why?'

'I suppose my happiness is mostly due to the fact that I'm working at a job I love.'

'A job you love?' Stan repeated. 'Do you *really* love it?'

'Of course I do.'

'Or is it just that your father *told you* that you should love it?'

Jenny laughed. 'Sometimes you do talk complete and utter nonsense, you know,' she said.

There was a knock on the door, then the door opened just wide enough for Elaine to pop her head round it.

'I don't know whether or not you'd be interested, Miss Brunskill, but there's something really quite gruesome on the front page of that newspaper,' she said, with obvious relish.

Jenny looked at the double-page advertisement once more, her eyes ablaze with pleasure, then reluctantly folded them together so she could take a look at the 'really quite grue-some' thing that Elaine had spotted on the front page.

'Oh, my God!' she groaned, when she'd read it.

'What's the matter?' Stan asked.

'They've found a woman's hand down by the river! It was in a plastic freezer bag!'

'Do they know *whose* hand it is yet?'

'Whatever makes you even ask a question like that?' Jenny Brunskill wondered.

Stan shrugged. 'Why wouldn't I ask it? What other question *could* I have asked about a severed hand?'

Elaine Dunston burst into the room again, without even bothering to knock this time.

'The police are here, Miss Brunskill,' she gasped.

'The police?' Jenny repeated, mystified. 'What on earth are you talking about, Elaine?'

'There's two of them – a detective sergeant and a detective constable. They're in the lobby. And they say that nobody can leave the premises until everybody's been questioned.'

'Did they give you any idea of what it might be all about?'

'No, they didn't. They said they wanted to speak to you about it first, but wouldn't it be awful if—'

'What it's all about, madam,' said a heavy voice from the doorway, interrupting Elaine mid-flow, 'is a severed hand.'

Even though it was still only a little after three o'clock in the afternoon, it already felt as if it had been a very long day indeed, Monika Paniatowski thought, as she looked down at the hand which Dr Shastri had just extracted from the refrigerated drawer.

It was, as Mike Traynor had said in the alleyway, clearly a *man*'s hand. The palm was large and the skin somewhat rough. The fingers were thick, and the fingernails were clipped short. There was black hair sprouting from both above and below the knuckles.

'As you have already surmised, this – unlike the lady's – is a working hand,' Dr Shastri said.

'And did the same person who cut off hers also cut off this one?' Paniatowski asked.

Shastri laughed. 'I am truly flattered by your unbounded confidence in me, my dear chief inspector,' she said, 'but you must accept that even *I* have some limitations.'

'Meaning that you can't say?'

'Meaning that, if backed into a corner, I might be willing to commit myself to saying that a similar cleaver was used in both cases.'

'But not necessarily the same one?'

'No, not necessarily the same one. Meaning also that the two amputations are similar enough for me to be willing to accept that they could have been carried out by the same person – though it would certainly not surprise me to learn that they had been the work of two separate attackers.'

'I see,' Paniatowski said, disappointed.

'However, you should not despair,' Shastri said cheerfully. 'After all, each cloud has its silver lining, it is always darkest before the dawn and every dog has his day.'

Paniatowski grinned. 'What have you found out?' she asked.

'Not much,' Shastri said airily. 'In fact, the merest of trifles. But it may just help you in your inquiries.'

'Spit it out,' Paniatowski told her.

Dr Shastri looked hurt. 'Now that you are the Big Chief, you are far less fun to play with,' she said. 'Very well, to cut a long story short, the first thing I discovered was a slight trace of ink on all the fingertips.'

'Ink?' Paniatowski repeated.

'Yes. It puzzled me at the time, and, to be honest with you, it still does. But then I stopped worrying about that, and became quite excited by what I found under the fingernails.'

'And just what *did* you find?' asked Paniatowski, who had resigned herself to playing Shastri's game.

'I found a white powder, and when I analysed it, I discovered that it was largely made up of polysaccharides – which is starch to an ignorant person like you – and also gluten.'

'In other words?'

'In other words, it is common flour – which leads me to believe that the man was a baker.'

'What it's all about, madam, is a severed hand,' the voice had said.

Jenny looked up. The man who'd spoken was in his late thirties. He had the square build of a rugby player, with dark, flashing, suspicious eyes, and lips which would find no difficulty in expressing contempt. He was accompanied by a slimmer, younger man with a thin, artistic face, who – had his hair been a little longer – could have been mistaken for a poet.

'I'm DS Walker and this is DC Crane,' the thickset man said. 'We'd like to ask you some questions about Tom Whittington.'

'Tom? He's our head baker.'

'You don't say? Now there's what I call a coincidence –
I'm here to talk about Whittington, and you actually know
him.'

The man was a brute, Jenny decided.

'Tom isn't here today,' she said.

'I know he isn't. It would be nothing less than a bloody
miracle if he was,' Walker retorted.

'You said this was about a severed hand.'

'And so it is.'

'But I've just been reading the evening newspaper, and that
said it was a *woman*'s hand which had been found.'

'You shouldn't believe everything you read in the papers,
madam, although, for once, they're right, and we *have* found
a woman's hand. But we've found a man's hand, as well –
one that used to be attached to the wrist of this Mr Whittington
of yours.'

'Oh, sweet Jesus!' Jenny gasped. 'Oh, Holy Mother of God.
Are you *sure* it's Tom's hand?'

'Take it easy, Miss Brunskill,' DC Crane said soothingly.
'Try taking a few deep breaths.'

What the bloody hell is the young idiot playing at? Walker
thought angrily. I don't *want* the sodding woman taking it
easy. She's more useful to me when she's on edge.

'You can go, DC Crane,' he said.

'But, Sarge . . .'

'Now!' Walker said firmly. 'You can wait for me outside.'

For a moment, Crane looked as if he was about to disobey
the order, then he turned and stepped back into the foyer.

'I asked you if you were sure it was Tom's hand,' Jenny
Brunskill repeated shakily.

'Did you know that this feller Whittington, who you're
telling me you employed as your *head baker*, had a criminal
record?' Walker demanded, ignoring the question.

'Yes, as a matter of fact, I did.'

'But you *still* gave him a job?'

'It isn't much of a criminal record. He stole a car, when
he was young. It was a foolish thing to do, but he's never
repeated it. He's not been in trouble for over twenty years.'

'So you say, madam, though in my experience a leopard
never changes his spots,' Walker said. 'But that's all pretty

much by the by. The fact is that Whittington *does* have a criminal record, and that means we've got his fingerprints – which, in turn, means that we know that he's now minus one hand.'

Jenny glanced across at Stan for some sign of support in her time of distress, but her brother-in-law was gazing fixedly at the wall, and seemed to be in another world.

'I think you're being very callous and insensitive about the whole situation,' she complained to Walker.

'Do you, madam?'

'Yes, I do. Tom's not just a name to us. He's someone we work with. In some ways, he's almost family.'

Walker's lip curled. 'Then that would be the *black sheep* of the family, wouldn't it, madam?'

Paniatowski glanced down at her wristwatch, and saw that it was already three twenty-five.

'I must go,' she said. 'There are quite a lot of bakeries in the Whitebridge area, and they'll need checking.'

'Give my love to Louisa,' Shastri said.

'I will,' Paniatowski promised.

'Give it to her today – before you forget.'

Paniatowski smiled. 'Is that another way of saying that however busy I am with this investigation, I should still find some time to spend with my daughter?' she asked.

Shastri smiled back. 'Oh, you are far too clever for me,' she said. 'You see right through me.' Her face grew more serious. 'Remember, Monika, she has no father, no aunties or uncles – there is only you.'

'I *do* remember,' Paniatowski replied. 'But thank you for reminding me of it, anyway.'

The phone rang, and Shastri picked it up.

'Yes? Yes, she is.' She handed the phone to Paniatowski. 'It's for you.'

'Who is it?'

'I did not ask and he did not say, but I suspect that it is probably one of your handsome young policemen, who, I have no doubt, looks upon you as almost as he might look upon a goddess.'

Monika took the phone from the doctor.

'DCI Paniatowski,' she said.

'Go to Brunskill's Bakery,' said a man's voice.

The voice didn't sound at all natural, Paniatowski decided. Either the man was talking through a handkerchief, or else he was finding some other way to distort it.

'Who am I talking to?' she asked.

'Go *now!*' the man said.

'I shall need a name before I can . . .' Paniatowski said.

But the man had hung up.

There were only two of them in Jenny Brunskill's office now – Jenny herself and DS Walker.

'This is the way we're going to play it, Miss Brunskill,' Walker was explaining. 'I'll ask you a few questions, and you'll give me a few answers. It shouldn't take long at all. Once we've got that out of the way, I'd like you to vacate the office if you don't mind, so that I can use it to question your staff, starting, I think, with that Polack who was with you when I arrived.'

'Are you referring, by any chance, to my brother-in-law, Stanislaw?' Jenny Brunskill asked.

'Yes, if that's his name,' Walker agreed easily. 'But I think I'd find it easier just to call him Stan, like you do.'

'No doubt you would find it easier,' Jenny said icily. 'But it would be more *appropriate* for *you* to call him *Mr Szymborska*, especially considering the fact that he is not *merely* one of my staff, as you so readily seem to assume, but is a part-owner of this business.'

'Szym . . .' Walker said experimentally. 'Szym . . .' He grinned. 'No, I think I'll just stick to Stan.'

'You said you'd use my office to question the staff *if I didn't mind*?' Jenny said.

'Yes?'

'Suppose I *do* mind? Suppose I don't want you questioning *my* staff in *my* office? Suppose, for that matter, that I don't want to answer any of your questions myself?'

'You'd be well within your rights,' Walker said. 'But you have to ask yourself one question. And it's this – if you refuse to cooperate, what conclusions am I likely to draw from that?'

'Why should I *care* what conclusions you draw?'

'Because I'm the police, madam,' Walker said, his voice suddenly hardening. 'And though I can be through this place like a dose of salts if I choose to, I think you'll find that if you force me to take a roundabout route – which will include getting warrants issued – then it might take two or three days to complete the job, during which time no work will get done in the bakery at all. Besides,' he added, 'I'd have thought you'd be willing to do anything you could to help us catch the man who cut off Tom Whittington's hand.'

'You're right, of course,' Jenny admitted. 'Catching this terrible man *is* what really matters. So what would you like to know?'

'Let's start with the obvious question,' Walker suggested. 'Have you got any *other* jailbirds working here?'

'Tom never went to jail,' Jenny said. 'He was given a suspended sentence and three years' probation.'

Walker sighed heavily. 'All right, if you prefer it that way, have you any other employees with *criminal records*?'

'Two or three.'

'Which is it?'

'Three.'

'So you've actually got *four* jailbirds working for you.'

'In this company, we pride ourselves on giving people who've made a mistake a second chance.'

'Have any of these "second chancers" of yours ever been done for violence?' Walker asked.

'No.'

'Any of them who've *not* been done for violence, but who you feel could turn very nasty, given the right circumstances?'

'Certainly not. We like to encourage a happy working atmosphere here in Brunskill's Bakery, and that kind of person – anyone prone to violence – would simply not fit in.'

Walker sighed again. 'I have to say, you're not being very helpful, madam,' he told her.

'So what would you like me to do in order to be *more* helpful?' Jenny wondered. 'Tell you that Billy the cake mixer often looks at me in a funny way, as if he'd like to beat me up?'

'Only if it's the truth, madam,' Walker said. '*Does* he often look at you in a funny way?'

'No, of course he doesn't. He's a perfectly sweet boy. That's why I gave him the responsibility of looking after the bakery cat.'

'Then why bring his name up at all?'

'I was just trying to make the point that . . .'

'Unless, deep down – subconsciously, shall we say? – there's something about him that *does* worry you.'

The office door swung violently open, and Walker looked up to see Paniatowski framed in the doorway.

'I'd like a word with you outside, Sergeant!' she said.

Walker raised his eyes towards the ceiling, in a gesture of mock despair towards a vengeful god.

'Yes, ma'am, I'm sure you would like a word with me, and I'd like one with you, so if you could just give me a few minutes to finish off this—'

'Now!' Paniatowski said.

Walker rose heavily to his feet. 'I'm sorry about this, Miss Brunskill,' he said. 'I won't be long.'

'If I was you, Sergeant, I wouldn't go putting any money on that,' Paniatowski told him.

EIGHT

'This isn't right,' Sergeant Walker complained to his new boss, as he stepped into the foyer of the administration block and closed Jenny Brunskill's office door behind him. 'It isn't . . .'

'I think we'd better go outside,' Paniatowski said.

'Why?' Walker asked – furious, willing to take issue on almost anything that was said to him. Then he saw Elaine, the secretary, apparently absorbed in what she was reading at her desk, but with her ears flapping like a circus elephant's. 'All right,' he agreed.

They walked out on to the forecourt. The staff car park was just ahead of them, and the loading bay to the left. To the right was a public telephone box, and Paniatowski found herself wondering if this was the box that the call to the mortuary had come from.

'I really don't think you should have done that, ma'am,' Walker said morosely.

'You don't think I should have done *what*?'

'Spoken to me in the way you did, in front of a member of the general public. A male DCI would never have—'

Walker stopped abruptly, as if he'd suddenly decided that he was pushing things just a little *too* far.

'Yes?' Paniatowski asked.

'We're supposed to be working as a team,' Walker continued, in a tone which was a strange mixture of the aggrieved and the conciliatory. 'We're supposed to put up a united front when we're dealing with civilians.'

'Then why don't *you* start acting like you're a *member* of that team?' Paniatowski demanded angrily.

'Sorry, ma'am?' Walker replied, as if he had no idea what she was talking about.

It had been a mistake to lose her temper, Paniatowski realized, because it was just what Walker had wanted. Now, from his viewpoint, she was being the typical hysterical woman, and that made him feel as if *he* had the upper hand.

'What brought you to this bakery in the first place?' she asked, in a much calmer voice.

'I came in my Ford Escort,' Walker said. He waited for Paniatowski to explode again, and when it became plain that she wasn't about to, he continued, 'The reason I'm here is that I've identified the hand as belonging to somebody who *works* here.'

'And why didn't you let me know that you'd developed such an important lead?'

'Tried to, ma'am, but you weren't in your office, and nobody at the station seemed to know *where* you were.'

'I was at the mortuary,' Paniatowski said.

'Oh!'

'Which, given the discovery of the second hand, shouldn't have been *too* hard for you to work out.'

'Didn't think of that, ma'am,' Walker said.

'Anyway, even if you couldn't find me, why didn't you call me on my radio?' Paniatowski asked.

'I tried that as well, ma'am. I couldn't get through to you.' Walker laughed. 'But that's hardly surprising, is it?'

'What?'

'Well, since you were at the mortuary, you were in a *dead* zone.'

'I like a man with a good sense of humour,' Paniatowski said, between clenched teeth.

'Do you, ma'am?' Walker asked.

'Yes, I certainly do. So you will let me know if you come across any, won't you?'

He was lying about radioing her, of course, she thought. He had stumbled on a lead and rushed down to the bakery in the hope that he could solve this case on his own – thus making his new boss look a complete bloody fool.

As if the case *could* be solved that simply!

As if the killer, who had planned everything so well so far, would *allow* it to be solved so simply.

She realized there was one important question she had still not asked. 'So what *was* the lead which led you to this bakery?'

Walker smirked complacently. 'Fingerprints.'

'Fingerprints?'

'We took the man's hand and fingerprinted it, and then we matched the prints against our records, and came up with a name.'

'You fingerprinted it *before* the medical examiner had had the opportunity to examine it?' Paniatowski asked incredulously.

'Yes, ma'am.'

'Let me be clear on this. First you contaminated the evidence, and *then* you handed it over to the doctor?'

Walker shrugged. 'I wouldn't say we contaminated it, exactly. When we'd finished, we wiped the ink off.'

Well, that certainly explained the ink stains that Dr Shastri had found, Paniatowski thought.

Was Walker really as stupid as he seemed? she wondered. Could *anybody* be as stupid as he seemed?

'And once you'd matched the fingerprints, you came straight here?' she asked.

'That's right, ma'am.' Walker paused. 'Well, not straight here, of course. As I've already explained, the first thing I did was to spend quite a lot of time trying to contact you.'

'What did you hope to achieve by coming here without me? Was it your plan to have the killer in handcuffs before I even knew what was going on?'

'Yes, of course it bloody was!' the sergeant's eyes said.

'No, ma'am, it wasn't that at all,' Walker told Paniatowski. 'The way I saw it, I was just taking a bit of the donkey work off your shoulders and placing it on to my own.'

'So you *didn't* expect to find the killer here?'

'Now that's a different question entirely, if you don't mind me saying so, ma'am. I wouldn't be at all surprised if the killer *does* work here.'

And neither would I, Paniatowski thought – because most murder victims are killed by someone they see nearly every day.

'Would it be all right if I got back to interrogating the witness now, ma'am?' Walker asked.

'No, it wouldn't,' Paniatowski replied. 'I'm taking over the questioning myself.'

'That's just not bloody fair,' Walker muttered, almost under his breath.

'What was that, Sergeant? Something about it not being fair?'

'No, ma'am. I was just wondering, since you're taking over the lead I developed, what you wanted *me* to do.'

'I want you to find out if the uniformed branch have un-covered anything useful from the house-to-house search yet. And I want to see you in the Drum and Monkey at seven o'clock sharp. Got that?'

Walker nodded. 'Got it, ma'am. But did you just say *seven* o'clock in the Drum and Monkey?'

'Yes. Why?'

'It just seems a bit early to be thinking of rounding off the day, that's all. I believe that when Mr Woodend was in charge . . .'

'I *know* what Mr Woodend did, because I was with him,' Paniatowski said, keeping her temper under control – but only just. 'And perhaps, when we're further into the investigation, the meetings at the Drum will be held later. But *tonight's* meeting is at seven o'clock.'

'You're the boss,' Walker said.

'Yes, I am,' Paniatowski agreed. 'There's one more thing before you go, Sergeant.'

'Yes, ma'am? And what might that be?'

'You've made a number of mistakes today, not the least of which are contaminating evidence and failing to keep me informed of developments in the investigation. I could issue a reprimand for both those actions – and maybe I will.'

'That's your decision to make, ma'am,' Walker said flatly.

But what the expression in his eyes said was, 'You won't be issuing any reprimands, *ma'am*, because even if you *can't* control your own men, you don't want *your* bosses *thinking* that you can't – especially on your first day in the job.'

A small conference room adjoined Jenny Brunskill and Stan Szymborska's office, and it was in this conference room that Monika Paniatowski began taking the first steps in repairing the damage which had clearly been done by DS Walker's bull-in-a-china-shop routine.

'I thought it might be useful to interview you together,' she said, speaking to the two of them, across the conference table. 'Then, if one you forgets something, the other can fill in the gaps. But it isn't essential that we do things that way, and if you would prefer to be interviewed separately . . .'

Stan and Jenny exchanged rapid glances.

'We have no objection to a joint interview,' said Jenny,

taking on the role of spokesman. 'Stan and I work together all day, every day, and we have no secrets from each other.'

Everybody has secrets, Paniatowski thought – from their friends, from their partners, from their business associates, and probably even from their cats and dogs – but now was not the time to point it out.

She studied the two people opposite her.

Jenny Brunskill was a little younger than she was herself, she guessed. It would have been an exaggeration to say she could have become a beautiful woman, however hard she'd tried – but with even a *little* more care, she would certainly have been a rather pretty one.

She had silky reddish-brown hair, which would have looked wonderful if, instead of choosing to have it cropped like a boy's, she'd allowed it grow naturally. She had nice eyes, too, and even applying a smidgeon of make-up to them would have enhanced their natural qualities spectacularly.

It was almost, Paniatowski thought, as if she'd taken a conscious decision not to make the best of herself – as if her appearance was intended to be a clear and unequivocal statement that appearances didn't really matter to her.

Or maybe not, she corrected herself. Maybe appearances *did* matter to her, and maybe the look she had now – a look which almost screamed self-contained office manager – was *exactly* the one she had sought.

And she was probably a *very good* office manager, Paniatowski decided. For while she was not the kind of woman you would ever put at the head of an expedition through the Amazon jungle, you would certainly want her to be in charge of supplies en route.

Stan Szymborska was another case entirely. Where Jenny took great pains to show off her competence, he wore a quiet mantle of confidence. Where she would be painstaking, he would show flair. He was passing through that stage in life in which good looks gently transformed themselves into a distinguished appearance. Paniatowski wondered how his wife felt about this transformation from Greek god into Roman senator. For her own part, she found it very easy – *too* easy – to imagine herself in bed with him.

'Tell me about Tom Whittington,' she said.

'What do you want to know?'

'How long had he been working here?'

'Fifteen years,' Jenny said, without hesitation. 'It was my father who first employed him.'

'And did he get on well with all your staff?'

'Oh, yes,' Jenny said.

But Stan did not look quite so sure.

'Would you agree with that assessment of him, Mr Szymborska?' Paniatowski asked.

'He was our head baker – and a good one,' Szymborska said, as if that explained it all.

'Yes?'

'You do not get to be a good head baker with knowing how to run a tight ship. Away from work, he was shy and self-effacing, but once he put on his apron, he became a different man – a man who was quite definitely *in charge*.'

'So he wasn't exactly *popular*?'

'He was not disliked, if that is what you're suggesting. A few of our workers might have resented him, once in a while, but they would probably all agree that he was fair, as well as firm.'

'Was he married?' Paniatowski asked

'No,' Jenny Brunskill replied.

'Had he *ever* been married?'

'No.'

'So he lived alone?'

'Yes. He has – he *had* – a flat near the town centre. He was buying it with a loan which the company countersigned.'

'Did he have a current girlfriend?'

Jenny shrugged. 'We talk about the people who work in the bakery as a family,' she said. Then she glanced at Stan Szymborska, and continued, 'Or maybe that's just the way *I* talk about them. But I still think I'm right. We *are* a family, though perhaps not that *close* – not that *intrusive* – a family.'

'So what you're saying is that you don't *know* about his love life?' Paniatowski asked.

'Yes, that's what I'm saying,' Jenny agreed. 'Are you . . .' she continued, with a catch in her voice, 'are you absolutely certain, Chief Inspector, it's *Tom*'s hand that was found?'

'I'm afraid there's no doubt about it.'

'But it seems so . . . so very unlikely. People like Tom Whittington don't get *murdered*.'

'There were no indications that he was in any kind of trouble, were there?' Paniatowski asked.

'None,' Jenny said.

And, this time, she got an unqualified nod of agreement from her brother-in-law.

'Do you have any photographs of Tom which you can easily lay your hands on?' Paniatowski asked.

And the moment the words were out of her mouth, she thought, Oh my God, did I really say that – lay your *hands* on?

But Stan and Jenny had not noticed – or perhaps decided it might be better to *pretend* they hadn't noticed – and instead were discussing the problem she had set them.

'Tom, as Stan has already told you, was quite shy,' Jenny said. 'He certainly wasn't one for having his picture taken. But I suppose there might be a photograph of him in his personnel file.'

'Even if there is, it will be fifteen years out of date,' Stan pointed out. 'What about the photograph we had taken on the last works' outing?'

'That's clever,' Jenny said, standing up. 'I've got a copy in the office. I'll go and get it.'

She left the conference room, and returned, less than a minute later, with a framed group photograph.

'Is this any good?' she asked.

Paniatowski examined the photograph. It had been taken in Blackpool, as evidenced by the fact that the Tower was clearly visible in the background.

It had been in Blackpool that she and Charlie Woodend had first worked on a case together, a million years ago, she thought.

She turned her attention back to the photograph. As in school photographs, the group pictured had been arranged by hierarchical considerations, so that the senior staff were in the foreground, and the more junior stood on benches behind them.

'That's Tom,' Jenny said, pointing to a man in the front row.

Whittington was standing next to Stan Szymborska, as befitted his position in the company, and the first thing that Paniatowski noticed was how alike the two men looked.

They could have been brothers, she told herself.

Then she examined the photograph again, and decided that she'd been wrong. They were not quite close enough in looks to be mistaken for siblings, but they were undoubtedly handsome in the *same kind* of way, and the main distinction between them was that Stan was unquestionably older.

Her eyes rested next on the two women who were flanking the two men. There was no question here – even if they weren't standing side by side, as Stan and Tom were – that they were sisters, though one sported a cropped pageboy hairstyle, while the other had allowed her hair to cascade over her shoulders and thus display itself in its full glory.

Paniatowski looked at the picture again. This was a company outing, she reminded herself – which meant that everyone in the photograph worked for Brunskill's Bakery.

And that was when she felt her stomach perform a sudden and violent somersault.

NINE

A full two minutes had passed since she had first noticed the sisters in the photograph. Two minutes – or maybe even three – and Paniatowski was still not sure how to broach the matter which would quite possibly shatter the lives of the other two people in the room for ever.

'You seem very interested in the picture,' Jenny Brunskill said, sounding perhaps a little unnerved by the intensity of Paniatowski's concentration. 'Is there anyone else you'd like me to point out to you?'

There was no easy way to deal with the subject, Paniatowski decided – no way to cushion the blow, if blow there was to be.

'Is that your sister?' she asked, pointing at the woman with the long hair, standing next to Tom Whittington.

'Yes, that's our Linda.'

'And she works here too, doesn't she?'

Jenny smiled. 'That's right, she does. And not just *works* here. She's the *real* big cheese – the managing director.'

With her stomach continuing to perform aerobatics, Paniatowski said, 'I'd like to see her, if I may.'

But she already knew that wouldn't be possible, because if Linda Szymborska had been in the building, she would – as managing director – have made her presence known the second the police arrived.

'I'm afraid that Linda's not here today,' Jenny said. 'She was feeling sick, so she's stayed at home. Isn't that right, Stan?'

'She's . . . she may be at home *by now*,' Stan Szymborska said.

'What do you mean? *By now*?' Jenny asked. 'She was there when you left this morning, wasn't she?'

'No,' Stan admitted. 'She wasn't.'

'So where *was* she?'

'We'll talk about this later,' Stan said awkwardly.

'No!' Jenny insisted firmly. 'We will not talk about it later – we'll talk about it *now*.'

'We had a slight disagreement, and she stormed out of the house,' Szymborska told her.

'When? This morning? Over breakfast?'

'No, the argument was last night.'

So now the 'slight disagreement' had become an argument, Paniatowski noted.

'Last night!' Jenny repeated, incredulously.

'Yes,' Stan Szymborska agreed.

'Then I really don't understand what you're saying. Surely, after she came back . . .'

'She *didn't* come back.'

'Not *at all*?'

'No. I thought she'd only be gone for an hour or so, but she still hadn't returned when I was getting ready for bed, so I just assumed that she was still annoyed, and had checked into a hotel.'

'Does she often stay away all night after you've had a row?' Paniatowski asked.

Szymborska shook his head. 'No, she doesn't. In fact, she's never done it before.'

'I don't know what caused this row of yours, but you'd better make up pretty damn quickly,' Jenny said sternly. 'The last thing we need is for two directors of the company to be at each other's throats.'

She still didn't get it, Paniatowski thought. She still hadn't managed to join up the dots.

'I'm going to show you both a photograph,' she said aloud. 'I want you to be prepared for a shock.'

She slid the photograph of the woman's severed hand across the table to Stan and Jenny.

'Why are you showing us this?' Jenny wondered. 'You don't think . . . Oh God, you don't think . . .?'

'If you could just look at it very carefully,' Paniatowski said, in a soothing tone.

Jenny Brunskill gave it the briefest of glances. 'It's not her hand,' she said. 'It's *nothing like* her hand.'

'Please look at it again,' Paniatowski urged.

Jenny did. 'If it's Linda's hand, where's her engagement ring?' she demanded aggressively. 'Where's her *wedding* ring?'

'Mr Szymborska?' Paniatowski asked.

'I don't know,' Stan Szymborska mumbled. 'I want to say it isn't, but I just don't know.'

'Of course you know!' Jenny said, in a voice which was almost a scream. 'You're her husband. Don't you think you'd recognize your own *wife*'s hand when you saw it?'

Szymborska rose shakily to his feet. 'I think I have to phone home immediately,' he said.

'That's right,' Jenny agreed. 'You phone home. You talk to Linda, and put an end to all this ridiculous speculation.'

Szymborska lumbered into his office.

'It's not her, you know,' Jenny told Paniatowski. 'I *know* it's not her. If it was, I could tell straight away.'

But when Stan returned, two minutes later, even she must have begun to have her doubts.

'She isn't there,' Szymborska said flatly.

'Then she must have arrived back at home after you left, and gone out again since,' Jenny said.

'I spoke to the housekeeper. Linda hasn't been home all day.'

'That doesn't mean *anything*,' Jenny said. And then she kept repeating the words, until they became a chant in which hope battled against despair. 'That doesn't mean anything, doesn't mean anything, doesn't mean anything . . .'

'Is there something in your wife's office that she – and only she – will have been especially likely to handle?' Paniatowski asked Stan Szymborska.

'I . . . I should think so. Why?'

It was just as she'd suspected it would be, Paniatowski thought – there was no easy way to say it, no magic formula which would make it easier to take.

'Because we'll need a set of your wife's fingerprints,' she told Stan Szymborska.

An hour had passed, but when Paniatowski re-entered the conference room, it seemed to her as if neither Jenny Brunskill nor Stan Szymborska had moved an inch since the last time she had seen them.

She opened the file she was holding, and looked down at the forensic report which she already knew by heart.

'I'm sorry,' she said, 'but I'm afraid there's no doubt about it. It's Linda's hand.'

'Oh God!' Jenny gasped. Then a look of desperate hope filled her eyes, and she said, 'But that doesn't have to mean she's *dead*, does it?'

'Miss Brunskill . . .' Paniatowski said softly.

'It doesn't, does it?' Jenny asked, appealing to her brother-in-law. 'It doesn't have to mean she's dead!'

'What do *you* think, Chief Inspector?' Szymborska asked heavily.

'Anything's possible,' Paniatowski replied, choosing her words with care. 'But it would be wrong of me to offer you much hope.'

'You're right,' Jenny moaned. 'She's dead. She *has* to be dead. But how could it happen? Why would anybody *do* such a thing to her?'

'I don't know,' Paniatowski admitted.

'But you're a chief inspector!' Jenny said, with a new note of hysteria seeping into her voice. 'You're *supposed* to know these things! It's your *job* to know these things!'

Stan put his hand on his sister-in-law's shoulder.

'I'm sure Chief Inspector Paniatowski's doing all she can,' he said gently. 'And neither of us should do or say anything that will make her job more difficult for her.'

Jenny took in a deep gulp of air, and nodded.

'Is there anything we *can* do?' she asked.

'There is one thing,' Paniatowski told her. 'It won't be easy, but it would help.'

'Anything,' Jenny promised.

'Don't tell anyone that we've identified the hands as belonging to your sister and Tom Whittington.'

'But there are people who need *to know*,' Jenny protested. 'There are relatives and friends to be informed. People who really cared about Linda. They've a *right* to be told.'

'I know they have,' Paniatowski agreed. 'But I still don't want you to tell them *yet*.'

'Why?'

'Because it's highly probable that naming the victims is just what the killer both expects and *wants* us to do.'

'How can you say that?' Jenny asked. 'How can you possibly know what's in his mind?'

'I just know,' Paniatowski said, flatly.

'But *how*?'

'Are you sure you actually *want* me to tell you?'

'Yes!'

Paniatowski sighed. 'He could have just buried his victims. If he had, we'd have known they'd gone missing, but nothing more. Instead, he chose to send us their hands, which means that while he doesn't want to make it too easy for us, he still wants us to find out who they are.'

'I still don't see why . . .'

'He'll be expecting us to release the names, and when we don't, he'll start getting nervous. And *because* he's nervous, he might make a mistake which will lead us to him.'

There was more to it than that, of course.

In some ways, the potential witnesses in a murder investigation were rather like the audience in a theatre.

The audience followed the action on the stage, and thought they knew what was going on – thought they understood the whole world of the play. And then the lighting changed, and so did their perceptions.

The innocuous table in the corner of the set, which they had ignored up to this point, was suddenly the focus of their attention. And they knew that this table mattered – that it was significant. And even if it wasn't true – even if the only reason the table had been illuminated was because some lighting man had accidentally hit the wrong switch – they would cling to the idea of the table's importance, and feel strangely let down if it did not fulfil the hopes they had invested in it.

And so it was with a murder investigation. The more light that was thrown on the case, the more the potential witnesses built up their own stories about it – and the less the value of the statements they made.

They would tell you what they thought you wanted to know – rather than simply answer the questions that you had put to them.

They would force to the forefront of their brains an avalanche of information that they had decided would be helpful – and in the process would bury the information which really mattered.

At best, this would make them less effective as witnesses – at worst, they would become an actual impediment to the investigation.

But there was no point in telling Jenny Brunskill any of

this, Paniatowski thought. She would have found it hard to grasp under normal circumstances, and in her current situation it would sound like nothing more than meaningless babble.

'You do understand what I've been saying, don't you?' she asked. 'I want you to tell *no one* what I've just told you.'

'I understand,' Stan Szymborska said, in a flat, dead – yet firm – tone.

'And you, Miss Brunskill?'

'I understand too,' said Jenny Brunskill – but with far less conviction.

TEN

It was a little after quarter past seven in the evening, and the team – Paniatowski, Beresford and Walker – were sitting at their usual table in the public bar of the Drum and Monkey.

'There's absolutely no room for complacency in this investigation – or indeed in any investigation,' Monika Paniatowski said, 'but given what we were up against from the start, we've not done too badly for the first day.'

It was the sort of thing Charlie Woodend would have said, she thought, because – as the leader of the team – he'd have felt it was his duty to rally the troops. And that was why *she* had said it, too. But she was not sure that she had displayed either the authority or the conviction that Charlie would have done in her place. And besides, there was at least a small – treacherous – part of her which kept saying that even if they *had* made progress, they would have made more if Charlie had been in charge.

'We now not only know the names of the two victims,' she said, forcing herself to continue, 'but we've established a connection between them – that they both worked in Brunskill's Bakery.'

'Yes, you have to say that luck's certainly been on our side so far,' Walker commented.

But he didn't mean that at all, Paniatowski thought.

What he'd actually *wanted* to say was, 'If we have made a good start, then that's all down to me – because I'm the one who led us to Brunskill's Bakery in the first place.'

But he *couldn't* say that, could he? Not without reminding the others of the corners he'd cut, and the breaches of discipline that involved.

So all he'd done had been to draw the picture – and let Paniatowski and Beresford fill in the caption for themselves.

'Can I ask a question, ma'am?' the sergeant asked.

'You don't need to ask my permission,' Paniatowski told him. 'That's not how we work on this team – especially when we've left the office behind us and we're in the Drum.' She paused to light up a cigarette. 'So what was it you wanted to ask, Ted?'

'I was just wondering why we hadn't arrested the Polack yet,' Walker said. Then he remembered – belatedly – that *Paniatowski* wasn't exactly a Lancashire name, and quickly added, 'What I mean is, I was wondering why we hadn't arrested Mr Szym . . . Mr Szym . . . why we haven't arrested Stan.'

'Do you think he's our man?' Paniatowski asked.

'No question about it in my mind. After all, he is the husband, and he doesn't have an alibi for any of the time between leaving the bakery last night and turning up for work this morning.'

'No, he doesn't,' Paniatowski agreed.

'And, as you know yourself, ma'am, in cases like this, it's nearly always the husband who did it.'

That was true, Paniatowski thought – very depressing, but true enough nonetheless.

'Let's face it,' Walker continued, 'you've got to really hate somebody to cut their bloody hands off, haven't you – and where else do you find that kind of hatred but in marriages?'

'How do you see Tom Whittington's death fitting into the scheme of things?' Paniatowski wondered.

'Oh, that's an easy question to answer,' Walker said. 'He was Linda Thingy's lover.'

'Linda *Szymborska*'s lover.'

'That's right.'

And that, too, was probably all too depressingly true, Paniatowski thought. It was only too easy to see how Linda would have been attracted to Tom, who was – whichever way you looked at it – little more than a younger version of the man she'd chosen to marry.

'So it was a crime of passion?' Beresford asked.

'Absolutely,' Walker agreed.

'But crimes of passion are normally committed in the heat of the moment,' Beresford said.

'Ah, I see what you're getting at, Inspector,' Walker replied. 'Since we know that the note Stan sent to Traynor will have taken him some time to prepare, it can't have been in the heat of the moment at all.'

'Exactly,' Beresford agreed.

'So it's more of a *cold* passion we're talking about here.'

'A cold passion?'

'One that probably has much more to do with pride than it does with love.'

'That makes sense,' Beresford said, reluctantly. 'But what was the point of the pantomime *after* the murder?'

'What pantomime?'

'Why did he cut their hands off?'

'Maybe that's what they do in Poland when they find out that the wife's been having it off with somebody else.'

'What exactly do you think Poland is like?' Paniatowski asked, angry over what she saw as an attack on the reputation of a country she had not lived in since she was a small child. 'Do you see it as some kind of exotic Third World country, Sergeant?'

'Well, no, not exactly exotic,' Walker said.

'And why did he draw attention to what he'd done?' Beresford asked, like a dodgy plasterer hurriedly smoothing over the cracks. 'Why phone the press after he'd dumped the first hand, and send a note to Mike Traynor, telling him where the second hand was?'

Walker shrugged. 'Who knows? You have to remember that foreigners just don't *think* like us.' He realized that he'd put his foot in it again. 'I didn't mean you, ma'am. You're different, aren't you?'

'Am I?' Paniatowski asked.

'Of course you are. You've been living here for so long that you're *almost* English.'

'Stan Szymborska's been living here a long time as well,' Paniatowski pointed out. 'He was stationed here during the war, and *after* the war – weighed down by the medals he'd won as a fighter pilot – he came back.'

'I'm not disputing he did his bit in helping to defeat Hitler,' Walker conceded, 'but that doesn't mean he wasn't capable of killing his wife, does it?'

'No,' Paniatowski agreed, 'it doesn't.'

'And if you recall, ma'am, I did point out this morning, right after the first hand was discovered on the river bank, that I thought there was a *military* mind behind it.'

Yes, there was no disputing that, Paniatowski thought.

'If Linda Szymborska *was* having an affair with Tom Whittington,' she said aloud, 'then someone will have known about it, however careful they've been about not being seen together.' She turned to Beresford. 'And we need to find out *who* that someone is, Colin.'

'You're thinking they must have had a secret rendezvous somewhere?' Beresford asked.

'Exactly.'

'I'll have all the hotels in a twenty-mile radius checked out first thing in the morning.'

'In that case, you'll need this,' Paniatowski said, placing a plain brown envelope on the table.

'What is it?'

'A photograph of Brunskill Bakery's annual outing to Blackpool. I want you to have copies made and shown to all the hotel receptionists.'

Beresford studied the picture for a moment. 'Individual photographs would probably be better,' he said.

'But we haven't *got* individual photographs yet,' Paniatowski told him. 'In fact, given that Tom Whittington appears to have been both shy and a bit of loner, we don't even know if there *is* an individual photograph of him. Besides, look on the positive side of things.'

'The positive side?'

'If a receptionist at one of the hotels can pick out two people from a *group* – rather than from individual photographs – it's a pretty good indication that we're on solid ground.'

'You've got a point,' Beresford agreed.

'Another priority is to check out Tom Whittington's flat and Linda Szymborska's house,' Paniatowski said. 'I'll see to that myself. And we also need more information on Linda and Stan's marriage. If we ask him about it, I've no doubt he'll claim that it was a marriage made in heaven, and that – until last night – there was never a cross word between them. And Jenny Brunskill will probably tell us the same – because she's a loyal little thing. So what we need to do is talk to people who don't have quite as much invested in the perfect-marriage theory.'

'I'll handle that,' Walker offered.

Oh no, you won't, Paniatowski thought. I don't want you jumping into anything as delicate as that with your size-nine boots.

'There's another job I have in mind for you,' she said. 'I want you to be in charge of the search.'

'The search? For Linda Thingy's and Tom Whittington's bodies?'

'That's right.'

Walker sighed heavily. 'If that's what you really want, ma'am. You're the boss, and I'm here to do no more than your bidding.'

'But I take it from your sigh that you're not very enthusiastic about the idea yourself?'

'If I'm honest, ma'am, no, I'm not. As I see it, it'll be a waste of resources which could be more usefully employed elsewhere.'

'In what *way* will it be a waste of resources?'

'I'd have thought that was obvious.'

'Not to me, it isn't.'

'We have almost no chance of actually finding the bodies, because they could be anywhere in Lancashire by now – or maybe even further afield than that,' Walker said.

'They could be – but I don't think they are,' Paniatowski told him. 'It takes time to move bodies around, and given that both of the victims must have been killed after they left work—'

'It's true, they were, but that's more than twenty-four hours ago now,' Walker interrupted.

'. . . and that Stan, if he *is* the killer, has been in his office for most of the day, that time simply hasn't been available.'

'He could have shifted them overnight,' Walker said.

'Could he?' Paniatowski asked.

'I don't see why not.'

'If you'd just murdered two people, would you put their bodies – still leaking all kinds of unpleasant fluids – into the boot of your car and drive through central Lancashire in the dark with them?'

'Maybe.'

'I wouldn't, because even assuming you could *fit* both of them into the boot, think of the risk you'd be running. You might have an accident. People do – even careful drivers. You might be stopped by a random police roadside check – and there are plenty of those around, now that the traffic units are clamping down on drunk-driving.'

'That's true, but . . .'

'Our killer's planned out everything far too carefully to be willing to take that kind of chance. So I think the bodies are still here – somewhere in Whitebridge. And having heard my arguments, don't you agree, Sergeant?'

'It's possible,' Walker said reluctantly.

'And given the careful man we think he is, the odds are that he chose to commit the *actual murders* somewhere he knew he could safely leave the bodies once it was all over,' Paniatowski continued, 'because even moving them a *short* distance involves an element of risk.'

'Which means that you won't just be finding the bodies,' Beresford added supportively, 'you'll also be uncovering the scene of the crime – which is far more significant.'

'Because we all know that *however* careful they are, murderers almost always leave at least one clue at the crime scene,' Paniatowski concluded. 'Isn't that true, Inspector Beresford?'

'It is, ma'am,' Beresford concurred.

'And you'd agree with that, too, wouldn't you, Sergeant Walker?' Paniatowski asked.

'Yes, they usually do,' Walker conceded.

Paniatowski glanced down her watch, and then knocked back her remaining vodka.

'Right, that's it,' she said, standing up. 'We've done all we can for one day, we already know what we've all got to do tomorrow – and I'm going home.'

'There's just one more thing, ma'am,' Walker said.

'Yes?'

'You will remember that it was me who first suggested Stan as a suspect, won't you?'

'Oh yes,' Paniatowski promised. 'I'll remember.'

ELEVEN

Lily Perkins had been Louisa Paniatowski's nanny from the time Monika had adopted the four-year-old until her sixth birthday party, which was the occasion that the little girl chose for her historic announcement.

'I don't need a nanny any more,' she said, with deadly seriousness, after the candles had been blown out, the presents had all been opened and her guests were finally gone.

Paniatowski looked at the girl worriedly, and even the subject of the conversation herself, who was standing at the other end of the room, seemed somewhat concerned.

'You're not upset with Lily, are you?' Monika asked.

'Course not,' Louisa replied in an offhand way which indicated that she thought that was just the kind of stupid question you could expect from grown-ups. 'I love Lily – but I'm *too old* for a nanny now.'

Paniatowski relaxed. 'So you are,' she agreed. 'I'm sorry, Lily, but you're just going to have to go.'

'Go?' Louisa repeated, her lower lip already starting to tremble.

'Or how about this for an idea?' Paniatowski said quickly, before the tears could begin to fall. 'We give Lily the sack as your nanny, and we hire her to do our cooking and cleaning for us?'

'That *is* a good idea!' Louisa agreed, with obvious relief.

And so Nanny Lily had been banished from the house forever, and Housekeeper Lily had immediately taken her place.

Lily Perkins finished polishing the cooker hob and turned around to inspect the rest of the kitchen. She'd done a good job on it, she decided, a job that would satisfy even the most demanding of employers – so it would certainly more than satisfy Monika, who left half her mind in police headquarters and hardly even noticed what the house looked like.

There was the sound of a key turning in the front door, and

Lily stripped off her rubber gloves and made her way to the hall.

'Thank the Lord you're home,' she said, as her employer stepped across the threshold.

'Why? What's the matter? Is something wrong?' Paniatowski asked, with obvious alarm.

'Al-Jebra,' Lily said darkly.

'Al-Jebra?'

'You know! It's like doing normal sums, but you use letters instead of numbers.'

Algebra! Paniatowski thought, with relief.

'It was all right when Louisa was in primary school,' Lily continued. 'Then all I had to do was help her decide what crayon to use to colour things in with, and I was quite good at that. But I tell you, Monika, the stuff that she's bringing home now gives me a blinding headache. I've explained to her I'm well out of my depth – but, even so, I do so hate to disappoint the little lass.'

Paniatowski smiled. Lily was a real treasure, she thought, and though the woman might not be much in the brain stakes, she was full of common sense and had a heart as big as a double-decker bus.

Lily was already reaching for her coat from the hallway rack.

'If I rush, I'll just be in time for bingo,' she explained. 'To tell you the truth, I was fully resigned to missing it tonight.'

'I told you I'd be home by eight.'

'So you did.'

'Well, then?'

'But what with you starting a new job, and there being a new murder to investigate, I took all that with a pinch of salt.'

'I said I'd be home at eight and I *am* home at eight,' Paniatowski said defensively. 'I'm trying to turn over a new leaf.'

'Hmm,' Lily said, unimpressed. 'A new leaf, you say.'

'A new leaf,' Paniatowski repeated.

'Well, we'll see how long *that* lasts, won't we?' Lily asked sceptically, as she headed through the door.

Louisa was sitting at her desk, her pencil clutched tightly in her hand and her tongue pensively licking the corner of her mouth as she tried to penetrate the mysteries of Al-Jebra.

She really was a beautiful child, Paniatowski thought, watching her from the doorway – her skin was olive brown, her eyes were dark pools, and her hair was as jet-black as the coat of an Andalusian stallion.

She looked *so much* like her natural mother, and Paniatowski often found herself wondering just how much Louisa actually remembered of the woman who had been murdered by mistake.

She wondered, but she didn't ask, because since the child had never brought the subject up herself, she didn't feel brave enough to bring it up either.

Louisa sensed her presence, and looked up, smiling.

'You're home early, Mum,' she said.

'I'm trying to turn over a new leaf,' Paniatowski said, for the third time in as many minutes.

Louisa rolled her eyes in disbelief.

'Right,' she agreed. 'You're turning over a new leaf. And there really *is* a Father Christmas.'

'Don't make me feel guilty,' Paniatowski pleaded silently. 'Not tonight. Not on my first day in a job that I'm not even sure I can handle.'

'Cheer up, Mum,' Louisa said. 'It *was* only a joke, you know.'

Paniatowski forced herself to smile.

'I know that,' she said. 'Of course I do. So, tell me, how's the homework going?'

'It didn't make any sense at first, but I think I understand it now,' Louisa said seriously. 'You can check it, if you like.'

'I'd be more than delighted to,' Paniatowski said, pulling up a chair and sitting down beside her. 'In fact, I'd be honoured to.'

Louisa giggled. 'You do lay it on a bit thick sometimes, Mum, you know,' she said.

Yes, I suppose I do, Paniatowski thought. But that's because I'm trying to be both mother and father to you – and there are times when I think I'm not up to either job.

'By the way,' she said aloud, as she checked through Louisa's homework, 'I've got a message for you.'

'Who from?'

'Dr Shastri. She sends her love.'

Louisa looked puzzled. 'Do I know any Dr Shastri?' she asked.

'Of course you do. She's the police doctor.'

'Oh, Auntie Putibai!' said Louisa, as the penny dropped. 'Is that her name?'

'Didn't you *know* that's her name?' Louisa asked quizzically.

No, Paniatowski admitted, I didn't.

In fact, she'd be willing to bet that there was no one in the Mid-Lancs Constabulary who *did*.

She had worked with Dr Shastri for over ten years, and they had become friends – at least to the extent that the doctor's familiar-yet-distant attitude ever allowed anyone to become her friend – but Shastri had never volunteered her name, and, as time went by, it had grown increasingly difficult, not knowing it already, to ask what it was.

Besides, it didn't seem quite right that Shastri *should* have a first name, as if she was just an ordinary mortal like the rest of them.

The mention of 'Auntie' Putibai had got Louisa thinking of other pseudo-relatives.

'Do you know what?' she asked.

'What?'

'I do miss Uncle Charlie. I know he's only just gone, but I *already* miss him.'

And so do I, Paniatowski thought. So do I.

Detective Constable Jack Crane was sitting on a stool in his bedsit, with a well-thumbed book of Andrew Marvell's poems open on the small kitchen table in front of him.

As he read, his lips moved, not because they needed to, but because he liked the feel of them as they formed themselves around the words.

> An hundred years should go to praise
> Thine eyes, and on thy forehead gaze

Being both a university graduate *and* a policeman was not an easy furrow to plough, he thought with that small part of his mind which was still refusing to be absorbed by the poem.

His old university friends – still mindlessly quoting the words of Marx and Kropotkin, even three years after leaving their ivory tower – looked down on him as some kind of traitor.

And his colleagues in the Force? They didn't even *know* he'd been to university.

> For, lady, you deserve this state,
> Nor would I love at lower rate.

It had been a conscious decision on his part to keep his academic background a secret from the people he worked with, and it was one he had never regretted taking, because the simple fact was that most bobbies – and not just Neanderthals like Sergeant Walker – distrusted a man with an education. And when even a grammar-school education was looked on with suspicion, a man with a 1st Class Honours degree in English Literature would have to be a *complete* fool not to keep quiet about it.

While his lips continued to mouth Marvell's words, his mind turned to the murder investigation in which he, as a detective constable, would be playing a minor role.

He already knew much more about the case than most of the other junior offices involved in it, because, unlike them, he had been at the bakery with Walker, and so had learned the identity of the two victims.

He wondered if Linda Szymborska and Tom Whittington had been lovers, and decided that they probably had.

> The grave's a fine and private place,
> But none I think do there embrace.

And where were the bodies now?

Not in a fine and private place. That much was certain.

But wherever they were, he would be one of the people who would be looking for them.

'It's a crappy job, but you expect to be given crappy jobs when you're working for a crappy boss, don't you?' Detective Sergeant Walker had asked him over the phone.

But Crane didn't see it like that at all. Finding Linda and Tom might not provide the solution to the case, but there would at least be some satisfaction in knowing that he would be bringing two people who died for their love a little closer to their final dignified rest.

He slammed the book shut, suddenly angry with himself.

Two people who died for love!
He was just as bad as his old friends at university, he told himself. The only difference between them was that while they spouted *political* claptrap, *his* claptrap was romantic.
Died for love!
How did he know they had even *been* in love? What gave him the right to automatically think of them as 'star-crossed lovers'?

It could have been no more than *lust* that held them together – the hot and gasping coupling of two people who couldn't stand each other personally, but formed a perfect union in the bedroom.

'Maybe I shouldn't be a policeman at all,' he said, still angry with himself. 'Maybe I should catch tuberculosis and become a poet!'

'I'm not complaining about having to look after your mother, Colin,' said Mrs Taylor, in a voice thoroughly drenched with complaint, 'but I was under the impression that you were putting her into residential care today.'

'Yes, I was going to,' Colin Beresford admitted. 'But then something went wrong.'

'Went wrong? What do you mean?'

He couldn't bring himself to tell her that he'd forgotten – couldn't admit that, but for his oversight, Mrs Taylor would have had the afternoon and early evening to herself.

'I think it must have been some sort of administrative mistake at the home,' he said.

'Well, they'd better get it fixed soon, whatever it is,' Mrs Taylor told him, severely. 'Because looking after your mother is like looking after a child – *worse* than looking after a child.'

And as she spoke, she glanced across at the subject of this conversation, who was sitting on the edge of the sofa, drooling down her blouse and gazing blankly into space.

'I'll ring them first thing in the morning, and tell them to hurry the process along,' Beresford promised.

Mrs Taylor's eyes filled with suspicion. 'Are you sure you really *want* to put her in a home?' she said.

'She *needs* to be in a home,' Beresford replied.

'That's not what I asked you, Colin, and you know it. Do you *want* to put her in a home?'

Of course he didn't. She was his mother – or, at least, what was *left* of his mother. And despite all the evidence to the contrary, he kept hoping that if he tried just a little bit harder, she would show some signs of being her old self again.

'I know you never expected to be looking after her today, so I'm more than willing to pay you a bit more than usual,' Beresford said weakly.

'It's not a question of money, Colin,' Mrs Taylor said. 'It's a question of what looking after your mother *involves*. I'm not a trained nurse, you know. I used to be a hairdresser, which – unlike this one – is a very *clean* job.'

'I know,' Beresford said.

'And I'll tell you this much for nothing, Colin,' Mrs Beresford continued unrelentingly, 'I'm not prepared to keep being her nursemaid for much longer.'

'I know. I can understand that.'

'And it's not just me. Nobody on the street is willing to do it – however much you offer to pay them!'

Beresford turned towards his mother.

'Save yourself, Mother!' he pleaded silently. 'Do something – just *one* thing – to show that there's a little of your old spark left!'

His mother looked vaguely in his direction – though he had no evidence she was actually looking at *him* – and replied with a loud bodily noise.

'She's messed herself again,' Mrs Taylor said, not quite hiding her disgust. 'She's doing it more and more often now. She's got to go, Colin – there's no two ways about it.'

'Yes, she has,' Beresford said, as he felt a tear run down his cheek.

TWELVE

Sergeant Ted Walker looked, with disgust, around the tiny living room of his tiny rented flat.

It was a shithole, he told himself, not for the first time – a real honest-to-God *shithole*.

The wallpaper was faded and peeling off the wall, the carpet was frayed at the edges, the window leaked when it rained, the cold-water tap in the kitchen dripped persistently. And while he knew that all these things could be easily fixed, he didn't really see the point in bothering, because that would just make the place an *improved* shithole.

He had had a nice home once – a pleasant semi-detached in a quiet cul-de-sac. And then his wife – the ungrateful bitch that she was! – had run away with a door-to-door insurance salesman called Byron Jones.

A door-to-door insurance salesman! A *Welsh* door-to-door salesman!

Not a fighter pilot or a heavyweight boxer – that, at least, he could have understood – but a weedy little bastard who tramped the streets, collecting a pound here and one pound fifty there.

His mates – when he had still had some – had really been very good about the whole thing.

'You're better off without her,' they'd told him.

'She must have been mad to leave you for that little creep,' they'd said consolingly.

'Wouldn't be surprised if she didn't come crawling back on her hands and knees any day now,' they prophesied.

Yes, the men had been good.

But not the women!

Not the wives of those mates of his!

They had looked on him with contempt – which was bad.

Or as if he had become nothing more than a figure of fun – which was even worse.

He didn't know exactly *what* had brought about this change in their attitude.

Perhaps Doris had said something to them herself, before she ran away with the weed.

Perhaps they had needed no encouragement, but had cooked it up all by themselves – in their own nasty, poisonous little minds.

But however it had got there, he'd known what they were thinking – because he could see it in their eyes.

'You'd have thought he was quite good in bed, wouldn't you? But he can't have been, or she'd never have left him.'

'There mustn't be much lead in *his* pencil.'

'I doubt he can even get it up at all.'

'Well, you were all wrong, you bloody cows!' he shouted now, his voice bouncing off the walls of his shithole living room. 'You couldn't have been more wrong.'

Of course he could bloody get it up! Any time he wanted to! It was just that in the last couple of years with Doris, he hadn't got it up very often.

He shouldn't have been surprised that the women had turned on him like that, he told himself. What else should he have expected?

Because all women – women everywhere, and women throughout time – had always taken pleasure in crushing men's balls. They loved it. It was what they lived for.

And Chief Inspector Monika Paniatowski – with her tight figure and her superior bloody attitude – was a world-champion ball-crusher if he'd ever seen one.

But she'd taken on more than she could handle this time. He wasn't some whining little puppy, like Beresford, lying at her feet and yearning for a pat on the head or a few words of encouragement. He was a *real* man, and he wouldn't be pushed around.

Oh, yes, indeed, Doris would soon learn that it had been a big mistake to tangle with Sergeant Ted . . .

'I didn't mean Doris,' he told the wall. 'I meant Monika. That's who I meant – *bloody* Monika!'

It was almost midnight. Stan Szymborska was asleep, but not at rest. He twisted and turned, and sometimes he emitted a soft groan. If Linda had been there beside him, she would

have known what was happening – would have understood
that he was having *the* dream again.

But Linda was *not* there – nor ever would be again.

*In his dream, Stan is back in the prisoner-of-war camp. In
German, it is called a* stalag luft *– which means that it is
reserved exclusively for airmen – and it is divided into four
sections, one for the British, one for the Canadians, one for
the Americans and one for the Poles.*

*The British, Canadian and American prisoners are fed an
adequate if monotonous diet, and sometimes there is a Red
Cross parcel to add a little variety. They are allowed to
'associate in all kinds of ways', and so there are football
matches and educational lectures, bridge tournaments and
chess knockouts. And though these prisoners feel it is their
duty to escape – and will do so whenever the opportunity
presents itself – they are willing to admit their life in the
camp is boring, rather than difficult.*

*It is different for the Poles. They are regarded by the Nazis
– and especially by Colonel Schiller, the camp commandant
– as being less than human. Their section of the camp is
dirtier and meaner than the rest of the complex. Like all the
other prisoners, they are not – in accordance with the Geneva
Convention – made to work, but unlike the rest, they are not
allowed to play, either.*

*When the other prisoners are given potatoes, they are given
potato peelings. When the Red Cross parcels arrive, none of
them finds its way across the wire to the Polish section. And
when winter comes, and the other prisoners are issued with
fuel for the pot-bellied stoves which dominate their huts, the
Poles miss out again, though even if they* were *given fuel, they
would have nothing to burn it in – because they are not allowed
stoves, either.*

*Stan, who has been in this camp for six months, some-
times catches himself wondering whether conditions are any
better for the Poles in other camps. But when this happens,
he quickly tells himself that such speculation is pointless. It
doesn't matter how Poles are treated elsewhere. He must
deal with conditions as he finds them – and try to survive
if he can.*

Despite the difficulties – or perhaps because of them –

*morale is high in the Polish 'ghetto'. What little the prisoners
have, they share, and when one man is weakened through
illness, the others give him a portion of their own meagre
rations, in the hope that, with more food, he will become
strong again.*

*It is early in the seventh month of Stan's confinement that
things start to go wrong.*

*One night, Józef outlines a plan he has thought up for their
escape. It is a good plan, and it might just work, but it is
never implemented, because the next day the guards come and
take him away, and he is never seen again.*

*Another night, Piotr – drunk on the vodka they have
managed to produce from their potato peelings – amuses the
whole hut by telling scurrilous stories about Hitler's sexual
failure with women. And the next day, he is gone too.*

Stefan, the unofficial leader of the hut, calls a meeting.

'There is a traitor in our midst,' he says gravely.

*Most of the others nod in agreement, because it is a
conclusion they have already reached themselves.*

*Only Tadeujz – thin, nervous, Tadeujz, who has bulging
eyes like a wild hare's – seems uncertain.*

'We must find this traitor,' Stefan says.

'And how . . . how will we do that?' Tadeujz wonders.

*'He will not have betrayed us unless there was something
in it for him,' Stefan says. 'Like Judas in the Bible, he will
have been given his thirty pieces of silver. And he will have
stored his blood-money in this hut, for where else could he
have put it?'*

*'Perhaps they have not paid him at all,' Tadeujz says.
'Perhaps he will get his reward later.'*

*'Perhaps that is so,' Stefan agrees. 'But you will all consent
to a search of your personal possessions anyway.'*

*'Maybe the Germans used hidden microphones to hear what
we have been talking about,' Tadeujz says, almost frantic now.
'We should search the rafters for microphones.'*

*'Each man will submit to the search, while the others look
on,' Stefan says undeterred.*

'Not me!' Tadeujz protests. 'I refuse.'

'And we will start with Tadeujz,' Stefan says coldly.

They find half a chocolate bar hidden in his bedding.

It is not much in the way of evidence, but since none of the

*other fliers have seen a chocolate bar since before they were
shot down, it is more than enough to convict him in their eyes.*

*'It's been planted on me!' Tadeujz screams. 'It must have
been put there by the real spy.'*

*'So now you think there's a spy after all, do you?' Stefan
asks.*

'Yes! But it isn't me. I swear it isn't me.'

*Two of the other men grab his arms, pinioning him, while
a third wraps a gag around his mouth.*

*'Take him over to the centre of the hut,' Stefan says. 'I want
his hands on the table – palms down.'*

*'Palms down?' Stan repeats to himself. 'Why would he want
Tadeujz's hands on the table palms down?'*

'What are you going to do to him, Stefan?' he asks.

'Wait and see,' Stefan tells him.

*He goes over to the corner of the room, and carefully jiggles
one of the boards in the wall until it comes free.*

*Tadeujz, who has his back to these proceedings, attempts
to twist round to see what is going on, but the men who are
holding him do not allow him to.*

*Stefan puts his hand into the space behind the board – and
when he brings it out again, it is holding a hatchet.*

The black rat was six inches long, and two and half years old.
With luck on its side, it could live for another two and half
years, though – statistically – the chances were that it would
be dead within six months. The black rat knew none of this.
But it *did* know there were other living things – non-rats –
which had periodically posed a threat to its survival, and
were therefore to be avoided at all cost.

There were none of these non-rats in the old bakery which
the rat had chosen to make its home. Here it was safe, and if
it scurried across the floor, it was not through fear but simply
because that was what rats did.

Even so, it exercised caution, choosing to make a detour
around the large metal structure which human beings would
have recognized as a car – and not just any car, but an *E-type
Jag* – on the off-chance that something dangerous lurked
beneath the chassis.

The objects of the rat's journey were to be found just beyond
the car, lying on the ground. One of these objects was over

ten times the rodent's length, the other over eleven times. But the rat did not know – or care about – that, either.

What *did* interest it was that both objects were a source of easily obtainable food, and now that it had reached them it was working out – in its little ratty mind – which one it would choose.

Its decision to select the woman had nothing to do with her sex – of which, once again, the rodent was ignorant. Rather, it was motivated by ease. For while both corpses had stumps which had once been connected to hands, the woman also had extensive facial lacerations, which made harvesting the juicy meat so much simpler.

THIRTEEN

Annie looked smart in her nurse's uniform, Charlie Woodend thought, gazing fondly at her across the breakfast table.

Very smart – and *very* competent.

And caring, too. She definitely looked *caring*.

She must surely be an inspiration to her fellow nurses, and it was beyond doubt that her patients would think she was wonderful and all the young doctors would immediately fall in love with her.

That was his opinion, at any rate – and his opinion should count for something, because, having spent nearly thirty years in the Police Force, he had learned how to become almost *frighteningly* objective.

'You're starin' at me, Dad,' Annie said accusingly. 'An' I bet you've not heard a word I said.'

'I heard it all,' Woodend replied indignantly, perhaps half a second before he realized that his daughter was quite right, and – indulgent father that he was – he had no idea what she'd been talking about.

'You heard it all?' Annie repeated sceptically.

'Definitely,' Woodend replied, 'but could you be just a *little* indulgent to your poor old father for once, an' say it again?'

'I've pulled a double shift,' Annie said. 'I didn't want to – what with you only being here for a few days an' all – but we're very short-handed in the hospital at the moment, so I couldn't really turn it down. Will you an' Mum be all right on your own?'

'We'll be fine,' Woodend assured her.

Annie seemed far from convinced. 'This isn't Whitebridge, you know,' she said. 'It's *London* – the big city!'

Woodend smiled. Why did the young think that only *they* could handle things? he wondered. What did they think their parents had been doing before they were born, if not experiencing life?

'I was poundin' the streets of this city an' collarin' villains

when you were still in nappies,' he said. 'An' by the time you
started primary school, I knew the East End like the back of
my hand.'

Now I'm starting to sound like a borin' old fart, he thought.
An' I've only been *retired* for two days!

'I'll get back as soon as I can,' Annie promised, heading
for the door. She turned again, before stepping out into the
corridor. 'There's a newspaper on the table, if you want to
read it.'

'Thanks, love,' Woodend said – but she'd already gone.

The newspaper was lying face down, and so it was the back
page – the sports results – which he read first.

Whitebridge Rovers were doing very well, he noted.

Well, that was just typical of them, wasn't it? For over a
decade he'd faithfully turned out every other Saturday –
investigations allowing – to watch them get thrashed by the
visiting team. And now, when he was finally moving away,
they'd suddenly decided to improve!

He flipped the newspaper over, and saw the screaming headline of the front page.

Hands of Horror!

There was a further, smaller headline beneath it.

Terror stalks Whitebridge
By Mike Traynor, Special Correspondent

'Put it down, Charlie,' he told himself.

But even as the thought was crossing his mind, he was
beginning to scan the article.

'I thought I'd hidden that,' he heard his wife say, from the
bathroom doorway. 'Where did you get it from?'

'Annie gave it to me.'

'Well, obviously I didn't hide it well *enough*,' Joan said.
'And now, I suppose, the damage has already been done.'

'There's been a particularly nasty murder back home,' he
said. '*Two* nasty murders, as a matter of fact.'

'Yes, the damage has been done,' Joan confirmed. 'I *know*
there've been two murders, Charlie. That's *why* I hid the
paper.'

'An' Monika's been given the case.'

'Well, why shouldn't she have been? She *is* a chief inspector now, if you remember.'

'I do remember,' Woodend agreed. 'The thing is, it says here that she's got DS Walker for a bagman.'

'So what?'

'Well, he's not a bad bobby, in his own way, but he's what you might call a male chauvinist pig.'

Joan laughed. 'Male chauvinist pig?' she repeated. 'You want to be careful, Charlie – you're starting to sound frighteningly modern.'

'But you get the point, don't you?' Woodend asked earnestly. 'He's simply not the man Monika needs at the moment.'

'Don't underestimate her,' Joan warned. 'She's a clever lass, and she'll soon learn how to handle him.'

'I think I'd better just give her a quick call,' Woodend said, trying to sound casual.

'You'll do no such thing, Charlie Woodend,' Joan said firmly.

'She might want a bit of advice.'

'Well, if she does – an' I do say *if* – she's got the number, an' she only has to ring you.'

'But she might feel a bit awkward about doin' that.'

'An' how awkward do you think she'll be likely to feel if you ring her up *without* her askin' you to? If I was in her shoes, *I'd* take that as a sign that you'd got no confidence in me. An' that's the very last thing that Monika needs to feel at this moment.'

His wife was right, he thought. He *hated* the fact that she was right – but she was.

'She'll do a good job,' he said. 'Why wouldn't she? I've taught her all I know.'

'Well, there you are, then! Happy now?'

'Yes.'

But he wasn't.

In three days' time he would be starting his new life in Spain, and could finally leave Whitebridge CID behind him. But he hadn't quite left it behind *yet*, and he wasn't sure what troubled him more – the thought that Monika needed his help and wasn't getting it, or the possibility that she didn't need his help *at all*.

* * *

Sid Roberts was sitting by himself in the police canteen, tucking into one of those northern animal-fat-based breakfasts which – while they may well be bad for the heart – are scientifically proved to provide an excellent stomach lining for any man contemplating sinking a few pints of best bitter later in the day.

Roberts was pushing sixty. He had a shock of white hair, and a complexion which looked as if it had been constructed out of sandpaper. There was a popular saying around the HQ that he'd been a uniformed sergeant since Adam was a lad. But Monika Paniatowski, watching him from the doorway, didn't buy that at all. If Roberts had been on foot patrol in the Garden of Eden, in her opinion, Adam would have been given a clip round the ear and sent on his way – and the forbidden fruit would have stayed on the tree, where it belonged.

Still, there was no disputing the fact that Sid had been there a long time, and there was not a single member of the Whitebridge force who could remember a time when he *hadn't* had those three stripes stitched on his sleeve.

Several times, over the years, his superiors had suggested he apply for a promotion, but he'd always rejected the idea. He liked being a sergeant. He liked the perspective on his home town that the rank gave him. And while life might be said to be passing him by, it certainly didn't do so without him noticing every little detail of it.

Paniatowski walked over to Roberts' table. 'Mind if I take a seat, Sid?' she asked.

Roberts looked up from his eggs and fried bread. 'You're more than welcome, ma'am.'

'Ma'am?' Paniatowski said, with a smile on her lips.

'Ma'am,' Roberts repeated.

'Why don't you call me Monika, just like you did back when you were training me up?' Paniatowski suggested.

Sid Roberts shook his head. 'Nay, lass, that wouldn't be right. You're a detective chief inspector now, an' the proper respect for rank is one of the cornerstones of good policin'.'

Paniatowski grinned. 'You do know you're talking complete bollocks, don't you, Sid?' she asked.

'Everybody talks *a bit* of bollocks now and again, ma'am,' Roberts replied mildly.

'Yes, they do,' Paniatowski agreed. 'But the difference between you and most of the others is they don't *realize* they're doing it, and you do. Proper respect for rank! Cornerstones of policing! Bollocks of the first order! Remember, Sid, I've worked with you. I've watched you put *chief superintendents* in their place. I've seen them walk away from an encounter with you with their heads bowed, feeling as if they were about five years old.'

'I think you must be confusin' me with somebody else,' Roberts said seriously, though there was laughter in his eyes. 'So what can I do for you this mornin', ma'am?'

'Tell me about the Brunskill family.'

'The ones who own the bakery?'

'That's right.'

'How far do you want me to go back?'

'Begin with the father.'

Roberts nodded. 'The Brunskill family fortune started, like most family fortunes in this town, with the mills.'

'He was a mill worker?'

'Nay, lass, Seth Brunskill was a pie maker, but his *business* was with the mill workers. At first, when he didn't have a pot to piss in, he used to load an old hand-barrow up with pies and sell them at the mill gates at dinner time. He did so well that eventually he could afford to buy himself a horse an' cart, an' after that he splashed out on a motor vehicle.'

'And from then on, the business went from strength to strength,' Paniatowski said.

'Who's tellin' this story, ma'am – me or you?' Roberts asked sharply.

'Sorry,' Paniatowski said, bowing her head contritely.

'He got to the point – I think it must have been somewhere around 1953 – when he could afford to employ other people to do his sellin' for him. An' it was about that time, too, that his wife topped herself.'

'She committed suicide?'

'That's right.'

'Does anyone know why?'

'Not officially, but if you was to ask me to guess, I'd say it was because livin' with a mean-spirited bastard like Seth Brunskill had become such a strain that she simply didn't feel she could carry on any longer.'

'It must have devastated her daughters.'

'I very much doubt it. They took their lead from the way their father behaved, you see, and *he* regarded his wife as no more than a redundant baby-making machine.' Roberts took a sip of his tea. 'Now where was I? Oh yes, after he'd buried his wife, one the first things he did was to buy his new bakery . . .'

'The one Brunskill's have now?'

'Nay, lass, that's the *new* new bakery. The one I'm talkin' about is down on Brewer's Street. Anyway, for the next few years, it didn't seem he could put a foot wrong, but then the business started to go into decline.'

'Why?'

'Because Seth, bein' the man he was, refused to move with the times. There were no such things as supermarkets when he started out, you have to understand. Everybody went to the corner shop, because there was no choice in the matter. But by the early sixties, the supermarkets were everywhere, an' doin' big business. And Seth just wouldn't acknowledge that. People tried to tell him he had to change, but nobody ever had a higher opinion of Seth than he had of himself, an' he simply wouldn't listen. By the time he died, which will have been six years ago now, the bakery was totterin' on the edge of bankruptcy.'

'And then his daughters took over,' Paniatowski said.

'An' then his daughters took over,' Roberts agreed. 'They'd both been workin' in the bakery since they'd left school – Seth wouldn't have had it any other way – but up until the time he died, he'd been the *only one* takin' the decisions. Once he'd gone, of course, everything was different. The Brewer's Street premises were too small to run a modern bakery from, an' everybody but Seth had known that for a long time. So, within weeks, the bakery had moved to a new site. It cost an arm an' a leg, and the two sisters were up to their ears in debt, but gradually the business began to pick up again, an' now it's probably as strong as it ever was.'

'Tell me about Linda's husband,' Paniatowski suggested.

'Polish Stan – the delivery man?'

'What?'

'That's what they used to call him in the late forties, when he was runnin' his delivery service. An' there's another real success story for you. He started out with one clapped-out old van, doin' deliveries for anybody who wanted somethin' deliverin' – a sort of tramp steamer on wheels. He used to work every hour God sent. But it paid off. He bought another van, then another, an' by the time he sold his company he had quite a fleet.'

'So if he was doing so well with the delivery service, why did he sell the company?'

'He did it because he needed the money to buy his way into Brunskill's Bakery.'

'This was after Seth died?'

'No, it was a couple of years before.'

'So why did he want to buy into what, according to you, was a failing business? Did he do it to please his wife?'

'Linda *wasn't* his wife then. He didn't marry her until the year after Seth had popped his clogs.'

'But they'd been going out together for a while before that?'

'They may have been, but if they were, they kept it very quiet.'

'Why?'

'Seth Brunskill would never have approved of one of his daughters marrying a foreigner. To be honest with you, ma'am, I don't think he'd have approved of them marryin' anybody at all. They belonged to him, you see – just as much as the bakery did.'

'He really doesn't sound like a very nice man,' Paniatowski said.

'He wasn't. He was what nowadays you might call a "domestic tyrant" – which is just a fancy way of saying "bully".'

'Do you know anything about a man called Tom Whittington?' Paniatowski asked.

'Tom Whittington,' Roberts repeated, running the name around his filing cabinet of a head. 'I think I collared him about twenty years ago for nickin' a car. But, as far as I know, he's kept his nose clean since then. He works at the bakery, too, doesn't he?'

Well, he did, Paniatowski thought.

'That's right,' she confirmed. 'Is there no more you can tell me about him, Sid?'

'Not a dicky-bird.'

'You wouldn't, for example, know if he'd been having an affair with a married woman?'

Roberts smiled. 'They say I know a hell of lot, ma'am . . .'

'And so you do,' Paniatowski said.

'An' so I do,' Roberts agreed. 'But even *I* don't know everythin'.'

FOURTEEN

When Jack Crane had set out from home that morning, it had been with a determination to leave the fanciful poet back in the bedsit and bring only the hard-bitten *Detective Constable* Crane to police headquarters with him. And, so far, it was working out very well, he thought, as he sat facing DS Walker across a table at the opposite end of the police canteen to where Monika Paniatowski was having her chat with Sid Roberts. So far, he'd not been able to detect even a hint of a university man in himself.

A folded map of Whitebridge lay tantalizingly on the table between them. Crane's fingers just itched to open it up, but it was Walker's map, and the sergeant was showing no inclination to look at it yet. In fact, though Walker's body was in the room, his mind seemed to be wandering freely, and – if the expression on his face was anything to go by – it was not a pleasant wander at all.

Walker took a sip of his tea, then a puff of his cigarette, and Crane – who was finding the waiting almost unbearable – decided to throw caution to the wind.

'So where do you want us to start looking, Sarge?' the detective constable asked.

Walker took another sip of his tea, then placed his mug down squarely in the centre of the map.

'Well, aren't you bright-eyed and bushy-tailed this morning?' he asked sourly. 'Just can't wait to get stuck into the job, can you?'

There was really no satisfactory answer to that, Crane thought, and so he decided to say nothing at all.

'She's going about it in entirely the wrong way, you know,' Walker said, not even bothering to specify who 'she' was.

'Is she, Sarge?'

'Yes, she most certainly is. What she wants us to do is to find the bodies. Right?'

'Right.'

'So the easiest way to give her what she wants – the logical

way – is to pull Stan What's-'is-name in for questioning, and
sweat it out of him. But ma'am isn't having any of that. Ma'am
doesn't *want* to do it the easy way.'

'There's no guarantee that even if we did pull Szymborska
in, he'd—' Crane began.

'And, of course, sending us off on a wild-goose chase has
another advantage for ma'am,' Walker interrupted him. 'It's
a way of keeping me out of her hair while she follows up
the more *promising* leads – which she only has because *I*
identified the bodies for her.'

It was true that the stunt Walker had pulled with the fingerprints had meant they'd been able to quickly identify Tom
Whittington, Crane thought. But the examination of the hand
had also revealed baking powder under the fingernails, so it
was more than likely the DCI would have discovered his identity herself by the end of the day. And it had been Paniatowski,
not Walker, who had worked out that the woman's hand
belonged to Linda.

So, all in all, the sergeant was being rather unfair – but
only a fool would think to point that out.

'I'm not trying to be funny, but I think you're being overly
pessimistic, Sarge,' Crane said.

'You think I'm being *what*?'

Mistake! The university man had not been left at home at
all! Instead, he found a way to smuggle himself on to the
journey to work. And now, once at work, he was recklessly
sticking his bloody head above the parapet.

'I think there's a very good chance that, if we approached
the job properly, we *actually* could find the bodies,' Crane said.

'Oh, do you?' Walker said. 'And would you mind explaining
to your poor thick old sergeant just *how* we "approach the
job properly"?'

'Well, we can start by deciding which areas we can *rule
out* of the search,' Crane suggested.

'And how would we do that?'

'We're agreed that the murderer wouldn't want an audience
while he was chopping off the hands, aren't we?'

'No, I'm not sure that we are,' Walker said.

'Aren't you?' Crane asked, incredulously.

'No, I'm not. *I* think that *he* probably thought that the more
folk there, the merrier it would be. He probably even sold

tickets for it.' The sergeant grimaced. '*Of course* he wouldn't want a bloody audience! Any idiot knows that.'

'What he'll actually have wanted is to commit the murders as far away from any other people as possible,' Crane pressed on. 'So we can rule out all areas where there's a heavy population density.'

'A heavy population density?' Walker repeated. 'Do you mean somewhere where there's a lot of people?'

'That's right.'

'So why didn't you just bloody say so?'

'Housing estates are out,' Crane ploughed on. 'So are public places like bus stations, which might have been deserted at the time of the murders, but certainly wouldn't have been the morning after. The same is true of working factories. So what are we left with?'

'You tell me,' Walker said.

'*Abandoned* housing and *derelict* factories.'

'Brilliant!' Walker said.

'Do you really think so, Sarge?' Crane asked

And the moment the words had left his mouth, he knew he'd made another mistake.

'Brilliantly *bleeding obvious*,' Walker said. 'Do you really think that none of that had crossed my mind?'

'Well, no, Sarge, I . . .'

'But what's *also* crossed my poor, tired mind is that there are thousands of abandoned houses and hundreds of derelict factories in this dump of a town that we call home, so we could be searching for ever and *still* never find what we were looking for.'

Walker moved his mug to the corner of the table, opened the map and spread it out.

Crane saw, to his chagrin, that the sergeant's mind had not only been working on the same lines as his, but that Walker had actually marked on the map most of the areas that he would have marked himself.

Chagrin! he thought. That's another of those words I should have left at home.

'There'll be eight of you on the job,' Walker said, 'and so I've decided to divide you into four teams of two, each with its own sector.' He paused. 'Do you like that word, DC Crane? *Sector*?'

'Yes, Sarge, I . . .'

'It's very modern, isn't it? Very up-to-the-minute policing. You must have been surprised to hear it come out of *my* mouth.'

'Look, we seem to have got off on the wrong foot this morning, and if that's my fault, I'm very sorry,' Crane said.

'The search will start with the most likely places first,' Walker said, ignoring him. 'And them likely places will be here,' he stabbed his finger at the map, 'here, here and here.'

'You've err . . . not included Brewer's Street in any of the sectors you've marked,' Crane pointed out hesitantly.

'And I suppose you think that I *should* have included it, do you?' Walker growled.

'Well, yes, Sarge, I do. You see, historically, Brewer's Street's connected to the Brunskill family, and that might mean—'

'It's connected *historically*, is it!' Walker asked. 'How? Did Brunskill the Conqueror land his Viking boats on Brewer's Street? Did Henry the Eighth Brunskill have one of his wives' head cut off there?'

'I only meant that Brunskill's old bakery was on Brewer's Street,' Crane said, in a subdued voice.

'So what?'

'So it's home ground to them. And when you're thinking about doing something that will completely shake up your world, you often feel more confident if you can do it on ho—'

'Tell me, Detective Constable Crane, if you were going to commit a murder, would you do it in your own front parlour?' Walker asked, shaking his head in disgust as he spoke.

'Well, no,' Crane admitted.

'Then maybe you'd do it in the front parlour of the house that you *used* to live in?'

'No, not that, either.'

'Why not?'

'Because there'd be a . . . a . . .'

'A direct link to you?'

'Yes.'

'And that's just how the Polack's mind will have been working. Nobody shits in their own backyard unless they're complete idiots – and Stan, for all he might be a murderous bastard, is far from being that.'

'I suppose you might have a point, Sarge,' Crane conceded.

'Thank you,' Walker said. 'You don't know what it means for an old, worn-out bobby like me to hear a few words of faint praise from a bright young feller such as yourself.'

I've put my foot in it *again*, Crane thought.

'I didn't mean . . .' he said.

'Of course, if DCI sodding Paniatowski had said the same thing, you'd think she was a bloody genius.'

'I really never meant to offend you, Sarge,' Crane said weakly.

'Then you'd better pick your words more carefully in future,' Walker advised him. 'Now are you quite clear about how this operation will be run, because you're the one who'll be running it.'

'Me!' Crane exclaimed.

'You,' Walker agreed.

'But shouldn't you be the one who's actually coordinating the whole thing, Sarge?'

'In theory, yes, I should,' Walker agreed. 'But rather than wasting *my* time by chasing after some will-o'-the-wisp, I intend to make much better use of it.'

'Doing what?'

'Following up some of the juicier leads that ma'am's been trying to snatch away from me.'

Colin Beresford looked down from the podium at his team. There wasn't one of them over twenty-four, he thought.

Or twenty-five, max.

They said you were getting old when policemen started to look younger, but at least most people only saw younger policemen now and again, whereas he was *surrounded* by the buggers.

He turned towards the map which had been pinned onto the blackboard beside him.

'We'll be checking out all hotels, pubs with accommodation and bed-and-breakfast establishments in central Lancashire,' he said. 'But that's a massive job, as you'll appreciate, so we'll be starting with the places we're most likely to get a result – which, in this case, are the country pubs. Do any of you know *why* they're the most likely?'

One of the constables raised his hand in the air.

Jesus! Beresford thought. Does he think he's back in school or something? And *if* he does, is that because – God help me – I sound so much like a bloody teacher?

'When I've asked a question like that, there's no need to ask my permission to answer it,' he said. 'Got that?'

'Yes, sir,' the constable replied. 'We'll be checking the country pubs first because that's where people normally go for dirty weekends.'

He sounded like an authority on the subject, Beresford thought, and wondered whether he really was, or if he was still a virgin.

Then he wondered how his new team would react if they knew *he* was still a virgin himself.

But enough of thinking!

'Yes, it's where people *do* normally go for dirty weekends,' he said. 'The more off the beaten track these places are, the less likely the couple using them are to run into anybody they know.' He grinned. 'Not that that always works out as planned, by any means.'

The constables laughed, and he realized that they probably thought he was talking from personal experience.

Well, he certainly hadn't meant to give that impression, had he? But there was nothing he could do about it now.

'The only photograph we have for you to show around at the moment is of the Brunskill's works outing to Blackpool,' he continued, holding the photograph up. 'You are to ask the people you're interviewing if they recognize anybody on it. What you are *not* to do – under any circumstances – is to guide your potential witnesses in any way. If they can pick out your targets, that's great. If they can't pick them out, leave it at that.'

'Maybe the people who we show the picture to will *need* a little help from us, sir,' one of constables said.

'You've not been in plain clothes for very long, have you, son?' Beresford asked.

And he was thinking, I can't believe I said that. I can't believe I actually called him *son*!

'No, sir, I haven't,' the constable admitted.

'Well, when you've had a little more experience, you'll see the sense in what I'm saying. We have to think well beyond the investigation – to the trial. We have to think about how the defence brief is likely to treat your eye witness. "Did you recognize the man in the photograph immediately?" he'll ask. "Well, no, not immediately," the witness will admit. "So when *did* you recognize him?" "When the detective asked me if I was *sure* I hadn't seen him." You get the point?'

The assembled constables nodded. And not *just* nodded – nodded enthusiastically, as if they really appreciated what he'd said.

Bloody hell, I've become a Wise Man, Beresford thought. When did *that* happen?

'There's one more thing before I send you out,' he said. 'I'm not going to tell you not to drink on the job, because we all do. It's one of the perks of not being in uniform any more.'

The constables laughed again. This time, he'd have been disappointed if they hadn't.

'But I want you to watch how *much* you drink,' he warned. 'You'll be on licensed premises for most of the day, and getting pissed without even noticing you're doing it will be a doddle. But if you *do* get pissed, that's it, as far as I'm concerned. No warnings! No second chances! You'll spend the rest of your careers with the Mid-Lancs Constabulary shuffling papers around in one of the offices. Believe me, you don't want that.'

And from the looks on their faces, it was clear that they *did* believe him.

So there he stood – a man who the men serving under him believed in; a man whose advice they took, and maybe even noted down.

And a man who'd still done nothing about getting his mother into residential care, he reminded himself.

FIFTEEN

Paniatowski looked up at Chorley Court from the car park beside it – and could not stop herself from shuddering.

The Court was a mile from the town centre, and had been Whitebridge's first experiment in private high-rise living. But it had been a tentative experiment at best, the architects and engineers having lost their nerve at the last minute and deciding that instead of the eighteen storeys planned, they would cap it at twelve.

Thus, they were left with a building which, if it had been located in central Manchester, would have been regarded as little more than a pipsqueak. But this was *not* Manchester, thriving commercial capital of the north-west. This was Whitebridge, a declining mill town where previously the tallest structures had been the grim factory chimneys, and, for that reason alone, Chorley Court rapidly became something of a local landmark, which was pointed out to visitors with a good deal of civic pride.

Paniatowski had in lived in the Court herself, but had moved out eight years earlier, when Louisa had come into her life – when Louisa had *rescued* her life – and had never been back since.

She had no happy memories of the place. She had not really known any of the other owners, nor – she suspected – had they known each other. It had never been a community, in any sense of the word, but had served its residents in much the same way as the cave had served Stone Age man – by providing them with a reasonably secure bolthole in which to sleep at night and lick their wounds.

Now, looking up at the building, she was surprised to discover that she could no longer be sure which of these flats had been hers.

She lit a cigarette and began to walk across the forecourt towards the foyer. And as she walked, she found herself wishing that Tom Whittington had used the loan which

Brunskill's Bakery had counter-signed to buy a flat somewhere with less painful memories attached to it.

She found the porter/caretaker behind his desk in the lobby.
He was a man in his early sixties. His false teeth were not
quite the right size for his mouth, and though his uniform
jacket was quite presentable, the holed grey cardigan he wore
under it somewhat marred the effect.

Paniatowski told him what she wanted, and he led her to
the back of the foyer, where the lifts were located.

As he stabbed at a button to summon one, Paniatowski said,
'I think I'll take the stairs instead.'

The porter/caretaker sniffed disapprovingly. 'The flat you
want is on the ninth floor,' he pointed out.

'I don't mind,' Paniatowski replied. 'I could use the exercise.'

But that wasn't it at all, she told herself.

She wasn't going to take the stairs for the benefit of her
calf muscles. She was doing it order to postpone the moment
when she finally arrived at Tom Whittington's door.

'Where do you want me to start?' DC Mellor asked DC Crane,
as they stood facing the row of derelict terraced houses which
had once been a living, breathing road called Paradise Street.

'You could start at this end, and I could start at the other,
and we'll meet in the middle,' Crane said. 'How does that
sound to you?'

'Fine,' Mellor said easily. 'Whatever you want. You're the
boss.'

The words echoed in Crane's ears as he walked along the road.
'You're the boss.'

And he supposed that, given Walker's abdication of his
responsibilities, that was exactly what he was.

It felt strange to be the senior member of the team, he
thought – strange, but far from unpleasant.

The closer he got to the far end of the street, the more he
found himself dwelling on what his sergeant had said earlier.

'You don't shit in your own backyard,' Walker had
proclaimed, with absolute certainty.

It had sounded convincing at the time, but thinking about
it now, Crane was not quite so persuaded.

Most murders *did* happen in a domestic setting, he told
himself, and while the old bakery couldn't be considered in

any way domestic, it was at least *familiar territory* to both
the two victims and their probable murderer.

He decided to run a couple of possible scenarios through
his mind.

*Stan suggests that he and Linda should visit the old bakery.
Linda doesn't really see why he should want to do this, but
he is so insistent that she decides to humour him.*

*Once they are inside, Stan looks around him and says, 'This
is where we first got to know each other. This is where we
first fell in love. Those were happy days, weren't they?'*

'Yes,' his wife admits. 'They were.'

*'There was a romance about this old place, which the new
bakery – with all its cleanliness and efficiency – can never
recapture,' Stan continues.*

*And Linda, who is starting to be concerned now – who may
even have guessed what is coming next – tries to cool things
down by saying, 'Oh, I don't know about that. We certainly
produce a lot more bread at the new place than we ever could
have here.'*

*But Stan is not to be put off. 'That happiness we knew is
still in the air here,' he says. 'Do you think that if we take
really deep breaths, we can draw that happiness into our lungs?
Do you think that we can recapture what we once had?'*

*'I don't know what you're talking about,' Linda says – but
she does, and now she is quite worried.*

*'I want you to give up Tom Whittington,' Stan says, finally
coming out into the open. 'Will you do that for me?'*

*Worry has become fear, and Linda is tempted to say that
yes, she will give up Tom and come back to him. But what
would be the point of that? It would be a lie. And Stan would
know that it was a lie.*

*'I can't give him up,' she says. 'It's not you I love any longer
– it's him.'*

And then she sees the hatchet in Stan's hand!

Too fanciful! Crane told himself, in disgust.

Far too fanciful!

The poet raising his ugly head again, and squeezing the
policeman out of the picture completely.

Well, how about something much more down-to-earth?

*Linda and Tom are mad for each other, burned up with a
passion they have no way of controlling. The occasional night*

in a hotel is not enough for them. The odd afternoon session,
when Stan is out of town, does not even begin to slake their
raging thirst.

So where can they go when they can stand the pressure no
longer? Where they can be absolutely sure they will not be
interrupted?

They remember they still have a key to the old bakery, and
one night Tom sneaks a mattress into it. And it is while they
are lying back on this mattress, exhausted from their love-
making, that they realize that they are not alone – that hovering
over them is a man with a meat cleaver.

Better, Crane decided, but though this scenario was grit-
tier, there was still a fancifulness lying among the grit.

So perhaps Sergeant Walker – the experienced bobby, the
veteran police officer – had been right all along. Perhaps the
last place you *would* expect to undercover the scene of this
particular crime was in the old bakery.

But just say he was *wrong*! Just think what a feather in his
cap it would be for the young detective constable who was
proved to be *right*!

And the beauty of it was that *whichever* way it turned out,
he personally couldn't lose, Crane thought. If the bakery was
the place where the crime had been committed, he could shout
it from the rooftops. If it wasn't, all he had to do was keep quiet,
and no one would ever know how just *how* fanciful he'd been.

He would definitely go to the old bakery, he decided. He
would go first thing the following morning, before the proper
search – the official search – had even begun again.

The porter/caretaker was waiting for Monika Paniatowski at
Tom Whittington's front door, and was breathing as heavily
as if *he*'d been the one who'd walked up nine flights of stairs.

'You didn't mention *why* you wanted to look around the
flat?' he said, with artful casualness.

So he had not yet made the connection between the second
severed hand and the visit by the police, Paniatowski thought.
But he probably would soon – and even if he didn't, all would
become clear to everyone when she gave her late-afternoon
press conference.

She had thought long and hard before taking the decision
to release the names. She didn't want to do it – it was too

early in the drama to drench the stage with light – but she had reluctantly decided that she had no choice.

The problem was Jenny Brunskill. She, like her brother-in-law, had promised to say nothing, but Paniatowski had little confidence in that promise.

It would not have been more than an hour, she guessed, before Jenny Brunskill had rung a friend, and – after swearing her to secrecy – had tearfully poured out the whole tragic tale. And the friend, in turn, would have rung another friend and extracted the same promise – so that already, even this early in the morning, there were probably at least a score of people who already knew that Linda Szymborska had been murdered.

And the process would both escalate and mutate. Jenny's account would grow in the telling, and by the time a hundred people got to hear it (and that would not take *too* long), it would be distorted beyond belief.

Better to nip it in the bud, then – even if that did make investigating the case more difficult.

The caretaker coughed. 'I said, you didn't mention why you wanted to look round the flat,' he repeated.

'No, I didn't,' Paniatowski agreed. 'If I remember rightly, all I *did* do was show you the warrant which gives me the right to carry out the search.'

The caretaker rubbed his nose pensively. 'Mr Whittington isn't in any sort of trouble, is he?' he persisted.

'Can you think of any particular reason why he *might* be?' Paniatowski countered.

The caretaker shrugged to indicate that he couldn't, and opened the door. 'Want me to come in with you?' he asked hopefully.

'I can manage.'

'I can show you how things work.'

'I'm searching the place – not thinking of buying it.'

'Only trying to be helpful,' the caretaker grumbled.

Then he turned and walked reluctantly back to the lift.

This was like taking a journey back in time, Paniatowski thought, as she stepped into Tom Whittington's hallway – and it was not a particularly pleasant journey, at that.

Her first sight of the lounge came as a shock. She had expected it to have the same basic layout as her old flat – and so it did – but what she had not expected was how much the furnishings would remind her of the furnishings she had once owned.

She wondered why it should seem so familiar, when, to all intents and purposes, it was not the same at all.

The three-piece suite, for example, was of an entirely different colour and material to hers.

The coffee table had a tiled surface, instead of wood veneer. And yet . . .

And yet she still could not overcome the strong feeling of eerie familiarity.

And suddenly, she thought she had it! It was that the furniture was there to simply fulfil a function – and nothing more.

Tom Whittington hadn't agonized over which three-piece suite would best express his personality. He had needed somewhere to sit, and so he had gone down to the nearest furniture shop and had bought whatever it had in stock at the price he was prepared to pay.

Just as she had done herself!

She crossed the room to the kitchen, which was tucked away in a corner. When she'd lived in the Court, she had rarely cooked. And why should she have? What would have been the point of lavishing time and effort on a meal she would end up eating alone?

She opened one of the cupboards and peered inside. There were only a few pans, and even they looked as if they had hardly ever been used. She opened the fridge and found only milk and orange juice.

It was already becoming clear that Tom Whittington's attitude to catering was virtually identical to her own. In fact, she thought, they seemed alike in so many ways.

She wondered if he had been as lonely as she had – if he had thrown himself into his work because it was the only thing which gave meaning and purpose to his life. And if he *had* been that lonely, whether the aching emptiness inside him had resulted in him embarking on a dangerous affair with his boss – an affair that had cost him his life.

From the vantage point of the kitchen counter, she surveyed the lounge.

The room was far from tidy. In one corner, there was a heap of discarded clothing. At least half a dozen newspapers were strewn across the floor next to the sofa. And several coffee cups, some already growing fur, lined the mantelshelf.

There was nothing unusual in any of this, Paniatowski

thought. If anything, it was typical of the kind of bachelor who, without a mum to look after him, quickly allowed himself to fall into bad habits.

So why did it jar?

She ran her finger along one of the kitchen shelves, and got her answer. It had been dusted recently.

She checked the rest of the fitments in both the kitchen and the bathroom, and discovered that everything was sparkling.

The furniture, too, had been recently polished.

So what kind of sense did that make? she wondered.

Why would Whittington have cleaned his flat from top to bottom, yet neglected to tidy up the old newspapers and dirty laundry?

It didn't make any kind of sense *at all*, she thought, answering her own question.

She began a slow and methodical search of the flat. It was pretty much as she'd expected. There was a small bookcase containing a couple of dozen popular paperbacks, none of which, she found when she checked them, had been used to hide anything. There was a small stereo system, and a stack of long-playing records, but nothing was hidden in the record sleeves either.

Whittington seemed to have received no mail other than bills and special offers, nor was there any other indication – apart from a packet of condoms in the bathroom cabinet – that he knew anyone else in the entire world. It was a depressing life he seemed to have led, and Paniatowski thanked God that it wasn't *her* life any more.

It was only when she was giving the place one final look-over – and decided to move the sofa to see if there was anything underneath – that she hit pay dirt. Lying under the sofa was a headscarf with the Liberty's label. It looked genuine – and running it through her fingers, she decided it *was* genuine.

A Liberty silk scarf!

How many women could have persuaded themselves that they were entitled to such an indulgence?

And of those who did, how many would have been care-less enough to leave it behind in someone else's flat?

Paniatowski could only think of one.

SIXTEEN

On the street of expensive detached houses, surrounded by their own beautifully manicured grounds, the slightly battered Ford Escort stood out like costume jewellery in Tiffany's window.

It didn't bother DS Walker that he was being so conspicuous. In fact, he *wanted* Stan What's-'is-name to know that he was being watched – wanted the Polish bastard to feel the noose tightening around his neck.

Not that nooses tightened around *anybody*'s neck any more, he thought regretfully.

The good old days of criminals plunging to their deaths – their necks broken and their bowels opening – were long gone. The bleeding-heart liberals had seen to that.

But who knew, maybe the pendulum would swing back once again, and the judges could joyfully take their black caps out of mothballs.

Walker had no definite or carefully worked-out plan for collaring the Pole. But he was certain that if he stayed there long enough, Stan would come out of the house and do something suspicious – or at least do something that could be *argued* to have been suspicious – which would give him all the excuse he needed to pull his suspect in.

And once he had him in the interview room – war hero or no war hero – the man would crack.

Walker smiled as he imagined the look on the face of that other bloody Pole – DCI Paniatowski – when he handed her the investigation on a plate.

Pissed off? That wouldn't come near it.

He glanced down at his wristwatch, and saw that it was already eleven thirty-five.

Why didn't the bastard come out, he wondered.

Probably because he was putting on a show – pretending to be in deep mourning for the poor bloody woman whose hand he'd cut off.

As if *that* was going to fool anybody!

Still, if he wasn't coming out, he wasn't coming out, Walker told himself – and since the pubs were already open, it was pointless to stay there in the vague hope that he would.

He turned the ignition key in the Escort, slipped into gear and pulled away from the kerb.

The Chorley Court porter was back behind his desk, with a Player's No. 6 cigarette in his hand and a martyred look filling his face.

'Have you finished?' he asked.

'I've finished,' Paniatowski confirmed.

'An' have you made sure the door locked itself behind you?'

'It's locked.'

'Are you certain, because if it isn't, I'll have to . . .'

'I double-checked it,' Paniatowski assured him. She paused for a second. 'Do you remember Mr Whittington having many visitors?'

'I wouldn't know anything about that,' the porter replied, looking away.

He had been rebuffed – excluded from the mysteries of the police investigation – and as a consequence he was being awkward, Paniatowski thought. If she was ever going to get his cooperation, she would have to throw him at least one small titbit.

She glanced over her shoulder – the better to increase the drama surrounding the coming revelation – then whispered, 'You mustn't tell this to a soul, but he's been murdered.'

'Murdered!' the caretaker gasped, and the expression which came to his face said that while he had been hoping for a bit of juicy gossip, he had never expected it would be *this* good.

'Do you remember reading about a man's severed hand in the papers this morning?' Paniatowski continued, still conspiratorial.

'Yes?'

'It was his.'

The porter nodded sagely. 'I thought it must have been,' he said, conveniently ignoring his very recent astonishment.

'So now you see how vital your answers to my questions might be?' Paniatowski asked.

The caretaker puffed out his chest, and nodded again – self-importantly this time.

'Mr Whittington didn't spend that much time here, but when he did, he kept himself pretty much to himself,' he said.

The more I learn about him, the more he sounds like the me that I used to be, Paniatowski thought.

'Yes,' the porter continued, 'it would be fair to say that he didn't *usually* have any visitors at all.'

'But *occasionally* he did?' asked Paniatowski, picking up on the emphasis, just as he'd expected her to.

'Yes, occasionally he did,' the porter said, with gravity. 'There was this woman who came here a few times.'

'What did she look like?'

'I couldn't say, exactly. You see, she always wore a head-scarf. And big sunglasses! In Lancashire! Now I ask you, how often do you need to wear sunglasses in *Lancashire*?'

'But even in the headscarf and sunglasses, you'll have got a general impression of her,' Paniatowski coaxed. 'How tall was she?'

'About medium height – maybe just an inch or two shorter than you.'

Which would make her just about Linda's height, Paniatowski thought.

'And how old would you say she was?'

'This is only a guess, but from the way she moved I'd put her somewhere in her thirties.'

Which, by what was probably *no coincidence at all*, was Linda's age.

She was still a long way from being able to claim she'd got a *positive* identification, Paniatowski thought – but she was certainly getting closer to it by the minute.

'What about her hair?' she asked.

'Couldn't see the colour, but I know it was long.'

'*How* do you know it was long?' Paniatowski asked suspiciously.

'You know how women's hair looks, when they just cram it inside the headscarf, instead of making a proper job of pinning it up?' the porter asked.

'Yes.'

'Well, that's how her hair looked – bunched up inside the headscarf.'

'But if it hadn't been bunched up, how long would it have been?' Paniatowski asked. 'Would it have reached her shoulders?'

'Easily,' the porter said.

'Tell me about the headscarf,' Paniatowski suggested.

'I only saw it from a distance.'

'But you must still have got some impression of it.'

The porter thought about it. 'Let me put it like this,' he said finally. 'I'm no expert on women's clothes, but I wouldn't have said it was the kind of headscarf you could have bought in Woolworth's.'

Paniatowski took an evidence envelope out of her bag, and held it up for him to see.

'Was this the headscarf that the woman you saw visiting Mr Whittington was wearing?' she asked.

'It might have been,' the porter replied. 'If not, it was certainly one very similar.'

'Can you remember the last time you saw the woman?'

'It must have been the night before last.'

The night that Tom Whittington and Linda Szymborska were murdered, Paniatowski noted.

'Do you have any idea of the actual *time* the woman was here?'

'I'd just finished watching *The Nine O'Clock News* on the telly, and was going round the place locking up. So that would make it . . . What? About nine thirty-five, would you say?'

'Something like that,' Paniatowski agreed.

The porter's mouth suddenly fell open, as if his train of thought, though slow and ponderous, had finally pulled into the station.

'Here,' he said, 'according to the paper, it wasn't just a man's hand that turned up – it was a woman's as well.'

'That's right,' Paniatowski agreed.

'And did the woman's hand belong to the woman in the headscarf – the one who was having it off with Tom Whittington?'

Of course it bloody did! Paniatowski thought.

'I'm afraid I can't comment on that,' she said.

DC Blake was known among his friends for both his off-beat sense of humour and his self-confidence. He was rather proud of the fact that he had been the one to introduce the term 'dirty weekend' in Inspector Beresford's briefing session, though a little embarrassed that, *before* being so worldly-wise, he'd raised his hand for permission to speak. Still, that could be glossed over later, and he knew from experience that by the time he'd re-told the tale for the third or fourth time, the hand-raising would have been transformed into a gesture designed to take the piss out of authority.

The Old Oak Tree Inn in Knorsbury had impressed him from the moment he had driven up to it. It had a heavy stone roof and mullioned windows. Ivy grew up the thick stone walls, and bees flitted between flowers in the immaculate gardens. It was, he decided, the kind of place you never really thought existed outside the world of chocolate-box tops – and if it was also the kind of place you used for dirty weekends, then dirty weekends were starting to look like a jolly good idea.

The receptionist at the Old Oak Tree was a serious-looking middle-aged woman with her hair drawn into a tight bun. No doubt that severe expression of hers melted when she was greeting the inn's guests, Blake thought, but it certainly showed no signs of melting for a mere detective constable, and the way she looked at *him* made him feel about seven years old.

'I'd like you to take a careful look at this photograph, if you wouldn't mind, madam,' Blake said, laying the picture of the Brunskill's works outing down on the counter.

'I am not a "madam",' the woman said haughtily. 'I am *Miss* Dobbs – and I would be grateful if that was how you addressed me.'

'Right,' Blake agreed. 'Sorry about that. So *could* you look at the photograph, Miss Dobbs?'

The receptionist took one pair of horn-rimmed spectacles off her nose and replaced them with another, almost identical, pair.

'This is a photograph of a charabanc outing – a day trip to the seaside,' Miss Dobbs said, in a tone which managed to convey her evident disdain for such working-class frivolities.

'Yes, it is,' Blake agreed.

'I would have thought that the least you could have done would have been to produce individual photographs of the person or persons who you were interested in,' Miss Dobbs said.

'Well, of course, we *could have* done that, but this is so much better,' Blake replied.

'Is it?'

'Oh, yes. It's called the Group Format Identification Procedure, and when they tried it out in America, it was very successful,' Blake explained, making it up as he went along, and feeling much better for having done so.

'I see,' Miss Dobbs said dubiously. Then she glanced down at the photograph, and added, 'Yes.'

'What?'

'You asked me if I could identify any of these people in the photograph, didn't you?'

'Yes.'

'And I can.'

She *recognized* someone. She bloody *recognized* someone, Blake thought. It was almost too good to be true.

The detective constable felt a powerful urge to 'help' the receptionist – just to make sure she got it right.

But then he remembered what Inspector Beresford had said, and – almost holding his breath – he asked, 'Which ones?'

'This man,' said Miss Dobbs, pointing to Tom Whittington, 'and this woman standing next to him,' she continued, indicating Linda Szymborska.

'How do you know them?'

'How do you *imagine* I would know them, Constable? They were guests at the inn.'

Blake was tempted to say, 'That's *Detective* Constable, Miss Dobbs,' but his nerve failed him at the last moment, and he contented himself with a simple, 'Ah, they were guests!'

'Are they married to one another?' Miss Dobbs asked, her lip already curled in anticipatory contempt. 'Or do they, as this photograph would seem to suggest, merely work together?'

Blake firmly intended to say that – this being a police matter – he could not give her that information, but even as the thought was passing through his brain, he felt Miss Dodd's eyes burning into him and heard himself saying, 'They just worked together.'

'I thought so,' Miss Dobbs said triumphantly. 'You can always tell, you know.'

'Can you?'

'Indeed. Couples like them are always so much more affec-
tionate to each other than couples who are actually married.'

'But when they arrived, they signed in as a married couple,
did they?' Blake asked.

'Of course,' Miss Dobbs said severely. 'We do have our
standards, you know.'

'And when was it they stayed here?'

Miss Dobbs opened the register, and quickly flicked
through it.

'Two weeks ago,' she said. 'They only stayed for one night.
They signed in as Mr and Mrs Lord.'

Dick Whittington, Blake thought. *Lord* Mayor of London.

Well, it was nice to know that even adulterers could sometimes have a sense of humour.

'Is there anything more that you can tell me about them,
Miss Dobbs?' he asked.

'Very little indeed. After they checked in, we hardly saw
them again.' Miss Dobbs paused for a second. 'We offer pony
trekking here, you know.'

'No, I didn't know that,' Blake said, because that was clearly
what was expected of him.

'Guests can also hire bicycles or go on bird-watching ex-
peditions, and in the evenings, if there is sufficient demand,
I myself can sometimes be persuaded to give a short piano
recital in the main lounge. But *Mr and Mrs* Lord did not take
advantage of any of the wonderful facilities the inn has to
offer.' She sniffed, disapprovingly, 'I expect they thought they
had much *better* things to do with their time.'

If I'd been here for a dirty weekend when you were on the
desk, I wouldn't have *dared* not to sample the wonderful facilities, Blake thought.

'You didn't happen to notice what kind of car he was
driving, did you?' he asked hopefully.

'*She* was driving,' Miss Dobbs corrected him.

'I bcg your pardon?'

'It was *Mrs* Lord who did the driving. Probably – if I know
anything about women like her – to make him feel small.'

'And do you know what kind of car it was?'

'Certainly. It was a dark blue E-type Jaguar. A very flashy
vehicle, I've always thought, but then people like them just
love flashiness, don't they?'

SEVENTEEN

Jenny Brunskill was sitting behind her desk in her office. Her face was puffy, her eyes were red and she seemed to have become a much smaller woman than on the previous day.

'Are you sure it was wise of you to come into work today?' Paniatowski asked sympathetically.

Jenny shrugged, though it seemed to take her considerable effort. 'The business doesn't run itself,' she said.

'I know, but . . .'

'Some brutal madman has robbed us of both our managing director and our head baker. That only leaves the two of us – my brother-in-law and me – to keep the bakery running. And you can't expect Stan to do anything, when he's just lost his wife.'

'Linda wasn't *just* his wife,' Paniatowski reminded her gently. 'She was also your *sister*. And I think you should seriously consider the possibility that her death has been almost as much of a shock to *your* system as it has been to your brother-in-law Stan's.'

'Oh, it has certainly been a shock,' Jenny conceded, 'but by being here, I'm doing what Linda would have *wanted* me to do. The bakery was her life, you see. It's been *both* our lives, for as long as we can remember. Our father taught us well, and we never forgot the lessons we learned. Besides,' she gave another weak shrug, 'in a situation like this, it's best to keep your mind occupied with ordinary, run-of-the-mill things, don't you think?'

'How does Stan feel about the bakery?' Paniatowski asked.

'Stan?' Jenny repeated, as if she didn't quite know what the chief inspector was getting at.

'Does he have the same sort of commitment to the place that you and your sister have – that you *have*, and your sister *had*?'

'I'm afraid I still don't know what you mean.'

'Your brother-in-law used to run a very successful goods delivery business, didn't he?' Paniatowski asked.

'That's right, he did.'

'Yet he sold that successful business, and invested all his money in a bakery which was in real trouble.'

'Who told you that?' Jenny demanded, suddenly angry. 'Who said the bakery was in trouble when Stan bought into it?'

'Well, I should have thought that the very fact you needed to take in a new partner . . .'

'Sales had gone down, but that was nothing more than a temporary fluctuation which all businesses of this nature are prone to from time to time,' Jenny said. 'But we knew it wouldn't be long before folk realized that you can't beat good honest bread, and came back to us.'

The contrast between the first and second sentences couldn't have been more striking, Paniatowski thought. The first one, measured and smooth, belonged to Jenny, the bakery business manager. The second, rougher and almost belligerent, came straight from the dead mouth of Seth Brunskill.

'Linda and I weren't the *least bit* worried by the downturn in business,' Jenny said, as if it had suddenly become important to convince her visitor that this was the truth.

Paniatowski wasn't buying it.

'That does surprise me,' she said.

'It wouldn't have surprised you *at all* if you'd known our father,' Jenny countered. 'Both Linda and I knew he'd *never* allow the bakery to fail. He had built it up from nothing, you see – and he loved it as much as we did.'

'Even so, when Stan became a partner . . .'

'He knew a good thing when he saw it. He understood that by buying his way in when we were suffering temporary difficulties, he was ensuring himself a meal ticket for life.'

'*By the middle of the sixties they were in big trouble,*' Sergeant Sid Roberts had told Paniatowski. '*By the time Seth died, the bakery was totterin' on the edge of bankruptcy.*'

Some meal ticket for life!

'Don't get me wrong, I don't blame Stan for doing it,' Jenny continued. 'Any man in his situation would have grasped such an opportunity when he saw it. *Most* men in his situation would have demanded *much more* control over the business than *he* was willing to settle for.'

Jenny was performing a remarkable feat of mental gymnastics, Paniatowski told herself.

On the one hand, she was claiming the bakery hadn't been in trouble at all, while on the other she was more or less indicating it was in so *much* trouble that Stan Szymborska could have virtually taken over the whole thing, if he'd chosen to.

'I wonder if Stan's decision was based on anything more than mere business considerations,' Paniatowski said.

'What do you mean?' Jenny asked.

'Well, he did marry Linda, didn't he?'

'Yes?'

'So I was wondering if he perhaps bought into the business *because* he was in love with her.'

'There was nothing at all going on between Stan and Linda before Father died,' Jenny said emphatically.

'No?'

'No! It was only after Father passed on that my sister started to feel the need for a man.'

Or perhaps to feel the need for *another* man, Paniatowski thought.

'Possibly there *was* nothing actually *going on* . . .' she said aloud.

'There wasn't. I can assure you of that.'

'. . . but it doesn't necessarily mean that Stan couldn't have had *feelings* for Linda, does it?'

Jenny gave her a smile which, while weak and tired, was still undoubtedly superior.

'Stanislaw is Polish – as, I imagine, you are yourself,' she said. 'When did you leave Poland?'

'As a child,' Paniatowski said.

'As a *refugee*,' she added mentally. 'Fleeing with my mother, to keep ahead of invading Germans who, she was sure, would punish us for being the wife and daughter of a dead Polish army officer.'

'As a child,' Jenny echoed. 'Ah, that explains it.'

'Explains what?'

'Why you know so little about life in Poland. The Poles, you see, place great value on the family, and everyone's place in it – a value which, sadly, we no longer seem to share in this country.'

'I'm afraid I'm not quite following your argument.'

'It's really very simple. My father was the *head* of this

family, and Stan would never have gone against his wishes by *allowing himself* to fall in love with Linda.'

Was Jenny for real, Paniatowski wondered. Did she actually *believe* all this rubbish she was spouting?

Yes, she decided – Jenny probably did.

'As managing director, did Linda sometimes have to go on business trips?' Paniatowski asked.

'Occasionally.'

'And did these business trips of hers necessitate her staying away from home overnight?'

'Once in a while they did,' Jenny said, sounding puzzled. 'Why are you asking?'

'I was wondering if she happened to be away a week last Wednesday,' Paniatowski said.

Or to put it another way, she thought, I was wondering if she happened to be away when (according to the report that DC Blake had just made) a Mr and Mrs Lord checked in at the Old Oak Tree Inn in Knorsbury.

'Linda *was* away one night that week,' Jenny said. 'She went to a short conference of bakery managers in Leeds. But I can't remember exactly which night it was. I expect the details will be in her appointment book, which she always keeps on her desk, so if you'll give me a minute, I'll . . .'

Jenny froze.

'Take it easy,' Paniatowski said softly.

'The . . . the book's in her office but I can't . . . I don't want to . . .' Jenny mumbled.

'But you don't want to go in there yourself just yet?' Paniatowski supplied.

Jenny nodded. 'It's weak of me, I know, and maybe tomorrow I'll be able to face it . . .'

'You said the appointment book would be on her desk. Would you mind if I went and found it myself?'

'Of course not.'

'And while I'm in there, would you have any objection to my searching the office?'

'*Searching* it?' Jenny asked, alarmed.

'I need to look for evidence,' Paniatowski explained. 'Anything that might give me a clue as to who Linda's murderer might be.'

Jenny hesitated. 'You won't make a mess, will you? You'll leave everything as you found it?'

'Of course,' Paniatowski agreed.

And she was thinking, Linda Szymborska's only been dead for a little over twenty-four hours, and *already* her sister's turning her office into a shrine.

The moment Paniatowski stepped into Linda's office, she realized how wrong she'd been about Jenny's intentions for the place.

The evidence was all there.

The heavy teak desk – which most other firms would have got rid of years earlier.

The framed prize certificates which proclaimed that, generations ago, Brunskill's loaves had triumphed over other brands of bread which probably no longer existed.

The huge painting dominating the far wall.

There was no *need* to turn this place into a shrine – because it already *was* one.

She gave the portrait a closer inspection. In the great tradition of Lancashire tycoons, Seth Brunskill had had it painted in oils, and – also in that tradition – the man himself was giving the artist a hard stare, as if assessing whether or not he was getting value for money.

He had been a handsome man, with much the same sort of handsomeness as Stan Szymborska and Tom Whittington possessed, Paniatowski thought. That surprised her, although given that both his daughters were good-looking women – or rather, one was, and one *had been* – it shouldn't have done.

Perhaps her expectations of Seth Brunskill had been shaped by Sergeant Sid Roberts' sour view of the man, she told herself. And perhaps Roberts had been right – for while the features were undoubtedly strong and regular, there was no humour in the eyes, and no signs of compassion around the mouth.

She could not picture Seth dandling Linda or Jenny on his knee, or tickling one of them under the chin. On the other hand, it was easy to imagine him scowling at them when they had done something of which he disapproved – and Paniatowski could almost *hear* him saying that they had disappointed him, and they must try harder next time.

*   *   *

DS Walker was well into his third pint of best bitter when the man with the dandruff-flecked collar sat down next to him, uninvited.

'Detective Sergeant Walker?' the man asked, though it was not really a question at all. 'I'm—'

'I know who you are,' Walker said gruffly. 'What exactly do you want, Mr Traynor?'

'Just a few words.'

'Well, here's a *couple* of words for you,' Walker said, after taking a sip of his pint. 'Piss off!'

'You're not very keen on the press, are you?' Traynor asked.

Walker lit up a cigarette. 'Well, let's put it this way,' he suggested, 'if I was planning to push a line of people off a cliff, then reporters would certainly be *in* that line, right after lawyers and foreigners.'

'And where would detective chief inspectors be in the line?' Traynor wondered.

'What?'

'You don't much like DCI Paniatowski, do you?'

Walker shrugged. 'I've nothing against her.'

'And *I* don't like her, either,' Traynor said, choosing to treat the veracity of the comment with the contempt it deserved.

'Why's that?'

'Because she's had her chance to cooperate with me, and she's not taken it – which means that, in my book, there's a black mark against her name.'

'Is there any particular reason that you're telling me this, Mr Traynor?' Walker wondered.

'Have you ever heard the expression, "My enemy's enemy is my friend"?' the reporter asked.

'Might have done,' Walker said evasively.

'It's not a trick,' Traynor assured him.

'Then what *is* it?'

'It's an *offer*. If you help me, Detective Sergeant Walker, then I'll be more than willing to help you.'

Walker frowned. 'Would you care to spell that out?'

'Certainly. I'd very much like to know just how a big a cock-up DCI Paniatowski's making of her new job, and if you were to provide me with a few details, you could rest assured I'd make sure the rest of the world found out, too. Now, some people might call that kind of thing disloyal . . .'

'And what would *you* call it?'

'I'd call it loyalty of the highest order.'

'Would you?'

'Indeed. Because if DCI Paniatowski's not doing her job properly, then it's your duty as a member of the Police Force – and the well-being of that force is where your loyalty *truly* lies – to make the general public aware of that failing. And, of course – though I know this wouldn't sway you one way or the other – there might be a bit of money in it for you.'

'That sounds suspiciously like you're making an attempt to bribe me,' Walker said.

'I wouldn't put it quite like . . .'

'And if you think I'd be willing to betray my boss, then you don't know me at all.'

Traynor stood up again. 'I'm sorry,' he said, awkwardly. 'I seem to have made a mistake.'

'A big one,' Walker growled.

'No hard feelings?' Traynor said, offering his hand.

'Aren't there?' asked Walker, pointedly ignoring it.

Traynor began to walk slowly towards the door.

'I must be losing my touch,' he told himself. 'I really must. I could have sworn that Walker was just the sort of man who'd . . .'

And then he heard the sergeant call out from behind him, 'Hold on a minute, will you, Mr Traynor!'

The reporter turned around. 'Yes, Sergeant?'

'You forgot to leave me your business card,' Walker pointed out.

Traynor smiled in self-congratulation. 'Losing my touch?' he asked himself. 'Not a bit of it! I can still smell out the stink of human weakness from across a crowded room.'

'You're quite right, Sergeant,' he told Walker. 'I *did* forget to leave you my card.'

Jenny Brunskill was still sitting at her desk – still apparently absorbed in her work – but it was obvious she had been crying again.

'Did you find anything?' she asked Paniatowski hopefully. 'Were there any of the clues you were looking for?'

Paniatowski shook her head. 'No,' she admitted. 'But it was

a bit of a long shot anyway. And there are plenty of other lines of investigation that we've been following.'

'You *will* catch him, won't you?' Jenny Brunskill asked.

And, as always when she was asked that question, Paniatowski found herself struggling for an answer – because while she wanted to give the assurance which was being sought, she could not ignore the fact that there were some murderers who *did* get away with it.

'We're doing all we can,' she said.

Jenny smiled weakly. 'I believe you are,' she said. 'You're trying your best, and that's all any of us can do.' She paused for a second, then continued, 'Did you find Linda's appointment book all right?'

'Yes. It *was* Wednesday night that she was away.' Paniatowski lit up a cigarette. 'Why didn't you go with her to Leeds?'

'Oh, that sort of thing simply isn't my cup of tea,' Jenny said, almost apologetically. 'I look after the books, and Linda looks after – Linda *looked* after – the people.'

'So Linda went *alone*?' Paniatowski asked.

'Yes. Why would you ask that?'

'Well, I just thought that Stan might have gone with her.'

'He used to, but then Linda said that since she was always working so hard on those trips, there wasn't much point in taking him along.'

'Or, since it was a *bakery* conference, I thought she might have taken her head baker with her.'

'That kind of conference isn't about *baking* the bread,' Jenny said. 'It's much more to do with reviewing the baking industry as a whole, and finding ways to . . .' She suddenly stopped talking, and her face turned as white as flour. 'What are you suggesting?' she demanded. 'Do you think that Tom and Linda . . . that Linda and Tom could have . . .?'

'You must surely already have considered the possibility that they were having an affair,' Paniatowski said.

'Never!' Jenny said, in a voice which was now almost a scream. 'The idea never even occurred to me! And it *still* doesn't! Linda wouldn't do that to Stan! She wouldn't *dare* do it!'

'So on the Wednesday that Linda was in Leeds, Tom was in the bakery *all day*, was he?' Paniatowski asked.

Jenny looked away. 'I have work to do,' she said.

'*Was* Tom here all day?' Paniatowski persisted.

'No, as a matter of fact, he wasn't here at all that Wednesday.'

'You said that without even consulting your records,' Paniatowski pointed out.

'There's *no need* to consult them. I *know* it was the same day.'

'How can you be so sure?'

'Because of the way things happened that day.'

'Go on,' Paniatowski said.

'Linda was just about to set off for Leeds when Tom phoned in sick. She nearly didn't go at all, because, with Tom out, she thought she'd better work in the bakery herself. But I said we should be able to cope for just one day, and she said that in that case . . .' A look of horrified realization suddenly filled Jenny's face. 'Oh, my God,' she moaned.

'Was Tom often off sick?' Paniatowski asked.

'No, he was almost never . . . I can't remember the last time he . . .'

'So doesn't it strike you as awfully convenient that he should be sick on the same day as Linda was going to Leeds?' Paniatowski said softly.

'Tom *was* sick that day,' Jenny said desperately. 'I *know* he was sick. He *had to be* sick.'

EIGHTEEN

Sergeant Walker took a sip from the pint of best bitter, and smacked his lips with satisfaction.

They always said the first pint of the day was the best, he thought, and they were quite right. Not that this *was* his first pint of the day – strictly speaking, it was his fifth – but it was his first in the Drum and Monkey, and that had to count for something.

The night before, alone in his shithole of a flat, he had sunk to a bit of a low point, he realized, but now, after a few pints, the world was starting to look a much better place, and even his problems seemed more manageable.

'We're waiting, Sergeant,' said one of his bigger problems, who was sitting across the table from him.

'Sorry, ma'am, I was just getting all the details of my report straight in my head,' Walker replied. 'This is the area we've covered this morning,' he continued, pointing to shaded-in parts of the map which he'd spread out on the table. 'As you can see, I've concentrated my men on areas where there were abandoned buildings, because it seemed to me that the killer would have chosen somewhere he was unlikely to be interrupted.'

'Makes sense,' Paniatowski agreed.

'So we gave it our best shot, and I'm afraid we still didn't find anything,' Walker concluded.

'But at least you've narrowed down the area that's still left to be searched,' Beresford said encouragingly. 'And it will be narrowed down even further this afternoon, which means that by tomorrow—'

'Tomorrow?' Walker interrupted, wondering if his last two pints in the Green Man should have been accompanied by whisky chasers. 'Are you saying we'll still be searching *tomorrow*?'

'Yes,' Beresford replied, with a note of surprise in his voice. 'We'll certainly continue the search tomorrow, unless, of course, you strike lucky sometime this afternoon.'

'Tomorrow,' Walker repeated, as if he still couldn't get his mind round the idea. 'We'll still be searching tomorrow?'

'Is there a problem with that, Sergeant?' Beresford asked.

'No, sir, not exactly a problem, as such.'

'Well, then?'

'But I can't quite see why you'd think it might be necessary to continue the search.'

'It could be that I'd *still* like you to find the stiffs,' Beresford said.

'Fair point,' Walker agreed, nodding his head. 'Very fair point. But surely, once you've got Stan What's-'is-name safely under lock and key, he'll tell you exactly where you need to . . .'

'What makes you think that we're going to arrest Stan Szymborska?' Paniatowski wondered.

'Well, for a start, I did hear it on the grapevine that you were planning to hold a press conference in a couple of hours' time, ma'am.'

'I am.'

'And naturally, I assumed that you'd have Stan banged up by then, so you could have something to brag to the hacks about.'

'You think I should arrest Stan Szymborska just to make myself look good for the press?' Paniatowski asked incredulously.

'No, not *just* to make yourself look good, ma'am,' Walker said. 'That would be quite wrong. But since you're going to have to arrest him sooner or later, why not make it sooner?'

'Because we simply don't have enough *evidence* to make an arrest yet,' Paniatowski said.

'Don't we?' Walker asked. 'Look, ma'am, we know that he doesn't have any kind of alibi for the night of the murder. Right?'

'Yes, we do know that.'

'And we also know that his wife was having an affair with Tom Whittington – the *second* victim.'

'Agreed.'

'And, most damning of all – we know he's a bloody foreigner.' Walker paused, and grinned at Paniatowski. 'That last part was a joke, ma'am.'

'Of sorts,' Paniatowski agreed. 'Listen, Sergeant, I know you have a gut feeling that he's guilty . . .'

'It's a feeling that I've had from the very first moment I clapped my eyes on him, ma'am.'

'. . . and it's one that Inspector Beresford and I both share with you. Isn't that right, Colin?'

'Definitely,' Beresford agreed.

'But the fact is that without proof, we've no chance of making a case against him.'

'Unless he confesses,' Walker pointed out.

'He isn't *going* to confess,' Paniatowski said.

'Now, you see, that's just where you and I fundamentally disagree, ma'am.'

'It's in his military record that when he was shot down over Germany, he was interrogated by the SS,' Paniatowski said exasperatedly. 'Have you got that, Ted? The bloody *SS*! And if he didn't tell *them* anything, then he's certainly not going to tell you.'

'Maybe he *did* tell them something,' Walker said stubbornly.

'He'd never have been awarded all those medals if he had, now would he?' Paniatowski asked.

'Possibly not,' Walker agreed reluctantly.

'But you still think you can do it, don't you?' Paniatowski challenged. 'You still think that even though the SS – who were world champions when it came to extracting information from people – got absolutely nowhere with him, you can succeed.'

'Well, I'm certainly willing to give it a go,' Walker said gamely.

'It isn't going to happen,' Paniatowski told him. 'Do you understand that, Sergeant?'

For a moment it looked as if Walker was going to continue to argue, then he nodded his head.

'Whatever you say, ma'am,' he agreed. 'You're the boss, and we have to be guided by your judgement in these matters.' He glanced down at his wristwatch. 'Would you mind if I stepped outside for a couple of minutes? I want to contact my lads, just to see how they're getting on – and the radio reception's much better in the car park.'

'Go right ahead,' Paniatowski said.

Walker stood up, and walked to the door.

'If Stan Szymborska *is* the killer, how are we *ever* going to prove it?' Paniatowski asked Beresford.

'We need to break his non-alibi,' Beresford replied. 'We need witnesses who can testify that he wasn't at home at all – but was riding around Whitebridge behind the wheel of his wife's Jag.'

'You think that *is* what he was doing?'

'I don't know how he could have managed it otherwise. Let's say, to give us a workable example, that the bodies are currently residing in an abandoned warehouse on the south side of town.'

'All right.'

'He could either have killed his victims first and driven them there, or he could have driven them there – probably drugged or tied up – and then killed them. I suppose there's a *third* possibility, that he somehow persuaded Tom and Linda to *meet* him there, but I don't think that's very likely.'

'It's highly *unlikely*,' Paniatowski agreed. 'If I was having an affair, the last thing I'd be willing to do would be to go with my lover to an out-of-the-way place where I knew my husband was waiting for us.'

'So, whether he killed them before he took them to the theoretical warehouse, or killed them once they were there, he'd have needed a car.'

'Couldn't he have used his own car, rather than Linda's Jag?'

'He doesn't *own* a car. He has a motorbike,' Beresford said. 'And I can hardly see him driving his Honda 750 through the centre of Whitebridge with a corpse draped over his shoulder,' he added with a grin.

'He could have hired a car,' Paniatowski pointed out.

'He didn't. I've already had my lads check that out. Besides, if he didn't use the Jag, where is it? You can't leave a car like that on the streets of Whitebridge without it being noticed, and if it had been picked up by joy-riders, we'd have heard about it by now.'

'So you think he decided to hide the car in the same place as he hid the bodies?'

'Not necessarily. He could have left it somewhere else entirely. But whichever it was, I'm convinced he did hide it.'

'If you *could* find witnesses who could put him in the Jag, that would be a big breakthrough,' Paniatowski admitted. 'But I'm not prepared to pin *all* my hopes on that.'

'So what other lines of inquiry do you want us to follow?'

'I want a comprehensive background check on Stan Szymborska, going right back to the time he first settled in Britain. I want to know if he is actually the spotless hero he appears to be, or if he's ever been in trouble before. And if he has been in trouble, what *kind* of trouble? Was any of it violent – and if it was, was that violence directed against women?'

'We should probably talk to his old girlfriends – if he has any,' Beresford said.

'Oh, he'll have had them all right,' Paniatowski said confidently. 'A man like Stan won't have gone long without some kind of female companionship. We also need to talk to people who knew him when he was running his delivery service – and the people who've been working with him at the bakery.'

'Got it,' Beresford said.

'And since we're devoting most of our resources to Szymborska, we'd better pray that he really *is* our man,' Paniatowski said.

'He is,' Beresford said. 'It's gone beyond a gut feeling. We both *know* he did it, don't we?'

'Yes,' Paniatowski agreed. 'We both *know* he did it.'

Once out in the car park, Sergeant Walker made no attempt to establish radio contact with any of the constables he was supposed to be supervising, but instead walked quickly towards the nearest public telephone box.

It wasn't his fault that he was going to have to make this call, he told himself. Not in any way, shape or form. The blame rested entirely on Monika Paniatowski's shoulders.

She should have listened to him. She should have been *guided* by him. Because despite having a good mind – and he was forced to admit that her mind *was* quick and analytical – she clearly didn't know villains like he did.

And *because* she didn't know villains, she was making one big mistake on top of another.

It was as he was fumbling with the change from his pocket that he realized he was drunk.

But not *that* drunk, he told himself.

Not *so* drunk that he was doing something now that he might live to regret later.

He managed to insert the coins in the slot at the second attempt, and to dial the *Evening Chronicle*'s number largely without incident.

When he'd been connected, he said, 'I'd like to speak to Mike Traynor, ace reporter,' and then he giggled.

'Who shall I say is calling?' asked the woman on the switchboard, somewhat frostily.

'Never mind who it is,' Walker growled, his good humour deserting him as quickly as it had arrived. 'You just tell Traynor I've got a very big story for him, and he'll never forgive himself if he misses it.'

Traynor came on the line almost immediately.

'Who is this?' he asked.

'No names,' Walker said.

'Is it Sergeant—'

'I said no names, you bastard! Just shut up and listen to what I've got to tell you.'

'All right,' Traynor agreed.

'Chief Inspector Polack's holding a press conference in about an hour and a half's time. You'll be there, won't you?'

'Yes, I will, but—'

'Then before the conference starts, I think there's a couple of things that you should know.'

Walker spoke for two minutes, then slammed down the phone and stepped out of the box.

Once on the street again, he was surprised to discover that he was looking around, almost guiltily.

Well, he had nothing to feel guilty about, he told himself angrily.

His conscience was clear. What he'd done had been for the good of the Police Force and in the interests of justice.

And if it also served to bring DCI Paniatowski down, that was no more than a bonus.

NINETEEN

The press room in Whitebridge Police Headquarters had seating for twenty reporters, which, at any normal briefing, would have been more than adequate. But this was not a normal briefing – this was a *national* story which was being covered, and the room was full to overflowing.

Monika Paniatowski, on the verge of delivering her first-ever press conference, looked straight ahead – and tried to ignore the bright lights which the presence of two television camera crews had made necessary.

She cleared her throat.

'Thank you for coming, ladies and gentlemen,' she said. 'I would like to begin this press conference by releasing the names of the two victims of this shocking crime. They are Linda Szymborska, aged thirty-eight, who was the managing director of Brunskill's Bakery, and Thomas Whittington, also aged thirty-eight, who was the head baker in the same company.'

All the reporters were jotting down these details as she spoke, she noted. All, that was, apart from Mike Traynor. He had his arms ostentatiously folded across his chest, and a smirk on his face that was so wide the rest of his features seemed in imminent danger of being swallowed by it.

Paniatowski had already decided what details she would reveal to the press – and the order she would reveal them in – before she'd walked into the room, and once she started speaking again, she pretty much stuck to that plan.

Not bad, she thought, when she'd finished.

True, the briefing had lacked Charlie Woodend's flair, but it had been both clear and succinct enough to be more than satisfactory.

She took a sip of water from the glass on the table in front of her, and steeled herself for the next stage in the process.

'I am now open to questions from the floor,' she said. 'I will answer them as frankly as I can, but you must accept that I will inevitably be holding back *some* information in order not to prejudice the investigation.'

Mike Traynor's hand had shot into the air before she'd finished speaking.

For a moment, she considered ignoring the man who had damaged her investigation by leaking the story of a second hand to the nationals. But *only* for a moment, because to ignore him would be seen as a sign of weakness – and being seen as *weak* was the last thing she needed at that particular juncture.

'Yes, Mr Traynor?' she said.

'What's the connection between the two victims, Chief Inspector?' Traynor asked, almost innocently.

'I thought I'd already spelled that out more than clearly enough, Mr Traynor,' Paniatowski said. 'They were colleagues.'

'And that's all there is to it?' Traynor asked, in a tone which he was clearly hoping would sound surprised, but instead gave the impression of a man *pretending* to be surprised. 'There's no closer link between them than the fact that they happened to work in the same bakery?'

'None that we've yet established,' Paniatowski lied.

'Really?' Traynor asked.

'Really,' Paniatowski confirmed stonily.

'Well, I must admit I'm astonished to hear you say that, Chief Inspector,' Traynor told her.

'Are you?' Paniatowski countered. 'And why might that be?'

She should never have said it, she realized, the moment the words were out of her mouth. She should never – ever – have given him the opportunity to come back at her.

'Why might that be?' Traynor asked, obviously enjoying himself. 'Well, it *might be* because one of the officers closely involved in your investigation, a Detective Constable – ' Traynor glanced down at his notes – 'Detective Constable Blake, spent over half an hour this morning talking to the receptionist in a hotel which is *well known* for facilitating illicit nocturnal activities.' Traynor grinned. 'In other words, it's a place that people go to for dirty weekends. And it *might be* that while he was there, he established that certain persons connected with this case – I'll say no more than that – had spent the night at the inn, posing as man and wife.'

Where the bloody hell had he got *that* particular bit of information from, Paniatowski wondered.

And she was not alone in wondering. All the other journalists in the room were looking directly at Traynor now, and the atmosphere was crackling with feelings of envy and resentment.

'Would you care to make any comment on that, Chief Inspector?' Traynor asked.

'No, I would not,' Paniatowski replied. 'Next question,' she continued briskly, scanning the room for more hands.

But there *were* no more hands, because the pack had clearly decided that they were likely to learn more from listening to Mike Traynor's questions than from asking any of their own.

'Isn't it true that as a result of the evidence you've already gathered, there is one man who clearly stands out as a prime suspect?' Traynor pressed on.

'I have no idea what basis you have for asking that question,' Paniatowski replied, as she felt her stomach turn over.

'In fact, wouldn't it be fair to say that any *other* chief inspector on the Force would already have arrested him – and the reason you haven't done the same is because he's one of your own people?'

'My own people?' Paniatowski repeated. 'I really have no idea what you're talking about.'

But she did. She bloody did!

'I thought I'd already spelled that out more than clearly enough,' Traynor said, parodying Paniatowski's earlier comment. 'But if it will help you to fully grasp what I'm saying, then I'm perfectly willing to dot all the "i"s and cross all the "t"s for you.'

There was no easy way of getting out of this situation, Paniatowski thought. No easy way at all.

But she was damned if she was going to leave the podium and go scurrying away with her tail between her legs.

Her best course of action, she decided   the only course she was even *prepared* to contemplate – was to take whatever Traynor threw at her squarely on the chin.

'Let's hear what you have to say, Mr Traynor,' she invited. 'And let's have it in plain speech, shall we, without any of your usual nasty little innuendos or snide suggestions?'

Traynor smirked. 'Certainly, Chief Inspector. Always glad

to oblige. In plain speech, then, isn't it true that this prime suspect would have been in custody long ago, if it hadn't been for the fact that you're both *Poles*?'

Paniatowski's eyes filled with an angry red mist. How could the bastard suggest that? How *dare* he suggest that?

Get your temper under control! she thought savagely. Get a bloody grip on yourself, Monika!

But she knew she was fighting a losing battle.

She turned towards the uniformed constable who was standing on duty by the door.

'I want that man ejected from the briefing!' she said, knowing – even as she spoke – that she was making a big mistake, yet unable to *prevent* herself from doing it. 'I want him ejected right now!'

'Hang about – you can't do that!' Traynor protested. 'I'm a reporter. I've got the right to ask any questions I want to, and I refuse to be thrown out just because *you* don't like some of those questions I *do* ask.'

The constable had drawn level with Traynor, and, before taking any further action, looked up at Paniatowski to see if she'd changed her mind.

How *could* she change her mind, she asked herself. If she changed her mind now, she'd look an even bigger fool than she was looking already.

She nodded, and the constable bent down and took hold of Traynor's arm.

For a second or two, it looked to Paniatowski as if the journalist was thinking of making his body go limp, like the Vietnam peace protestors she'd recently seen on television. But that was not really Traynor's style at all. Besides, he probably thought that making a dignified exit – or at least, as dignified an exit as someone like him *could* make – would be much more impressive.

Traynor rose to his feet, and allowed the constable to guide him to the door, but once there he took the officer by surprise by suddenly swivelling round and calling out, 'What's the matter, Chief Inspector Paniatowski? Don't you believe in the freedom of the press?'

The constable re-established his grip – slightly more firmly this time – and bundled Traynor out through the door.

'As a matter of fact, I do believe in the freedom of the press,'

Paniatowski told the remaining journalists. 'I believe in it passion-ately. But it's a freedom which has to be used responsibly, for public information rather than for personal glory.' She paused for a second. 'I'll take more questions now.'

But no further hands were raised. The other hacks might not like Mike Traynor – in fact, they'd made it quite plain, only minutes earlier, that they didn't – but there were times when it was necessary to show solidarity, even with an odious man like him.

And this was one of them.

TWENTY

Paniatowski sat alone in her office, a cigarette burning down in one hand and the morning's reports from Beresford's team – unread – on the desk in front of her. It was more than an hour since the press conference had ended, but the pounding in her head – which had begun when Traynor had started to move in for the kill – still refused to go away.

A uniformed WPC appeared in the open doorway, stood there uncertainly for a moment and then coughed.

Paniatowski looked up, straight into the WPC's eyes, and was almost certain she saw pity in them.

So it had come to this! A female constable – an officer at the very bottom of the ladder that she herself had worked so very hard to climb – was feeling *sorry* for her.

'Yes, what is it, Margaret?' she asked wearily.

'I'm sorry to disturb you, ma'am, but there's a feller here who says he has to see you.'

'And does this feller have *a name*?' Paniatowski snapped.

'Yes, ma'am, but—'

'I'm sorry, Margaret, there was no call for me to speak you like that,' Paniatowski said contritely.

'It's all right, ma'am. I know you've been under a lot of strain.'

Pity again!

'What *is* his name?' Paniatowski asked.

'It's something Polish, ma'am. It's very complicated. I tried my best to remember it, but . . .'

'Is it Szymborska?' Paniatowski suggested.

'That's it,' the WPC agreed, with some relief.

'You'd better show him in, then,' Paniatowski said heavily.

Paniatowski was shocked at Stan Szymborska's appearance. Less than twenty-four hours had passed since she'd last seen him in the bakery, but in that short time he seemed to have aged at least ten years.

'Do you want me to stay, ma'am?' the WPC asked.

'No, thank you, Margaret, that won't be necessary.' Paniatowski turned towards her visitor. 'Do please take a seat, Mr Szymborska.'

Szymborska lowered himself carefully into the chair, like an old man who was afraid that he might slip and hurt himself.

'Can I get you a hot drink, Mr Szymborska?' Paniatowski asked, concerned. 'A cup of tea? Or perhaps coffee?'

'No thank you.'

'Or, if you would prefer it, I have a bottle of good Polish vodka in the drawer.'

Stan Szymborska shook his head 'At this particular moment, I do not think vodka would be a good idea for *either* of us,' he said.

The bloody nerve of the man! Paniatowski thought.

'If there's one thing I really *don't* appreciate,' she said, 'it's being told when a drink would – or would not – be a good idea for me.'

Stan Szymborska shrugged, almost imperceptibly. 'Then by all means pour yourself a drink if you want to, Chief Inspector,' he said. 'But I will not be joining you.'

She didn't want to drink alone, she thought.

And anyway, he was right. In her current mental state, it wouldn't be a good idea.

'Shall we get straight to the point of this meeting, Mr Szymborska?' she asked crisply.

A thin ironic smile crossed Szymborska's lips. 'Yes,' he agreed. 'In fact, I have been waiting to get *straight to the point* for quite some time.'

This was her office, and she was a senior police officer, Paniatowski thought. So why did it feel as if Stan Szymborska was in charge?

'Why are you here?' she asked.

'I saw your press conference on the television,' Szymborska said, 'and it would seem from what I saw that I am your number-one suspect.'

'*I* didn't say that,' Paniatowski pointed out.

'No, you didn't,' Szymborska agreed. 'But the fact that you didn't *say* it doesn't mean you aren't *thinking* it. *Is* that what you think?'

'We naturally look very closely at the husbands of murder victims, especially when they don't have an alibi for the time at which the murder was committed,' Paniatowski said cautiously.

'Of course you do,' Szymborska agreed. 'You asked me why I am here. I am here to tell you that I would never have hurt my wife. I am here to tell you that I loved her.'

'You'd be surprised how many murderers claim to have loved their victims,' Paniatowski said.

'I would not be surprised at all, but that does not mean that they are not liars,' Szymborska countered. 'When you love someone – truly *love* them – you would never harm them, whatever they did to you. You would sacrifice your own life for them – even if you knew, deep down, that they were not worthy of such a sacrifice. You would do it not because you wanted to, or because felt you should, but simply because you had no choice in the matter.'

'And would you have sacrificed *yourself* for *your* wife?'

'Yes.'

'Whatever she'd done to you? However much she'd humiliated you, and made a public laughing stock of you?'

'Yes.'

I half-believe him, Paniatowski thought.

She didn't want to, but she couldn't help herself.

'*When* did you first fall in love with Linda?' she asked.

Stan shrugged again, as if he could see no point to the question.

'Why should that matter?'

'It matters because I'm trying to build up a picture of your relationship in my mind.'

'For what reason? Because you think that will make it much easier for you to pin the murder on me?'

'Because I think it will help me to discover the truth.'

Szymborska nodded. 'All right. I will believe you, though I can think of no reason why I should.'

'Thank you,' Paniatowski said, before she could stop herself.

'When did I fall in love with Linda?' Stan Szymborska mused. 'It must have been ten years ago, when the company I owned first started making deliveries for her father's bakery.'

'Jenny says you didn't fall in love with Linda until *after* her father's death,' Paniatowski told him. 'She says you had too much respect for Seth Brunskill to *allow* yourself to fall in love.'

'Ah, poor Jenny. She *would* say that,' Szymborska replied. 'But she's lying, is she?'

'No, she is not lying – she simply does not know the truth. She worshipped her father, and so she assumed that everyone else around him did, too. Linda suffered from the same delusion, but she's better now ... she ... she *was* better.' A sad smile came to Szymborska's face. 'You should have seen Linda when I first met. She was like a beautiful, delicate bird – but with a broken wing.'

'I take it from what you've just said that you didn't share the daughters' admiration for their father.'

'He was a swine of a man. I have known prison-camp guards with more humanity.'

'And yet you went into business with him?'

'Yes.'

'Why?'

'To spare my Linda from more suffering.'

'Would you care to explain that?'

'The business was failing, but that could not be Seth's fault,' Szymborska said. 'Nothing was *ever* his fault. So the blame had to rest with the girls, and every day, in every way he could think of – and believe me, he could think of many ways – he punished them for it.'

'I still don't see why you invested in the bakery,' Paniatowski confessed. 'You already had a successful business of your own. Couldn't you have simply told Linda how you felt, and asked her to marry you, then and there?'

'I could have done, but she wouldn't have listened.' Szymborska hesitated for a second. 'What do you know about prisoner-of-war-camp punishment cells?' he continued.

'Almost nothing at all,' Paniatowski admitted.

'When I was in the camp, there was a punishment cell which the Nazis kept exclusively for the Poles, who they regarded as less than human,' Szymborska told her. 'In fact, it was not really a cell at all – it was a metal box, out in the yard. I was sentenced to a week in it, once. It was the longest week of my life. There was no light in there, and no room to move. For the first day or so, I tried to hold on to something of the world I had left behind me. But by the third day, the *box* had become my world – the only world that seemed to have ever mattered.'

'Go on,' Paniatowski said.

'The cramps began on the first day, but the fourth day they had become truly agonizing. So I twisted and turned as much as I could, and sometimes, just once in a while, I managed to ease them.'

'It must have been terrible,' Paniatowski said.

'You are completely missing the point,' Szymborska told her bluntly. 'Such terms as "terrible" meant *nothing* inside the box. It was not *terrible* at all – it was just the way that things were, and you lived with it because there was nothing else you could do.'

'I understand.'

'I am not sure that you do – yet!' Szymborska continued. 'It was an offence to talk to the man in the box, and anyone caught doing it was likely to be placed in the box himself. Yet my comrades took the risk, and whenever they could, they whispered a few words of encouragement to me.'

'But those words meant nothing to you?' Paniatowski asked.

Szymborska smiled sadly. '*Now* you are starting to understand. As it happens, I didn't even *hear* those brave words – not because any physical barrier prevented it, but because of what was going on in my head. But even if I *had* heard, they would have made no sense to me.'

'You say they kept you in there a week?'

'A week. It doesn't sound *too* long, does it? But when the Nazis finally let me out, the other world into which they released me seemed all wrong. It was too bright. There was too much noise – too much happening. I wanted to go back into my box, where I understood the rules. But slowly, this feeling went away. Slowly, I came to terms with the real world again. And later, when other comrades had taken my place in the box, I would do as they had done, and risk the whispered words – even though I knew it would be pointless.'

How heroic, Paniatowski thought. How admirable!

And then she remembered that she was talking to the man who – whatever he had, or had not, done in the past – was now the chief suspect in a truly horrific murder case.

'I suppose that your wartime experiences are all very interesting in their own way,' she told him, almost having to force the words out of her mouth, 'but I don't see what they have to do with the matter we were discussing.'

'Don't you?' Szymborska asked, as if he knew that he had touched her – as if he knew that she was lying.

She felt a wave of shame sweep over her, but fought it back.

The man across the desk from her had, in all probability, cut off the hands of his wife and her lover, she told herself.

Yield no ground to him!

Give him no breaks!

'Perhaps you could explain to me why *you* think it's so relevant,' she suggested.

'Imagine if, instead of being placed in the box once you had grown up, you were born into it,' Szymborska said. 'Imagine if you had never known anything else. That was the situation that Linda and her sister were in – placed in the box by their father at birth, and never allowed to see the outside. *Of course* I could have asked her to marry me – whispered the words through the wall of the box – but she would not have heard them. And even if she had heard them, they would have made no sense to her. So I bought into the business, and I waited until she could be liberated from the box.'

'By which you mean you waited until her father died?'

'Yes, that is what I mean. I led her gently into the sunlight, using my hand to shield her eyes from the brightness. And then I waited again, as she grew accustomed to this new world. And only when she was finally ready – only when she had lost all desire to return to the box – did I ask her to marry me.'

'What about her sister Jenny?' Paniatowski asked. 'How did *she* escape from the box?'

'She hasn't escaped,' Szymborska said. 'And I don't think she ever will.'

When Paniatowski entered George Baxter's office, the chief constable was at his desk, with a pile of balance sheets stacked up in front of him.

'I'd have asked you to come and see me sooner, Monika,' he said, 'but for the last three hours I've been tied up in a finance meeting, so I've only just had a chance to review the video recording of your press conference.'

'Is that right, sir?' Paniatowski asked, noncommittally.

Baxter stood up and walked around his desk.

'Shall we sit down?' he said, gesturing at the two comfortable chairs at the other end of the office.

'If it's all the same to you, sir, I'd rather—'

'It wasn't a request,' Baxter interrupted her.

Once they were seated, facing each other across the coffee table, Baxter said, 'You are *aware* the press conference wasn't good, don't you?'

'Yes,' Paniatowski agreed, dully. 'I am aware of that.'

'In fact – and I have to be totally honest with you about it – you completely lost it in there, Monika. You were doing very well at the start – and then you completely lost it.'

'Do you know how *hard* it's been for me, working my way up through the ranks in a Force where most of the men believe that a woman's place is in the home?' Paniatowski demanded angrily.

'Yes, I do,' Baxter said.

'And when I finally make it, what happens? I'm accused of not doing my job properly, not because I'm a woman – though you could tell that half of those reporters were thinking that *as well* – but because I'm a *Pole*.'

'Nobody imagines it's been easy for you, but even so, you still should have handled it better,' Baxter said firmly. 'Charlie Woodend would have, you know. Charlie would have soon found a way to make Traynor feel like the slug he is, while at the same time reducing the rest of the hacks to fits of laughter.'

'I'm *not* Charlie,' Paniatowski said.

'No, you're not,' Baxter agreed.

'But that doesn't mean I can't do the job, does it?'

'No, it doesn't, *necessarily*. But you're still going to have to do something pretty decisive to put yourself back on the right track – pretty decisive and pretty damn quick.'

'Like what?'

'That's up to you.'

'But what do *you* think I should do?'

Baxter hesitated for a second, then said, 'You might *consider* arresting Stan Szymborska.'

Paniatowski shook her head.

'I'm not going to be led by the nose by snivelling loathsome hacks like Mike Traynor,' she said. 'I'm not going to arrest Stan Szymborska when there simply isn't enough evidence to make that arrest stick.'

'Are you sure that the amount of evidence you have is your *only* consideration?' Baxter asked.

'What other consideration *could* there be?'

'Have you stopped to ask yourself if you might not be blinkered by the fact that Szymborska – like your father – is a war hero?'

'That's not fair,' Paniatowski said bitterly. 'The only reason you know about my father is because I told you about him myself. In bed! You can't use that information against me now.'

'I can use any information I choose to use, if I consider it is relevant to something which is undermining the performance of one of my officers,' Baxter said. Then he smiled. 'There! Now do you see what you've done? You've got me talking like a stuffed shirt.'

'You can't keep switching around like that,' Paniatowski said, refusing to return the smile. 'Who are you at the moment? George Baxter, my ex-lover? Or my boss, George Baxter the chief constable?'

'I'm both. We're *all* several different sides of ourselves at the same time. And the only way we can handle that, with any chance of success, is by doing our best to ensure that the side of us which is most appropriate to our current situation is in control. That's why I think you should ignore your war-hero father – who you can hardly remember, anyway – and arrest Szymborska. If it turns out to be the wrong move, then I'll be willing to take my fair share of the flak – to take *more than* my fair share, in fact.'

'You make it sound like you're trying to protect me,' Paniatowski said.

'That's *exactly* what I'm doing,' Baxter agreed.

'But *who* are you trying to protect? Monika? Or DCI Paniatowski?'

'Both of you, as you should have realized by now. Given our history, that's the way it has to work – that's the only way it *can* work.'

Paniatowski was silent for quite a while, then she said, 'Are you *ordering* me to arrest Stan?'

'Of course not. This is your case, and – as long as it remains your case – you must run with it as you see fit.'

'Well, I'm certainly pleased we've got all that cleared up, sir,' Paniatowski said.

'So will you be arresting him?' Baxter asked.

'No, sir, I won't,' Paniatowski said firmly.

She was pacing her office again, but this time she was so distracted that she didn't always remember to avoid the furniture. It didn't matter. Though she had already barked her shins twice, she hardly even noticed the pain.

Was Traynor right when he'd said that the only reason she hadn't already arrested Stan was because he was a fellow Pole?

Was Baxter right when he'd told her that the real problem was that she was confusing the suspect with her father, who, if he'd lived, would only have been a few years older than Stan?

But more importantly – and much worse – had she allowed Szymborska to *play* her?

The simple dignity with which he'd talked about his time in the box and his courtship of Linda had almost brought her to tears.

Yet was any of it *real*? Or were the box and the love story no more than parts of the highly elaborate game which had started with the appearance of the two severed hands?

The simple truth was that she had lost confidence in her own judgement, she told herself.

And how was she to get that confidence back?

By talking to Colin Beresford?

No, that wouldn't be fair. She was the leader of the team. He should draw *his* confidence from *her*, rather than it being the other way round.

Almost without seeming to will it, she came to a sudden halt next to her telephone.

For a moment, she had no idea why – and then she understood.

She flipped open her address book, and dialled a number she'd thought she'd never need to call.

She heard the phone ringing at the other end of the line.

'Pick it up,' her mind screamed. 'For God's sake, pick it up!'

And then someone did.

'I'm afraid Annie's not here at the moment,' said a voice

she knew so very well it almost brought tears to her eyes, 'but if you'd like to leave a message, I'll see she gets it.'

She could see him quite clearly, almost as if he were standing in the room with her.

The big head, with the features which looked as if they'd been carved by a sculptor who'd got bored halfway through, and simply given up.

The square hard body, clad in the inevitable hairy sports coat.

The smell of him – meat pies and best bitter and cigarette ash.

The expressions which filled those half-finished features of his – amusement, puzzlement, anger and joy.

They'd been through so much together, the two of them. He'd *helped her* through so much.

'Help me *now*, Charlie!' she pleaded silently. 'Tell me what to do!'

'Is anybody there?' Woodend asked.

Paniatowski opened her mouth and closed it again, opened a second time and was on the point of speaking when something from within her forced her jaw to clamp closed.

'Hello?' Charlie Woodend said. 'Hello?'

It was now or never, Paniatowski thought. And quickly – before she had time to change her mind – she put the phone back on its cradle.

TWENTY-ONE

Sylvia Hope-Gore showed Beresford into her conservatory. It was a pleasant room. One end of it was clearly the social side, with a series of cane chairs and tables. The other end – the horticultural side – was given over almost exclusively to the cultivation of a number of green plants with slightly spiky leaves, which the inspector did not recognize.

'You sit yourself down, and I'll go and make us a nice cup of tea,' Hope-Gore said. 'You've no objection to herbal, have you?'

'None at all. I rather like it,' replied Beresford, who didn't think he'd ever drunk herbal tea in his entire life.

'Good,' Hope-Gore said. 'I stopped drinking what you might call "normal" tea ages ago – and so would you, if you knew as much about the conditions on the tea plantations as I do.'

Beresford was not at all surprised by the comment. He had done his research on Sylvia Hope-Gore, and was well aware that while most of the people in Whitebridge who knew about her would have been happy enough to describe her as a local celebrity, there was a substantial minority who would only have used the term if they could have added the word 'notorious' to it.

Miss Hope-Gore – she'd never married – had been born into minor landed aristocracy, but had rejected both her family and her class in the 1920s, when she'd become a communist. Since then, she'd attempted – with greater or lesser success – to be a constant thorn in the side of the local establishment. She'd been active in industrial strikes during the Depression, had organized rent boycotts after the war and had been a staunch champion of the rights of hippies to get (as she'd once put it), 'as much free love as they can afford'.

The old woman returned carrying a tray on which there was a teapot, two cups and saucers and a plate of biscuits.

'I'll help you with that,' Beresford offered.

'You most certainly will *not* help me,' Sylvia Hope-Gore

replied fiercely. 'Doddering I may well be, but I'm not yet quite so doddering that I can't handle a tea tray.'

'No, of course not,' Beresford agreed, as he watched the old woman's progress across the room with some anxiety.

Sylvia Hope-Gore carefully laid the tray down on the cane coffee table, which lay between two cane chairs.

'For goodness' sake, sit down,' she said. 'You're making the place look untidy, standing there like that.'

Beresford sat. 'I was noticing your plants,' he said. 'I don't think I've ever seen anything quite like them before. What are they called?'

'Oh, I don't know the scientific name for them,' Sylvia Hope-Gore said airily. 'I just call them *ganja*. Does that name mean anything to you?'

'No, I don't think it does,' Beresford admitted.

Sylvia Hope-Gore nodded. 'I suppose that's just as well,' she said. She indicated the tray. 'There's Rich Tea or Garibaldi biscuits. The choice is yours. Or if you'd prefer it, I've just baked some hash . . .' She stopped herself just in time. 'No, that probably wouldn't be a good idea,' she admitted.

She poured the tea and passed Beresford a cup. He took a sip, and tried not to grimace.

'Very nice,' he said.

'It's an acquired taste,' Miss Hope-Gore told him. She gave Beresford a hard stare. 'When you said earlier that you liked herbal tea, you were just humouring an old woman, weren't you?'

'No . . . I . . .'

'*Weren't you?*'

'I'm sorry,' Beresford said abjectly.

'There's no need to apologize,' Miss Hope-Gore said. 'It was rather *sweet* of you to pretend.' She sipped at her own tea with obvious relish. 'I used to be something of a radical, you know.'

'So I've heard.'

'Of course, I've slowed down a bit since my heyday, but when the need arises, I can still man the barricades with the best of them.'

'I believe you,' Beresford said.

And so he did.

'But we all change, whether we want to or not,' Miss Hope-Gore continued, a little wistfully. 'There was a time – and not *so* long ago – when I'd rather have pulled off my own arm than talk to the police.'

'But not any more?'

'No, not any more,' Miss Hope-Gore said wistfully. 'I don't get many visitors these days – it must be a week since I've talked to anyone but the milkman – so even a representative of the forces of fascist repression is welcome.' She smiled, almost coquettishly. 'Besides, you are a very *good-looking* boy.'

Beresford returned it with a smile of his own, which he hoped acknowledged the compliment without also issuing an invitation to pursue this line of conversation any further.

'If you don't mind, I'd like to ask you a few questions about Stanislaw Szymborska,' he said.

Miss Hope-Gore smiled fondly.

'Stan,' she said softly. 'I haven't seen him for years. But why would *you* be interested in *him*?'

'Haven't you read the papers?' Beresford asked.

Miss Hope-Gore shook her head. 'Not since the Labour Party sold us all down the river in '64. Is Stan in trouble?'

'That will depend on whether or not he's done anything wrong,' Beresford said cunningly. 'When did you first meet him?'

'It must have been just after the war. I was trying to get Polish refugees re-housed at the time – it was just awful the way the council treated them – and Stan was involved in it, too. As a war hero, of course, he could have been said to have already done his bit and simply rested on his laurels. But that wasn't his way. He was never the sort of man to just sit back and take whatever fate threw at him – he made things *happen*.'

But had he *made things happen* two nights earlier, when he may just possibly have learned of his wife's affair? Beresford wondered.

'How well did you know him?' he asked.

'It depends what you mean by *well*. Are you asking me, in your sweet boyish way, if we were lovers?'

'No, I . . .'

'Because if you are, then the answer is most definitely yes.' Miss Hope-Gore took another genteel sip of her tea. 'Have I shocked you?'

'No, of course not,' Beresford said.

He was lying. He already knew that Miss Hope-Gore was rumoured to have had affairs – her more salacious critics often claimed she'd had more pricks in her than a second-hand dartboard – but she must have been at least twenty years older than Szymborska.

'A man reaches his sexual prime when he's eighteen, but a woman has to wait until her forties,' Miss Hope-Gore said, reading his mind. 'And I wasn't always the wrinkled old hag you see before you now – you should have seen me before my tits dropped.'

'How long were you . . . were you together?' Beresford asked, wondering why the conservatory had suddenly become so hot.

'You mean, how long were we rutting like goats in heat?' Miss Hope-Gore asked, obviously enjoying his discomfort. 'How long were we making the beast with two backs? About three years, on and off. It was the most amazing sex I've ever known, and when we did split up, it certainly wasn't because we'd stopped enjoying each other in bed.'

'Then why?'

'It was purely for political reasons.'

'Political reasons?' Beresford asked, grasping at the words – so wonderfully free of sexual connotations – as a drowning man might grasp at a straw.

'Stan said that what the Russians were doing in Poland was wrong, while I, of course, claimed quite the opposite was true, because it was all being done in Comrade Stalin's name and Comrade Stalin simply could never *be* wrong. We were never going to agree on the subject, and so we went our separate ways. It was a very amicable parting, but then, you see, apart from the fury of the bedroom, our relationship had *always* been very amicable.'

'Fury of the bedroom,' Beresford repeated, accepting that, as much as he'd rather avoid the topic of their sex life, he wasn't going to be able to. 'Was he *violent* in bed?'

An amused smile played on Miss Hope-Gore's cracked old lips. 'Why do you ask?' she said. 'Hoping to pick up a few tips?'

'No, I . . .'

'Stan was energetic, rather than violent. In fact, I don't

think I ever saw him *really* lose total control of himself, even in the height of passion. Of course, that hadn't always been the case. There'd been a time when violence played a *central* part of his life.'

'You mean while he was serving as a fighter pilot in the Polish Air Force?' Beresford asked.

'Well, yes, I suppose I do mean that as well,' Miss Hope-Gore said.

'As well?'

'But I was actually thinking more of the time when he was in the prisoner-of-war camp. He had some terrible experiences then – so terrible that I don't think he's ever talked about them to another living soul.'

'Except to you,' Beresford said, wondering if she was just spinning him a line to make herself seem more important.

'No, he didn't talk about them even to me,' Miss Hope-Gore said.

'Then how do you *know* about them?'

'I don't really. Not in any detail. But I got a *flavour* of them, shall we say, from hearing what he said during his nightmares.'

'So he had nightmares, did he?'

'Haven't I just said that he did?'

'How often?'

'Fairly regularly. Not every night, by any means, but certainly at least once a week.'

'And these nightmares of his were *always* about his time as a prisoner of war?'

'Yes.'

'How can you be sure of that?'

Miss Hope-Gore smiled again. 'I think it was probably the fact that he kept repeating the words "German guards" and "camp commandant" that really gave it away,' she said.

'And he said that in English, did he?'

'He'd have to have done, or I'd never have had a bloody clue what he was going on about, would I?' Miss Hope-Gore asked, the smile still in place. 'He once told me that since he'd decided his future was to be in England, he always made an effort to try and *think* in English – and he seems to have succeeded to the extent that he dreamed in it, too.'

'So he got very agitated when he was dreaming about these prison-camp guards, did he?' Beresford asked.

'No, not at all. While he was mumbling on about *them*, he was quite calm. It was only when he got on to the subject of the hand that he started to become really distressed.'

'The hand?'

'That's right. He cut it off. Or he helped someone else to cut it off. I was never quite clear which.'

'Can you remember exactly what it was that he said about it?' Beresford asked.

'Shouldn't think so,' Miss Hope-Gore said cheerfully. 'At best, he was hardly coherent at the time, and that time *was* nearly twenty-five years ago.'

'Could you try?' Beresford pleaded.

'All right,' Miss Hope-Gore agreed. She closed her eyes. 'I got the impression he was arguing with someone called Stefan. Stefan wanted to cut the hand off, and Stan didn't. But in the end, Stefan talked him round, because Stan said, "It is the right thing to do. It is just." That sounds a bit melodramatic when *I* say it, doesn't it? But hearing it the way *Stan* said it – and picturing the circumstances in which he must have *originally* said it – I can assure you it didn't sound melodramatic at all.'

'I'm sure it didn't,' Beresford agreed.

Miss Hope-Gore opened her eyes again. 'And now I think about it, there was one word he kept saying over and over, especially as the nightmare was drawing to a close.'

'And what word was that?' Beresford asked.

'Betrayal,' Miss Hope-Gore said. 'Does that make any sense to you?'

'Yes,' Beresford said. 'It makes *a lot* of sense.'

Jenny Brunskill walked up the cobbled street in one of the older parts of Whitebridge like a woman on a mission. And that was exactly what she was on, she told herself – a mission.

She had never done anything like this before – never even *thought* of launching a commando raid into what could prove to be enemy territory.

In the past, Linda would have handled something like this, she thought, and she herself would have been quite content – even quite relieved – to *let* Linda handle it. But now Linda was gone, and so it was up to her.

She had reached her objective – a corner shop which was

located on the junction of two streets of terraced houses, and had windows looking out onto both of them.

She stepped out in the street to get a better look at it. There was a long metal sign over the door, and though the name of the shop – Handley's General Store and Off Licence – was clearly visible in the middle, it was dwarfed by the much larger advertisements for Embassy Filter Cigarettes which flanked it. On the pavement was a long trestle table, holding wicker baskets of fruit and vegetables, and a hand-written sign had been pinned to the corner of it, which asked customers to serve themselves and pay inside.

This was just the kind of shop which had been the back-bone of the bakery's business for so long, she thought, as she opened the door and heard a brass bell ring in the back room. And though she and Linda had expanded the selling base in the years since their father had so tragically passed away, it was *still* business they could not afford to lose.

And yet they *had* been losing it. A five per cent drop in sales here, a ten per cent drop there. Only a few loaves, when you looked at it one way, but a symptom of a serious problem when you looked at it in another.

Her initial plan had been to approach the shopkeepers directly.

'*How can you let us down like this?*' she'd imagined herself saying. '*After all the years we've worked together, how can you betray us now?*'

But that wouldn't work, she'd quickly realized. Not for *her*.

If her father had said something like that, the shopkeepers would have hung their heads in shame and almost begged him for his forgiveness. If Linda had said it, they would have at least looked sheepish, and then begun to toe the line again. But she was not her wonderful father, nor her strong sister. She was only Jenny – and they would just have laughed at her.

So if the direct approach would not uncover whatever conspiracy was afoot, she would have to be more oblique in her approach, she decided. And that was she was being now – more oblique!

She picked up a small wire basket, filled it with things she didn't really want and approached the cash desk.

The shopkeeper, a middle-aged man with a bushy white moustache and a red face, smiled at her.

'I don't think I've seen you in my shop before, have I, love?' he asked.

'No, you haven't,' Jenny agreed. 'I used to live in Accrington. I've only just moved to Whitebridge.'

'Accrington,' the shopkeeper repeated, as he began ringing up her purchases on the till. 'Well, if *that*'s where you've come from, you must be really congratulating yourself on moving up in the world.' He paused, wondering if he'd said the wrong thing. 'Just my little joke, love. No offence intended.'

'And none taken,' Jenny replied. 'You're quite right – Whitebridge *is* much nicer than Accrington.'

'Well, us locals like to think so, any road,' the shopkeeper said. 'I'm Ed Handley.'

'Pleased to meet you, Mr Handley.'

'Now, none of that,' the shopkeeper said, with mock severity. 'If you're going to become one of my regular customers – an' I certainly hope you are – you'd better start callin' me Ed.'

'All right,' Jenny agreed.

'An' what might your name be?' Handley asked.

She hadn't thought of that, she told herself in a panic. She'd never even *considered* the need for an alias.

'I'm Jenny,' she said. 'Jenny . . . Smith.'

Handley transferred her purchases to a brown-paper bag.

'Will there be anything else, *Jenny*?' he asked.

She took a deep breath. 'Yes, I think I'll take a loaf of Brunskill's thick sliced.'

'Can I make a suggestion?' Handley asked.

'Yes, I suppose so.'

'Why not try a Tompkins' large crusty loaf instead? I think you'll find it's much better bread.'

If he had spat in her face he could not possibly have offended her more, but Jenny forced herself to keep calm.

'If Tompkins' is much better, why are you still selling Brunskill's?' she asked.

'Well, to tell you the truth, it's more out of habit than anything else. But I've been slowly moving over to Tompkins', and now that Brunskill's is likely to close down, I'll be giving them all my business.'

Jenny shivered. It was like seeing your own obituary before you'd even realized you were dead, she thought.

'I didn't know Brunskill's *was* closing down,' she said aloud.
'Then you can't have been reading the papers, can you?'
Handley said. 'One of the owners of Brunskill's was murdered
the other night, and another of the owners – her husband, as
a matter of fact – is about to be arrested for the murder.'

'It . . . it didn't say *that* in the paper, did it?' Jenny asked.

'Well, no, not in so many words,' Handley conceded. 'But
if you read between the lines, it's there, clear enough. And
once he *is* arrested, the business is finished. After all, who
wants to buy bread from a firm that has a murderer in the
family?'

TWENTY-TWO

The shutters were down on the main entrance to the bakery, but when Paniatowski rang the bell at the side door, her ring was answered by a small late-middle-aged man in a boiler suit.

'I don't know who you've come to talk to, Chief Inspector Paniatowski,' the man said, 'but whoever it is, he's gone home.'

'Unless, of course, I've come to talk to you, Mr Monkton,' Paniatowski countered.

'An' have you?' Monkton asked.

'Yes.'

'Well, in that case, I suppose you'd better come through to my office,' the nightwatchman said.

He led her down the corridor along the back of the bakery, to a room dominated by industrial shelving and a workbench, into which he had still managed to cram a couple of battered armchairs.

'When I called it my office, I was bein' ironic,' Monkton said. 'Is that the right word, Chief Inspector? Ironic?'

Paniatowski smiled. 'You know it is.'

She had liked Len Monkton immediately. He was not physically prepossessing, but his eyes hinted at both intelligence and humour, and – without really trying to – he exuded an air of dependability.

They sat down, and Paniatowski said, 'Is it true that you've worked for the bakery right from the beginning?'

'That's correct,' Monkton confirmed. 'I started on the day it moved into the Brewer's Street, an' I've been with it ever since.'

'Which means that you've got more than twenty solid years' service behind you,' Paniatowski calculated. 'Well, that is certainly something to be proud of, isn't it?'

'Is it?' Monkton asked, looking at her a little strangely.

'I would say so.'

'Let's get one thing straight before we go any further,' Len Monkton said. 'There are fellers I know who think that the longer they work at a job, the more commendable they are. But I'm not *one* of them fellers, Chief Inspector. It seems to me that if long service is the key to self-respect, then the donkeys workin' on Blackpool sands must be burstin' with it.' He paused for a second. 'What I'm really sayin' is that while that particular line might soften up a lot of the men you want to question, it won't work on me.'

Paniatowski grinned awkwardly. 'You're right, it *was* a line,' she admitted. 'But I've learned my lesson, Mr Monkton, and I certainly won't try anything like that again.'

'An' while we're into straight talkin', I'll tell you somethin' else,' Len Monkton continued. 'If you're looking for somebody to bad-mouth Mr Szymborska to you, then you've come to the wrong place, because I'll not hear a word said against him.'

'He's a good boss, is he?'

'He's a good *man*, Chief Inspector. A *thoroughly* good man. An' while you might just possibly be able to talk me into believin' that the moon is made of green cheese – or even that Whitebridge Rovers have a fightin' chance of winnin' the FA Cup this year – you'll *never* persuade me that Mr Szymborska killed his missus an' Tom Whittington.'

'So who did?' Paniatowski asked.

'I don't know – but it wasn't him.'

'Why don't you tell me a little about the bakery in general,' Paniatowski suggested.

'Now why would you want me to do that?'

'Well, one possibility is that I'm hoping to trap you into saying something you don't *want* to say,' Paniatowski replied, smiling again. 'The other possibility is that I just want to build up a general picture of the place, because I think that might help my investigation. Why don't *you* decide which one it is?'

Monkton thought about it.

'Where would you like me to start?' he asked finally.

'Wherever you want to. I find that the beginning's usually as good a place as any.'

Monkton nodded. 'Seth Brunskill was one of them men who confuse bein' *lucky* with bein' *smart*,' he said. 'The simple truth was that he owed whatever success he had to just happenin' to be in the right place at the right time.'

'But he didn't see it that way?'

'Oh no, not Seth. As far as he was concerned, he was some sort of genius – which meant that not only did things always have to be done his way, but he had to do most of them himself – because nobody else could be trusted to do them *properly*. He was hardly ever out of the bakery. Didn't believe in holidays. Never took a day off. An' in the end, I suppose, that's what killed him.'

'Heart attack?' Paniatowski guessed.

'Heart attack,' Monkton confirmed. 'He wasn't exactly what you'd have called a *young* man when he died, but it's my firm belief that if he'd slowed down a bit – if he'd just been able to learn how to delegate a little – he might still have been alive today.'

And perhaps Linda would still have been alive, too, Paniatowski thought – still living in her tin box, but still *alive*.

'Tell me about Tom Whittington,' she suggested.

'He was an odd feller,' Monkton said. 'He was born a few doors down from where I live, and I've known him all his life. And yet I don't feel I ever really knew him at all.'

'Why's that?'

'Because *nobody* really knew him. He was an only child, you see – the son of two other only children – an' his mother died when he was ten. It was cancer that did for her. His dad, Fred, who'd been a bit of a bad bugger even before she popped her clogs, got even worse once they'd buried his wife. I think he blamed Tom for her death.'

'Why? If she'd died of cancer, it was nobody's fault.'

'True enough,' Monkton agreed. 'But as far as Fred was concerned, *somebody* had to be to blame, and Tom was the closest to hand. Anyway, things went from bad to worse, and it soon got so that he'd thrash the living daylights out of Tom at the slightest provocation. An' I think that was when Tom decided that the only way to protect himself was to make himself invisible. So that's exactly what he did. He made himself invisible. An' not just to his dad, but to everybody. You'd never see him out on the street, an' my kids – who were at the same school as he was – told me that when playtime came, he'd stay in a corner, all by himself.'

'I'm not disputing anything of what you've just said for a second,' Paniatowski told Monkton. 'But I am finding it difficult to understand how any boy who dedicated himself to not being noticed could end up with a criminal record for stealing cars.'

'Not *cars*,' Monkton said. 'It was just *one* car. An' he was *talked into* stealin' that.'

'How?'

'There were a couple of real tearaways who lived on our street. One was called Pete Higgins, an' the other was Brian Clegg. An' these two thought Tom was fair game for a bit of sport, so they pretended they wanted to be his mates. Some kids do that kind of thing, you know.'

'I do know,' Paniatowski agreed.

'Of course, though they were laughin' behind their hands at him the whole time, Tom was completely taken in by it all, an' for first time in years he started lookin' happy.'

'Bastards!' Paniatowski said.

'There's no doubt that's exactly what they were,' Len Monkton agreed. 'Anyway, there was this big dance bein' held over in Burnley, an' Pete an' Brian wanted to go to it. But they had no way of getting' there, you see, so they came up with the idea of nickin' this car.' Monkton paused. 'I only found out about all this years later, when I overheard Pete and Brian braggin' in the pub – an' by then it was too late to do anythin' about it.'

'Understood,' Paniatowski said.

'They got Tom to break into the car, but it was one of them who did the actual drivin', because Tom didn't know how to. He never did learn – not till the day he died.'

Which was why, when they went to the Old Oak Tree Inn as Mr and Mrs Lord, it was Linda behind the wheel of the Jag, Paniatowski thought.

'Anyway, as bad luck would have it – at least for Tom – the owner of the car turned up just as they were drivin' away. He rang the police immediately, an' even before they'd left Whitebridge they saw a police car comin' up behind them, with its lights flashin'. But they didn't panic – you have to give them that. What they *did* do was to pull straight into a side road, an' once they'd stopped the car, Brian an' Pete legged it.'

'But not Tom?'

'No, they'd told him to stay with the car, and because they were mates of his – an' he trusted them – that's what he did. So, naturally, he was the one the bobbies arrested.'

'What about the other two?'

'Oh, the bobbies couldn't even be bothered to chase after them. There didn't seem to be any need. After all, they'd got one of the gang, an' they were sure he'd soon give up the names of the others.'

'But he didn't?'

'He did not. They were his mates – the first ones he'd ever really had – an' you don't betray your mates, do you? I don't know how long it took him to realize he'd been played for a mug all along, but he must have realized it in the end, don't you think?'

'Yes, I do,' Paniatowski agreed.

'Well, after that, he became even more withdrawn. You'd hardly ever see him at all. I'd felt sorry enough for him before, but I began to feel *really* sorry for him then. That's why I got him a job at the bakery. It wasn't so much for the money he'd earn – it was just a way of gettin' him out of the house.'

'Miss Brunskill told my sergeant that the reason her father took him on was because he believed in giving people second chances,' Paniatowski said.

'Miss Brunskill *would* say that,' Monkton retorted. 'If she'd seen old Seth strangle a baby before her very eyes, she'd have found some way to convince herself that he'd only done it for the baby's own good.'

'So why *did* Seth Brunskill take Tom on?'

'Because he knew that since Tom had a criminal record, he could get him cheap. An' then – surprise, surprise – Tom turned out to be a natural at the job – a real bobby-dazzler of a baker. But he still kept himself to himself – he never came out of his shell again.'

Until Linda Szymborska came along, Paniatowski thought. Until she *seduced* him in much the same way as Pete and Brian had.

TWENTY-THREE

'W hat's the homework situation like tonight?' Paniatowski asked down the phone, with a jauntiness she certainly didn't feel. 'Any of that Al-Jebra, which has Lily so worried?'

'No, it's just geography tonight,' Louisa said. Then she added, with some disgust, 'We have to draw a *map*!'

Paniatowski laughed. Her daughter was marvellous with words, but maps and Louisa just did not get on.

'I should be home in about half an hour, so maybe we can do it together,' she suggested.

There was a long pause at the other end of the line, then Louisa said, 'There's no bingo tonight, so Lily doesn't mind staying with me.'

'Lily doesn't *have* to stay with you,' Paniatowski replied. 'I've just told you, I'll be home in half an hour.'

Another pause.

'Are you sure that's a good idea, Mum?' Louisa said, finally.

'What do you mean, am I sure it's a good idea?'

'They showed your press conference on the telly, Mum,' Louisa said reluctantly.

'I was awful, wasn't I?' Paniatowski asked.

'I . . . I wouldn't say you were *awful*, exactly,' Louisa said, obviously choosing her words carefully. 'And that nasty man who was asking you questions didn't help – he was really unfair.'

'Anyway, how has my press conference got anything to do with my coming home?' Paniatowski asked.

'I think you should go to the Drum and Monkey instead,' Louisa said seriously.

'What is this?' Paniatowski asked, pretending she thought the whole thing was a joke – though she knew full well it wasn't. 'Is my *own daughter* advising me to get drunk!'

'You need to talk to Uncle Colin,' Louisa said.

'It's always *nice* to talk to Uncle Colin, but why should I *need* to?' Paniatowski asked, continuing to play the game to the bitter end.

'You're in a mess, Mum,' Louisa said. 'Even I know that – and I'm only a kid.'

'Yes, I'm in a mess,' Paniatowski agreed.

'What you really need is to talk to Uncle Charlie about it,' Louisa told her. 'But Uncle Charlie isn't here any more, so Uncle Colin will have to do.'

After her talk with her daughter, Paniatowski didn't need anyone else to confirm that she'd 'lost it' at the press conference, but if she had, there'd been ample confirmation in the public bar of the Drum and Monkey that night.

It wasn't that the regular drinkers were looking at her in a strange or pitying way – it was more a case of them not looking at her *at all*.

But she knew what they were thinking.

Charlie Woodend would have handled Traynor better!

Charlie Woodend would have handled the investigation *better!*

If Charlie had still been in charge, the guilty man would have been banged up long before now!

Beresford's pint was sitting in its rightful place on the team's usual table. The inspector himself, however, was some distance from it, examining – with apparent fascination – what Paniatowski would have taken for a shoe-shine machine, but for the fact that it seemed to have a television screen mounted on its top.

She walked over to him, and tapped him on the shoulder.

'Well, that – whatever it is – certainly seems to have grabbed your attention,' she said.

'It's called Pong,' Beresford said enthusiastically. 'It was only installed this afternoon.'

He moved slightly to the side, so that she could get a better view. Not that there was much to see, she thought. The background was black, but everything else – two square zeros at the top, a broken white line running down the middle, a smaller white line at each end of the screen and a square dot which bounced back and forth – was white.

'It's what they call a video game, and it's based on ping-pong,' Beresford explained. 'Do you fancy a game?'

'Not really,' Paniatowski said.

'Oh, come on, boss,' Beresford urged her. 'It'll help to take your mind off things.'

Paniatowski sighed resignedly. 'All right.'

Beresford reached into his pocket and took out what the government was insisting everybody call a two-and-half new pence coin, but he knew was actually a sixpence in real money. He slid it into the slot.

'What are the rules?' Paniatowski asked.

'Simplicity itself,' Beresford told her. 'You turn that knob, and your bat moves up and down. The objective is to keep returning my serves.'

The square ball bounced across the screen, and Paniatowski missed it. The number at the top of Beresford's side of the screen changed from a chunky zero to a one.

'Gotcha!' Beresford said.

She didn't care, she realized. Though she was normally the most competitive of games players, she had no real interest in winning this one.

Beresford served again, and this time she managed to send the ball hurtling back at him.

'Now you're getting the hang of it,' Beresford said.

But what was the point, she wondered. What was the point of *anything*?

Her heart was not in it, but her reflexes refused to let her give up the struggle, and in the next half-minute she notched up five points to Beresford's four.

'Big tough woman!' Beresford said, with a grin on his face.

But she wasn't, she thought. She was wielding the bat in this game, but in the game that really mattered – the game being played out at police headquarters – she wasn't wielding anything at all. Instead, she was the ball, a helpless object being bounced back and forth between the press and the chief constable, between the suspect she didn't want to arrest and the evidence which suggested that perhaps she should.

At the end of the game she had won by eight points to six.

'Another?' Beresford suggested.

'No, thank you,' she said. 'That's quite enough excitement for one day.'

They walked back to the table, and sat down.

'Are you expecting Sergeant Walker to be putting in an appearance tonight?' Beresford asked.

Paniatowski shook her head. 'He left me a message to say

that he's suddenly come down with a bad case of the flu, and he's gone to bed.'

'A bad case of *spinelessness*, more like,' Beresford retorted. 'After the way he ratted you out to Mike Traynor this afternoon, he simply daren't face you.'

'We don't know for certain that it was him who ratted me out,' Paniatowski countered.

'Of course we do,' Beresford said dismissively. 'There were only three of us who knew enough of the story to brief Traynor like that, and since you and I didn't do it, it just has to be Walker.'

'You're right, of course,' Paniatowski agreed. 'But we'll never be able to prove it.'

'Whether you can prove it or not, you simply don't have any choice but to get rid of him.'

Paniatowski shook her head again. 'Can't be done. At least, not yet. The chief constable's made that perfectly clear.'

'Then when *can* it be done?' Beresford asked.

'Maybe when I solve this case,' Paniatowski replied.

Or *if* I solve this case, she thought.

'Give me some good news, Colin,' she continued. 'Tell me your team's uncovered something that will gladden my heart at least a little.'

'I don't think I've got much to offer in the heart-gladdening stakes, but here goes,' Beresford said. 'Several people we questioned remembered seeing a Jag in the centre of town on the night of the murder. Two of the witnesses said it was being driven by a woman, two more said there was a man behind the wheel and the rest weren't close enough to say *who* was driving.'

'So who *was* driving it?' Paniatowski asked. 'Linda – which would confirm that what Stan said about her leaving the house in a huff was the truth? Or Stan, who made up the whole story about her leaving, and was ditching the car in a desperate attempt to back it up?'

'We both know the answer to that,' Beresford said.

'Yes, we do, don't we?' Paniatowski agreed. 'What about Stan's movements on the morning after his wife's murder?'

'We haven't come up with a single witness who can place Szymborska either at the river bank *early* in the morning, or outside the newspaper offices later on. So even though we *know* he wasn't where he claimed to be on either occasion, we have no way of proving it.'

'You've searched his house?'

'Oh yes. We didn't even need to get a warrant to do it. He was most cooperative – said that if it would help us to catch his wife's murderer, we could tear the whole place apart. And we did pretty much take him at his word – but we still didn't find anything.'

No, you wouldn't have done, Paniatowski thought.

Because while Stan Szymborska might be an emotional man, he was also a careful and intelligent one, and he'd never have invited them in if there'd been anything to find.

'Do you remember how Charlie Woodend used to say that solving a murder was very like doing a jigsaw puzzle?' she asked.

Beresford nodded. 'The pieces are there,' he said, imitating Woodend's voice, 'and all you have to do is collect them up and fit them together.'

'Which should be easy in this case,' Paniatowski said. 'Because it's probably the least complicated puzzle we've ever come across. There are only three pieces to it, and they fit together so perfectly that it's almost impossible to imagine how any other piece *could* fit in.'

'That's true enough,' Beresford agreed. 'There's absolutely no room for any more on top of the box.'

'So let's examine them one by one, to see if that gets us anywhere,' Paniatowski suggested, with a hint of desperation to her voice. 'The first piece is Stan Szymborska. In his dreams, he's cutting off hands, which *may* just be a part of his fantasy life. On the other hand, given the dreams are set in a brutal prisoner-of-war camp where he was a prisoner himself, it's more likely that the dreams are actually a memory of something which really happened.' She paused to light up a cigarette. 'What else do we know about him?' she continued.

'That he's a very passionate man,' Beresford said. 'Even twenty-five years later, the thought of being in bed with him was enough to bring a smile to Miss Hope-Gore's lips. And we know he was deeply in love with Linda – so deeply that he was prepared to wait until after her father died before declaring that love to her.'

'The second piece is Linda. We know she was obsessed with her father. Stan said she'd escaped from that obsession with his help – that he took her hand . . .' Paniatowski shuddered. 'Took her hand!' she repeated. 'Now there's a bloody irony, if I ever heard one.'

'Go on, boss,' Beresford said, sounding a little worried.

'That he took her hand and led her out into the sunshine. But *I* don't think she ever escaped from that box of hers.'

'So you think Stan's lying?'

'No, I don't. I think he really believes it, because he *has* *to* believe it. But I've seen her office. It's not clean and modern, like the rest of the bakery. It's a throw-back to the days when her father was in charge – a shrine to his memory. She worked directly under that huge scowling picture of the miserable old bastard *every single day*, for God's sake. And what Stan *doesn't* know – or isn't prepared to admit – is that he looks a bit like the old man himself, which is probably why she agreed to marry him in the first place!'

'And when the marriage – for whatever reason – started to lose its magic for her, she began an affair with a man who also resembled her father,' Beresford pointed out.

'And that brings us neatly on to the third piece of the puzzle – Tom Whittington. The man was a loner – an outsider. But he wasn't a loner through choice, was he?'

'No,' Beresford agreed. 'When Pete Higgins and Brian Clegg offered him their friendship, he jumped at the chance.'

'He was even prepared to do things he knew were wrong, in order to *keep* that friendship.'

'And when Linda Szymborska decided she wanted to start an affair with him – which he also knew was wrong – he found it impossible to resist.'

'There's an almost tragic inevitability about the whole thing,' Paniatowski said. 'Put sulphur, charcoal and potassium nitrate together, add a match and you've got an explosion. Put Linda, Stan and Tom together, add an affair and you've got a bloody murder. We know *what* happened. We know *why* it happened. And we can't prove a bloody thing.'

'It's not *quite* as simple as that,' Beresford said cautiously. 'There are things we still don't know or can't explain.'

'Like what?'

'For example, we have no idea why Stan decided to leave

one hand in the bushes on the river bank, and place the other in a bin outside the newspaper office.'

'No, we can't explain that,' Paniatowski agreed. 'But I'm willing to bet that if we ever find out exactly what went on in that prisoner-of-war camp, we'll have the answer to that, too.' She took a sip of her vodka. 'How are we ever going to pin the murders on Stan?'

Beresford shrugged. 'By following standard procedures,' he said. 'By continuing to investigate as carefully and methodically as we can . . .'

'An approach which, so far, has got us precisely nowhere!'

'. . . and by hoping that, eventually, we'll get a lucky break.'

What Colin was saying made perfect sense, Paniatowski thought. Even the great Charlie Woodend himself had put his faith in lucky breaks occasionally. But he had never just sat back and *waited* for the luck to happen. Instead, he found ways to *encourage* it to appear.

'We need to do something that will stir up the stew pot,' she said aloud.

'Sorry, boss?'

'Another of Charlie Woodend's little theories was that looking for clues was a bit like staring into a stew pot. He said that when you look into the pot, you know that there must be all kinds of juicy things cooking away, but all you can actually *see* are the bubbles on the surface. So what you need to do, according to Charlie, is give the pot a serious stir, and see what rises to the top.'

'And you have an idea about what you might do to stir the pot?' Beresford asked.

'Yes, I do. It's just come to me.'

There was something about the way she said the words which immediately made Beresford feel uneasy.

'What does it involve?' he asked.

'Well, the first thing it involves is an early morning visit to Borough Councillor Polly Johnson JP.'

'I suppose you'd better tell me about it,' Beresford said, without a great deal of enthusiasm.

Paniatowski outlined her scheme, and when she'd finished, Beresford said, 'But you do realize, don't you, that you haven't any real grounds for doing that?'

'Yes, I do,' Paniatowski agreed.

'And you are aware that the whole thing could blow up in your face?'

'I am.'

'I'm still not convinced you've thought it through properly,' Beresford said. 'The press could decide that they'll go to town on it. And if they do, they could *crucify* you.'

'Well, you really are my little ray of sunshine tonight, aren't you?' Paniatowski said.

'And if there's *enough* of an outcry, even the chief constable won't be able to protect you,' Beresford pressed on.

'No, he won't.'

'I have to say that what you're proposing sounds like an act of desperation to me,' Beresford told her.

Paniatowski smiled thinly. 'Maybe that's because it *is* an act of desperation,' she said.

TWENTY-FOUR

Fred Handley always opened his general store at seven o'clock in the morning. There wasn't much passing trade at that time of day, but since he had to be there himself to take deliveries, he thought he might as well catch what little there was.

The woman's arrival, at seven-oh-three, surprised him, partly because it *was* so early, and partly because it was only a few hours since he'd *last* seen her.

'It's Jenny, isn't it?' he asked.

'That's right,' Jenny Brunskill agreed.

'So what brings you back so soon? Did you forget something when you were here yesterday?'

Jenny laughed, as if he'd made a joke.

'Oh no, nothing like that. But I've got some time on my hands, so I thought I'd take the opportunity to stock up a bit.'

Stock up? Handley thought. At this bloody awful time of the morning?

But he nodded encouragingly anyway, because he always approved *in principle* of people stocking up – just as long as they did it at *his* shop, rather than one of the big supermarkets.

'So what can I get you?' he asked.

'I think I'll just look around, if you don't mind,' Jenny said, slightly awkwardly.

'I don't mind at all,' he assured her. 'Make yourself right at home, love.'

He didn't expect her to be there for long, because in a shop the size of his, there wasn't much *looking around* to do. Yet Jenny seemed intent on making a thorough job of it, carefully studying each shelf before moving along to the next – and at half-past seven, she was still there.

'Are you looking for anything in particular, love?' Handley asked.

'No, like I told you, I'm just getting a feel for the place,'

Jenny Brunskill replied. 'Although now I come to think of it, I will be needing a loaf of your thick sliced bread.'

'Would that be Brunskill's or Tompkins'?' Handley asked, with a throaty chuckle.

Jenny smiled at him. 'Tompkins',' she said. 'You've got such a smooth tongue in your head that you've talked me into it.'

Handley reached to the shelf and put a loaf on the counter. 'It's there when you want it.'

'Is that fresh today?' Jenny asked.

'Of course it's fresh,' Handley said.

'But fresh *today*?' Jenny repeated.

'Well, no,' the shopkeeper admitted. 'But bread like this stays good for days, you know.'

'When will *today's* loaves be delivered?' Jenny persisted.

Handley checked his watch. 'I imagine it should be sometime in the next half-hour or so. But you don't want to . . .'

'I'll wait,' Jenny said firmly.

In her youth, Polly Johnson had always woken up as fresh as a daisy, sprung out of bed immediately and – much to her late father's annoyance – been singing at the top of her voice by the time she reached the foot of the stairs.

But those days were long gone. She was Councillor Polly Johnson JP now, and as both the years and her responsibilities had taken something of a toll, she liked, instead of jumping in with both feet, to ease herself gently into the day.

She was easing herself into it that morning when she heard a tap on her kitchen window, and looked up to see Monika Paniatowski.

Polly opened the door for her unexpected visitor.

'Nice to see you, Monika,' she said, doing her best to erase from her voice the grumpiness she still thought she was perfectly entitled to feel.

'Nice to see you, too, Councillor Johnson,' Paniatowski replied.

'Tea?'

'Yes, please, I'd like it with . . .'

'No milk, no sugar and a slice of lemon.'

'You remembered.'

Polly nodded. 'I'm like a mother to you.'

She went to the counter, selected a medium-sized mug and picked up her teapot.

'So it's like *that*, is it?' she asked, as she filled the mug almost to the top with the recently brewed, steaming black liquid.

'Like what?' Paniatowski asked innocently – far *too* innocently – from the kitchen table.

'On any other occasion, I'd have been "Polly" to you, but this morning I seem to be Councillor Johnson. I take that to mean this is an official visit, rather than a social one. Not that I really needed that clue to tip me off. At this unearthly hour of the morning, it could hardly be anything else but an official one.'

'It is partly official . . .' Paniatowski began.

'It's *entirely* official,' Polly Johnson corrected her, slicing off a piece of lemon and dropping it into Paniatowski's tea. 'And don't think I haven't noticed that, even though you've only been a chief inspector for a couple of days, you're *already* trying to use one of Charlie Woodend's old tricks on me.'

'I beg your pardon?'

'As well you might, my girl. You've turned up at a moment when you're certain that a poor old soul like me will be far from her sharpest.' Polly walked over to the table, and placed the mug of tea in front of Paniatowski. 'And the *reason* you've done that is because you want me to sign something which, if I had more of my wits about me, I'd probably baulk at.'

'I . . .' Paniatowski began.

'Charlie did exactly the same thing,' Polly Johnson continued. 'The only difference is that he used to turn up at around three o'clock in the morning, so I suppose you could be said to be at least *something* of an improvement.'

Paniatowski grinned weakly. 'It's a fair cop,' she admitted.

'So what *is* this outrageous thing you want me to sign?' Polly asked. 'Do you want to search the bishop's palace for drugs? Or maybe the Women's Institute, for those sex toys that they fondly imagine nobody else knows they have?'

'No, neither of those things,' Paniatowski said.

'Or maybe you woke this morning and decided, on a whim, that you fancied arresting the mayor for being an idiot in a public place – which, though easy enough to prove, is not *strictly speaking* a criminal act.'

'Not that either.'

'Has no one ever told you that if you want to get something out of somebody, you should laugh very loudly at their jokes – however weak those jokes might be?' Polly asked.

'Sorry,' Paniatowski said.

She hadn't even laughed at that last comment, Polly Johnson thought – and that was surely worth at least a mild titter. She must be really desperate.

The poor little thing!

'So what *do* you want?' she asked.

'I want you to sign this,' Paniatowski said, sliding the slip of paper across the kitchen table.

Polly read it quickly.

'Sweet Jesus!' she said. 'I take it you've got solid, well-documented grounds for making this request?'

Paniatowski grimaced. 'Not exactly. But I can have an X-ray taken of my stomach, if that would help.'

'What?'

'I've got a gut feeling, Polly. A strong one. And I need you to sign on the dotted line, so I can make my case.'

'Charlie Woodend used to have gut feelings, too,' Polly reminded her.

'I know.'

'And often – more often than not, in fact – they were spot on. But even so, it usually took a great deal more than one of his gut feelings for me to give *him* what he wanted. You see, unfortunately for you, Monika, when I was taking my oath as a JP, I forgot to keep my fingers crossed. And what that means is that there's only so far I can allow myself, in all conscience, to go.'

'And, God knows, I can *use* all the help I can get on this one,' Paniatowski said.

She didn't even hear me, Polly thought. She's so wrapped up in her own worries that she isn't even listening.

For perhaps half a minute, Polly sat there in silence, then she opened her handbag and took out her fountain pen.

'You are to regard this as a welcome-to-the-job present, Chief Inspector Paniatowski,' she said sternly. 'But I won't be this much of a pushover the next time you come knocking on my door – whatever time of day or night it is.'

'Understood,' Paniatowski said, nodding gravely.

Polly signed quickly – as if she wanted it over and done

with before she changed her mind – and when she put her pen down again, she shivered.

'That made me feel really quite odd,' she said. 'Do you know, I don't think I've ever signed an exhumation order before.'

There was a time when Brewer's Street would have been heaving with activity, even at that early hour of the morning. Moore's Brewery (after which the street was named) would already have begun its daily task of producing thousands of gallons of ale, and in Brunskill's Bakery (which made the bread, which made the sandwiches, which men scoffed down *after* drinking the ale) the ovens would have been working at full pelt. But the brewery had been taken over by an industrial conglomerate which produced a mere parody of real beer, and which – being more interested in Moore's market than in its traditions and facilities – had immediately closed the place down. Then the bakery had gone, moving to a site more suitable for Linda Szymborska's ambitious expansion plans.

DC Crane stood in front of the old bakery, thoughtfully jangling the keys which he'd picked up from the estate agents the previous evening.

Now he was there, all he had to do was open the door at the back of the building and step inside, he told himself.

Mission accomplished.

So why was he having doubts? Why was there a small part of his mind – possibly his subconscious, though he couldn't be sure – which kept urging him to return the keys and forget that he'd ever planned to enter the bakery at all?

It couldn't be that he was worried he'd get into trouble for disobeying Sergeant Walker's orders, because Walker hadn't explicitly told him *not* to come to the bakery.

Besides, the sergeant never need find out about it.

Then what *was* his problem? Was he worried that when he discovered the empty bakery was just that – *an empty bakery* – he'd feel a complete fool?

Possibly that *was* it, he decided.

But what was foolish about ruling the bakery out of the investigation? Wasn't the process of elimination one of the cornerstones of this kind of work?

There was no point in procrastinating any further, he thought.

He had come here with a purpose, and it was time that purpose was fulfilled.

'Walk away!' his subconscious – if that's what it was – screamed. 'You'll regret it if you don't!'

'Bollocks!' Crane said aloud, as he began to walk down the alleyway which led to the loading bay.

TWENTY-FIVE

The Tompkins' Bakery's bread-delivery man arrived at Handley's General Store at five minutes to eight.

Watching him from the back of the shop, Jenny Brunskill was forced to admit to herself that his uniform looked much smarter than the uniforms which Brunskill's men wore.

She should have noticed that before, she thought. It was her *job* to notice the little details which made all the difference. And now she *had* noticed it, she would make it her business to see to it that, within a month, Brunskill's men had uniforms which made Tompkins' men look positively slovenly.

The delivery man walked up to the counter, and placed his tray on it. 'A dozen?' he suggested.

'Not sure about that,' Mr Handley said dubiously. 'This is a small business, and I don't normally sell more than eight or nine.'

The delivery man laughed. 'You've still not quite sussed out the system, have you?' he asked. 'We don't care what you sell – we're much more interested in what you *don't* sell, if you know what I mean.'

'I know what you mean,' Mr Handley agreed.

'So take a dozen, and if you have to throw any of them away, well, *you* won't be the loser, will you?'

He wasn't talking like a bread-delivery man, Jenny thought – at least, not like any bread-delivery man *she*'d ever known.

'A dozen, then?' the delivery man asked.

'A dozen,' Mr Handley agreed.

'We might as well settle up for the week, mightn't we?' the delivery man suggested.

'If that's all right with you,' Handley agreed.

The bread man consulted his clipboard, then reached into his pocket, pulled out a couple of banknotes and laid them on the counter. 'I think you'll find that's right,' he said.

'Seems to be,' Handley agreed.

Jenny waited until the bread man had left the shop, then went over to the counter.

'Here you are,' Handley said to her. 'A loaf fresh from the bakery, just like you wanted.'

'And *you* only wanted to take nine, though you ended up taking a *dozen*,' Jenny said.

'You naughty girl,' Handley said, wagging his finger playfully at her. 'Didn't your mother ever tell you that you should never listen in on other people's conversations?'

'And didn't anybody ever tell *you* that when you buy something, it's customary for you to pay the seller for it, and not the other way around,' Jenny countered.

Handley's face darkened. 'Look, I don't know what your game is,' he said, 'but I want you to leave my shop right now.'

'Don't worry, I'm going,' Jenny told him. 'And as for the Tompkins' crusty loaf I asked you to put aside for me – well, you know what you can do with *that*!'

Even the most devoted of grieving relatives would have thought twice before appearing at the dear departed's graveside at eight o'clock in the morning, and the official party assembled around this particular grave had the cemetery to themselves.

'How the hell did you get things moving so quickly?' Beresford asked, as he watched the gravediggers at work.

'I called in a few favours,' Paniatowski replied.

'Including, I presume, some that were owed to you by our beloved chief constable himself?'

Paniatowski looked away.

'Well no, that was one of the favours that I *didn't* actually call in,' she admitted.

'What?' Beresford exclaimed. 'You're surely not trying to tell me that Mr Baxter gave his approval for a dodgy enterprise like this one without even having to be strong-armed into it?'

'The disinterment is perfectly legal, and I've got the papers in my pocket to prove it,' Paniatowski said flatly.

The pile of earth was growing on the canvas which the gravediggers had laid beside the grave, and if the corpse was literally six feet under they were probably halfway to reaching it.

'Let me see if I've got this right,' Beresford said, with growing incredulity. 'What you're saying – or rather, what you're *implying* – is that Mr Baxter doesn't even *know* about any of this?'

Paniatowski forced a weak grin to her face. 'I didn't want to disturb his beauty sleep.'

'I want to be quite clear about this,' Beresford persisted. 'Do you, *or do you not*, have authorization from the big chief?'

'As I've already told you, it's all perfectly legal,' Paniatowski replied, avoiding the question.

'But not authorized,' Beresford pressed.

'But not authorized,' Paniatowski agreed.

'Last night, when we were in the Drum, you talked about stirring the stew to see what bubbled to the surface,' Beresford said. 'But if you're doing all this entirely off your own bat, then it's not a stew pot you're stirring at all – it's a bloody cesspit.'

'That's certainly one way of looking at it,' Paniatowski agreed.

'It's the *only* way of looking at it, Monika,' Beresford countered. 'The shit will be flying in all directions – any minute now – and some of it's bound to stick to you.'

'Maybe,' Paniatowski said.

'There isn't any *maybe* about it. You deliberately went out of your way to blind-side the chief constable.'

'Charlie Woodend used to do that all the time.'

'Yes, he did. But Mr Woodend always knew what he was looking for when he pulled a stunt like this.'

'*Usually* knew,' Paniatowski corrected him.

'All right, usually knew,' Beresford conceded. 'But *you* have no idea *what* you'll find when you hand this stiff over to Dr Shastri.'

'True,' Paniatowski agreed. 'But there've been two murders, so why shouldn't there have been three?'

'Because we know the motive for the murders of Tom Whittington and Linda, and there isn't *any* possible motive here.'

He was right, Paniatowski thought, in a sudden burst of panic. It *had been* a crazy idea – an idea she'd never even have contemplated if she hadn't been both exhausted and desperate.

But it was too late to stop it now, she told herself, as she watched the gravediggers step back and the undertaker's assistants move in to lift the coffin from the grave.

'I think you'd better leave,' she told Beresford.

'Now why would I want to do that?' the inspector asked.

'Because if you leave now, you might still just be able to get away with claiming that you didn't know was going on – that I'd kept you as much in the dark about it as I kept the chief constable.'

'I think you're wrong there,' Beresford said.

'What do you mean?'

'I think that if I leave now, I'll have a *very good* chance of getting away with it.'

The undertaker's assistants had removed the coffin from what should have been its last resting place, and were about to take it to the waiting hearse – but Beresford still showed no signs of moving.

'Well?' Paniatowski asked.

'Well what?'

'You're still here.'

Beresford shrugged. 'If you're on a sinking ship, the least you can do is make sure the deckchairs are arranged nicely,' he said.

There were two ways to enter the old bakery's loading bay. The first, which had once been used by the bread-delivery vans, consisted of a set of high double gates, which were now heavily chained and padlocked. The second entrance was a small door next to the gates, which had been used by the bakery's staff, and the key that DC Crane had in his hand was to the smaller entrance.

He inserted the key in the lock, and felt an uneasy twinge when it actually turned.

He pushed the door open, and stepped inside. A little of the outside light filtered into the large loading bay, but not enough to really see very much at all. Crane, congratulating himself for having anticipated this problem, switched on the torch he'd brought with him, and aimed it across the room.

His beam of light picked out the shape of the car – and not just an ordinary, common-or-garden car, but an E-type Jag!

Crane felt his stomach clench up. It had all been a game so far, he suddenly realized – a light-hearted version of a Shakespearian tragedy which he had been playing in his head for his own amusement.

And while he'd argued to himself that it was possible this was the scene of the crime, he'd never *really* believed it would be.

Not until now!

He walked over to the car, ran his finger across the bonnet and examined the result with his torch. The finger had picked up some dust, but not a great deal, and he was willing to bet that the vehicle had not been parked there for more than a couple of days.

It was then he began to feel that he was not alone in the loading bay – to sense that there was some presence watching his every move.

'Come out, wherever you are!' he shouted, with all the authority he could muster.

There was no answer.

'This is the police,' Crane continued. 'There is no escape. We have the place surrounded.'

Christ! he thought. What a terrible thing to say. I sound like I'm in some cheap American cop show.

The silence continued.

'Stay where you are,' he ordered, then remembered that only seconds earlier he'd told whoever it was to come out.

During his training, it had been drummed into him that in situations like this he should always proceed with caution.

But that training had not taken place in a dark bakery delivery bay, in which a murder victim's car had been stored. It had not prepared him for the hair-raising sense of evil which seemed to be floating through the air. In other words, the training had been a complete waste of time.

He plunged into the darkness, the torch in his hand – held at chest level – cutting a thin path through the darkness.

'You can't escape!' he shouted, and was surprised to discover that even the sound of his own voice was starting to frighten him.

He was not expecting any obstacles to be in his way, and when he encountered one he was totally unprepared to deal with it.

Suddenly, he had lost his balance and was lurching forward. He put out his hands to break his fall, but even as they were making contact with the ground, his head collided with something hard and unyielding.

He had heard that a blow to the head could cause you to see stars, but was amazed to discover that it was actually true.

What the hell happened there? he asked himself, aware, even as the thought passed through his mind, that only a small part of his brain was working properly, and that the rest of it was off on some kind of sun-dozed holiday.

He tried to force himself to focus.

The object he had hit his head on had undoubtedly been metal, but the one that he had tripped over had not. It had been solid, but not as solid as a lump of iron. Not as sharp, either. It had been rounded, and – he was guessing here – it had probably been quite long.

He was wasting time, he told himself. If he really wanted to find out what had tripped him and what had assaulted him, he should examine them in the light of his torch.

He had dropped the torch, but he could see the beam shining into the darkness.

It was no more than a few feet away, he estimated. In order to retrieve it, he didn't even need to stand up.

And maybe it would be better *not* to stand up until he had the torch in his hand, and could see what he was doing.

He wriggled, moving his whole body closer to the torch, then stretched out his hand to grasp it.

But there was something in the way – a long, rounded object.

Was this what he had tripped over, he asked himself. No, that thing – whatever it was – was still somewhere behind him. This had to be another *thing*.

He inched his body a few inches further towards the torch, and let his hand climb over this new obstacle, like a mountaineer scaling a small mountain range.

As his fingers ran over the hard ridges, surrounded by a softer – and much more pliable – material, he finally realized what he was touching, and almost pulled his hand back in revulsion.

But that would never do. It wouldn't do at all. He was a policeman, after all. And policemen didn't scare easily.

'You need the torch!' screamed a panicking voice in his head. 'You *have to have* the torch!'

His fingers, exhausted by the climb, finally wrapped around the torch, and he was able to pull it back over the mound.

Now was the time to *see*, he told himself. Now was the time to confirm what he already suspected.

It was a body, all right.

A woman's body!

The beam of the torch picked out the details of her torso. Her blouse had been slashed to ribbons, and was covered with rusty-brown stains, which could only be blood.

There's no need to look at the head, he told himself. You don't need to see *that* at all.

But his arm refused to obey his brain, and the torch beam travelled up the woman's body, stopping only when it reached the face.

'Oh, my God!' he moaned.

Now he understood all the warnings his kindly, well-meaning subconscious had been flinging at him, and promised he would never ignore it again.

But there were more much pressing matters to deal with than his own foolishness.

He wanted to be sick – he really *wanted* to be sick – but he knew that if he *was* sick in his current prone position, he was in danger of swallowing his own vomit and choking on it.

He dropped the torch again, and levered himself up into a kneeling position. He was only just in time. His stomach demanded that he lean forward, and when he had obeyed it, it emptied its entire contents on the floor of the delivery bay.

TWENTY-SIX

Three police vans had arrived within minutes of DC Crane making his call, and the uniformed constables disgorged from them had immediately set up barriers, sealing off the whole area. A pick-up truck had appeared on the scene soon after, and was now awaiting the instruction to take the E-type Jag to the police garage. DCI Paniatowski's MGA was parked just inside the barrier, as were an ambulance and Dr Shastri's Land Rover.

And there were other people very much in evidence.

Lots of other people!

Lighting technicians setting up lighting.

Fingerprint experts dusting for fingerprints.

Detectives hoping to find something to detect.

And patrol officers on patrol.

The lower end of Brewer's Street had gone from being on the periphery of the investigation to its very centre, in less time than it would have taken to write the details down.

DC Crane, a blanket draped over his shoulders, was sitting in the back of the ambulance and drinking hot, sweet tea.

'I'm so ashamed of myself, ma'am,' he said, his eyes fixed firmly on the floor of the ambulance.

'Ashamed?' Paniatowski repeated. 'Why?'

'Because the minute I saw that poor bloody woman's face, I lost it completely.'

'And so would most people who suddenly found themselves in that kind of situation.'

'But we're not most people, are we, ma'am?' Crane asked. 'We're bobbies. We're supposed to be able to *handle* things. And I didn't.'

'You're being too hard on yourself,' Paniatowski told him. 'By playing a hunch, you've given us by far the biggest lead we've had in this investigation – and I won't forget that.'

'Thank you, ma'am,' Crane said.

'No, thank *you*,' Paniatowski replied. 'Are you going to be all right, DC Crane?'

'I think so, ma'am.'

Paniatowski nodded. 'Good.'

She climbed out of the ambulance, but once she was on the street she turned round to face the detective constable again.

'And thank you for the other thing, as well,' she said.

'The other thing, ma'am?'

'Sergeant Walker didn't bother to tell me that he had established an ID for the second victim. He didn't tell me he was going to Brunskill's Bakery, either. But somebody did. Somebody phoned me up and told me exactly what was going on. And that could only have been you, couldn't it?'

Crane took a sip from his plastic cup.

'It's very nice, this tea, ma'am,' he said. 'Very refreshing.'

Paniatowski smiled. 'I'll be keeping a close eye on you, DC Crane,' she promised.

The old bakery's loading bay was bathed in the blinding light of several powerful arc lamps. To the left, the superannuated baking table on which DC Crane had banged his head was being studied by the forensic team. To the right, Dr Shastri was bent over the two corpses.

Paniatowski crossed the bay, and came to a halt next to the bodies. Linda Szymborska's dead face stared up at her, the eyes filled with frozen horror.

Or surprise.

Or pain.

Or perhaps all three.

She turned to look at Tom Whittington, whose eyes were closed, and whose expression seemed to indicate no more than mild bemusement.

'Can you tell me which of the victims died first?' Paniatowski asked the doctor.

'Based on the activity of our busy little friends the maggot and the blowfly, I would say that the woman died a few hours before the man,' Dr Shastri replied. 'But at this stage, that *is* only a guess. I will be able to speak with more authority once I have sliced them both open.'

'I'd like to see the results as soon as you have them available,' Paniatowski said.

'Were I a clever detective chief inspector, rather than a simple dissector of cadavers, I think I would find the manner in which they died more interesting than the actual timing,' Dr Shastri said.

Paniatowski grinned. 'I *had* noticed,' she said, 'but I can see you're just bursting to explain it to me, so please feel free.'

'The woman, as is evident from the ligature marks on her arms and legs, was strapped to that baking table over there,' Dr Shastri said. 'The amputation of her hand – if amputation is the correct word for such butchery – was the first act of violence committed against her. Once that was accomplished, her killer launched a more frenzied and general attack, using, I am almost certain, the same weapon he had used to cut off her hand. And you can see the result of that for yourself – he literally hacked her to death.'

'It would have been messy,' Paniatowski said.

'Very messy indeed,' Dr Shastri confirmed. 'There will have been a veritable fountain of blood, and I have no doubt that the killer will have been covered in it himself. Most men would have found this experience truly revolting, and would have pulled back. But our killer did not. It is possible that his frenzy was such that he did not even notice the blood until he had achieved his aim.'

'But Tom Whittington's death was not like that at all.'

'No, it wasn't. He was strangled, and the lack of any signs of struggle suggests that he was already unconscious when that strangulation took place. And his hand, unlike the woman's, was not removed until after he was dead.'

'So he hardly suffered at all?'

'Correct. And then there is the way in which the victims were treated once they were dead. The man was laid neatly on the ground. His left arm, with the hand still intact, was laid across his chest. His right stump, in contrast, was placed by his side, where it wouldn't be so noticeable.'

'And the woman?'

'She died at the bench, struggling, no doubt, to break free of her bonds. But those bonds were very securely tied, and were strong enough to keep her upright, even when she was dead.'

'But we didn't find her tied to the bench.'

'No, you did not. The killer, I think, wanted to rob her of even what little dignity she had left, so he cut through the bonds and let her fall into a crumpled heap on the floor.'

It was as if the killer both hated *and* blamed the woman much more than he hated and blamed the man, Paniatowski thought.

And if that *were* the case, there was good reason for it, because it must have been obvious to Stan Szymborska that mild-mannered Tom was almost an innocent party in the affair, and that Linda had been the real instigator.

'When can I have the full reports?' Paniatowski asked.

'Later today,' Shastri replied. 'And once I have completed them, I will apply myself to the other little job you asked me to do.'

She had almost forgotten *the other little job*, Paniatowski thought, and given recent developments, she was no longer sure that it even needed to be done at all.

'There's no rush with the third cadaver,' she said, 'but I really do need the reports on these two pretty damn quickly.'

'You will get them as soon as is humanly possible – if not sooner,' Shastri promised her.

Paniatowski nodded, and walked over to the baking table to which Linda Szymborska had been strapped, and where the grisly amputation of her hand had taken place.

'Have you come up with anything I can use yet, Arthur?' she asked the technician examining the table.

'No fingerprints, ma'am,' the technician replied. 'Looks to me as if the table's been wiped clean. But there is *that*!'

He was pointing to the pool – almost a reservoir – of dried blood on the floor. And, more particularly, he was pointing to the large male footprints squarely in the centre of it.

Stan Szymborska must have observed the police cars approaching from his front window, and by the time they had reached the driveway in front of his house, he was already standing at the door.

There were still signs of the recent strain on his face, Paniatowski thought, but considering he almost certainly knew what was about to happen next, he seemed remarkably calm.

'Have you found my Linda's body?' he asked.

'What an interesting way you have of expressing things, Mr Szymborska,' Paniatowski said.

'Please do not play games with me, Chief Inspector,' Szymborska replied, with great dignity.

'I'm *not* playing games,' Paniatowski told him. 'I said you have an interesting way of expressing things because you *do*. Most men in your situation would have held on to the desperate hope that their wife was still alive. But not you! *You* didn't ask if we'd found *her*, *you* asked if we'd found her *body*.'

'Why should I put on a show for your benefit?' Szymborska demanded. 'Why should I pretend that I still have hope that my wife is alive, when I know that she is dead?'

'Yes, you *do* know she's dead – because you killed her!'

'That is not the reason at all. I know she is dead because I have seen so much of death that I can almost smell it.'

'Now that *is* a good line,' Paniatowski said. 'But you shouldn't be wasting it on me – you should save it for your lawyer.'

'Where was she?' Szymborska asked, ignoring the comment. 'Where was my lovely Linda?'

'She was in the old bakery,' Paniatowski said, feeling rage flaring up inside her. 'She was where *you* left her!'

Why was she getting so angry, she wondered.

Why had the dispassionate, official front, which she could normally display on these occasions, so completely deserted her?

It was because the crime she was dealing with now was so horrific, she told herself.

But she had seen horrific crimes before, and she knew that wasn't the answer – or at least not the *whole* answer.

She was angry with herself, she suddenly realized. Angry that even when her gut feeling had told her Stan Szymborska was guilty, there had been some small part of her – buried deep inside – which had refused to accept it.

And she was angry with Stan, for pretending to be the man he wasn't – a man who she could admire, a man who (she had almost found herself wishing) could have been *her* man.

'I did not kill my wife,' Szymborska said quietly.

'Didn't you?' Paniatowski asked – much calmer, much more *professional* now. 'I have to inform you, Mr Szymborska, that I have here a warrant which entitles me to search your house.'

'Is that necessary? Your men have already searched it once,' Szymborska pointed out.

'True, they have,' Paniatowski agreed. 'But we'll not be looking for the same things this time.' She glanced down as his feet. 'What size shoes do you take, Mr Szymborska?'

'Size eleven.'

Paniatowski nodded. 'That's what I would have guessed. And that's *just* the size of the footprint in the blood.'

Stan Szymborska was standing in his living room – if not exactly under guard then at least under escort – when Paniatowski walked in holding the pair of black patent-leather shoes.

He still seemed very calm. No, it was more than just calm, she decided – he seemed resigned.

'Do these belong to you?' she asked.

'I don't know,' Szymborska said. 'But I certainly have a pair which are very like them.'

'We found them at the back of your wardrobe. At the *very* back of your wardrobe.'

And when she had the name of the constable who'd missed them on the first search of the house, she thought, she'd give him the bollocking of his life.

'Did you hear what I said?' she demanded. 'We found these shoes in your wardrobe.'

'Then I assume that they must be mine.'

'When was the last time you wore them?'

Szymborska shrugged. 'I couldn't say for certain. But I think it was probably some time ago.'

'And after the last time you wore them, you gave them an especially thorough cleaning, didn't you?'

'I would not imagine it was *especially* thorough. I like to take care of my clothes, but I am not fanatical about them.'

'Really?' Paniatowski said.

She turned the shoes over, so that Szymborska could see the soles and heels, which had been attacked so vigorously with some kind of abrasive that, in some places, the leather had been shredded.

'I did not do that,' Szymborska said.

'Of course you did,' Paniatowski countered. 'But you'd have been much better off burning them, you know. Because however hard you try to get rid of it, blood always leaves a trace.'

'Whatever I say – however often I tell you that I loved my wife with all my heart – I will never convince you that I did not kill her,' Szymborska said. 'So why must we waste time going through this pantomime? You have come here to arrest me, so why not do it?'

'All right,' Paniatowski agreed. 'Stanislaw Szymborska, I am arresting you for the murders of Linda Szymborska and Thomas Whittington. You do not have to say anything, but anything you do say may be taken down and used in evidence against you.'

'This should never have happened,' Szymborska said. 'I should have hanged myself long before it ever got to this.'

It was while Stan Szymborska was being processed that WPC Margaret Hill informed Paniatowski and Beresford of Jenny Brunskill's presence in the building.

'She's been demanding to speak to someone in authority, ma'am,' the WPC said.

'And where is she now?

'She looked like she was about to start screaming the place down, so I thought it best to put her in one of the interview rooms.'

'You just did right,' Paniatowski said. She turned to Beresford. 'What do you think she wants?'

'She's probably come to ask for Stan Szymborska's head on a spike,' Beresford replied. 'Would you like *me* to talk to her, boss?'

Paniatowski considered the matter. On the one hand, the last thing she wanted was to listen to a hysterical rant from a woman who probably considered slow torture too easy a death for her brother-in-law. But on the other, she might just learn something – one tiny piece of significant information – which she could use to crack Szymborska's calm self-reliant shell and push him into confessing to the crimes of which he was so patently guilty.

'I'll see her,' she said. 'But if I'm in there for more than five minutes, send in the cavalry.'

Jenny Brunskill was in a *far* worse state than her brother-in-law. Her pageboy hair was a mess, as if she'd been tugging at it, furiously and unrelentingly. Her eyes were enlarged and wild-looking. And her hands, resting on the table, were twitching uncontrollably.

Paniatowski sat down opposite her. 'I know this is a very difficult time for you, Miss Brunskill,' she said sympathetically, 'but I promise you, we'll make it as painless as we possibly can. There's the identification of the body to be dealt with first. Legally speaking, you are required to do that, but since there's no doubt it's her, it should be enough for you to just sign the paperwork.'

'What?' Jenny Brunskill asked.

'I said that, though legally speaking you're supposed to make a formal identification of the body—'

'Did you know that Tompkins' Bakery has been bribing some of the small shopkeepers around Whitebridge to take their bread, rather than ours?' Jenny Brunskill interrupted.

'Oh, for God's sake!' Paniatowski exploded. 'Just what kind of woman are you, Miss Brunskill? Your sister's been murdered, and all you can worry about is bloody bread sales!'

'It's vitally important to keep the bakery going at all costs,' Jenny said. 'Now that she's dead, it will be Linda's monument, just as it has always been Father's, but that's not the—'

'Monument!' Paniatowski repeated angrily. 'It's not a hospital or a charitable foundation we're talking about here. It's not even a work of art. It's nothing but a bloody bakery!'

'You're right, it's not a hospital or a charitable foundation,' Jenny said, suddenly almost eerily calm. 'It *is* just a bloody bakery. But, as I was saying, that's not the point.'

Paniatowski sighed. 'So what *is* the point?'

'Warren Tompkins will do anything to take over our business. Anything at all!'

'You're wasting my time,' Paniatowski said.

'But don't you see?' Jenny demanded, with astonishment evident in her voice. 'Isn't it obvious to you?'

'Isn't *what* obvious to me?'

'Stan didn't kill Jenny and Tom at all – someone who was working for Tompkins did!'

'You've lost your mind,' Paniatowski said, with disgust.

'Think about it,' Jenny insisted. 'Think about *who* was killed. The managing director and the head baker. Why them? Because they were the cornerstones of the business!'

'They weren't killed because they were *bakers*,' Paniatowski said. 'They were killed because they were *lovers*.'

'I didn't believe you the first time you made that wicked, wicked suggestion, and I don't believe you now,' Jenny Brunskill told her. 'It's simply not true. It *can't* be true.'

'You need to get away from all this for a while, Jenny,' Paniatowski said softly.

'Get away?' Jenny Brunskill repeated, as if the words were totally meaningless to her.

'Getting away will allow you to find another perspective on what's happened. I promise you, you'll see things differently once you're somewhere else. So go, Jenny. Please! Spend some time with friends or relatives . . .'

'My only relative's been *murdered*,' Jenny said. 'And my only friend's been *arrested* for killing her. And now they're gone, who's left to run the bakery? There's only me.'

'Listen, Jenny . . .' Paniatowski began.

'When will you arrest the people at Tompkins' who murdered my sister?' Jenny demanded.

'They *didn't* murder your sister, and I'm not *going to* arrest them,' Paniatowski said firmly.

'Then I will make a complaint,' Jenny said. 'I'll complain at the very highest level.'

'I hope you do,' Paniatowski said.

And she meant it, because while it was not her place to try and have Jenny Brunskill sectioned under the Mental Health Act, *somebody* in authority should certainly see that it was done.

TWENTY-SEVEN

'Doesn't it bother you that you'll probably end up going to prison for the rest of your natural life?' Paniatowski asked Stan Szymborska across the table in the interview room.

'Yes, it bothers me,' Szymborska admitted, in a voice which was so flat and unemotional that it was almost robotic. 'But it does not bother me for any of the reasons you might imagine.'

'So you won't mind being locked up twenty-four hours a day?' Paniatowski asked, deliberately taunting the man in the hope of getting a reaction – *any* reaction – out of him. 'You won't mind not feeling a soft summer breeze on your face, and the sun on your back, ever again? You won't mind losing the right to make any choices of your own?'

'No,' Szymborska said.

And he put so much conviction into that one simple word that she almost believed him.

Again!

'It *will* bother you once you're there,' she said harshly. 'Believe me, it will bother you *then!*'

Stan shook his head slowly and sadly from side to side. 'You can only miss those things you still want,' he said. 'The part of my life I cared about came to an end with my Linda's death. I am already in prison. And what does it matter if I lose the right to choose for myself when there are no longer any choices I wish to make? Besides, though I will have been imprisoned for a crime I did not commit, I have done things in my life for which I *deserve* to go to jail.'

'Your sister-in-law, Jenny, thinks that you're innocent, you know,' Paniatowski said.

Szymborska smiled sadly. 'I knew she would.'

'How did you know? Was it because you, better than most people, know just how gullible she is?'

'No, it isn't because of what I know about her, it's because of what she knows about me – and she *knows* that I would never kill my Linda.'

'You care about Jenny, don't you?'

'Yes, I do care about her. Like my darling Linda, Jenny has a deep inner beauty.'

'But *unlike* your Linda's inner beauty, Jenny's was never allowed to emerge? Unlike your Linda, she's still living in the shadow of her father?'

'Yes. I tried to help her – but perhaps I did not try hard enough. And for that, I feel a guilt which I will carry with me to the grave.'

'You can help her now,' Paniatowski said. 'If you really want to, you can help her without even leaving this room.'

'How?'

'She thinks some of the people who work at Tompkins' Bakery were behind your wife's murder. Does that surprise you?'

For a moment, Szymborska was silent.

Then he said, 'No, it doesn't really surprise me – not when I stop to think about it. The bakery is Jenny's world, you see, and anything that happens in the *rest* of the world can only be explained in terms of the bakery.'

'But you'll admit that believing someone in Tompkins' Bakery had Linda killed is delusional?'

'Of course it's delusional.'

'Then help Jenny to escape from that delusion by confessing – by showing just *how* delusional the idea is.'

'If I confess, you'll stop looking for the real killer,' Szymborska said. 'And then my Linda will *never* get justice.'

'We've *already* stopped looking for the real killer – because we've got him in custody!'

'Perhaps you may think that now,' Stan Szymborska said calmly, 'but if I continue to maintain my innocence, you will find seeds of doubt starting to grow within you. And eventually – even though I have been convicted of the crime – you will open the investigation again.'

'Now that really *is* delusional,' Paniatowski said.

And yet, she thought, those seeds were already there, and his very certainty was starting to make them grow.

But it was all bollocks, of course, she told herself angrily. He was playing her now, just as he'd played her all along. Well, it was time to show him that he couldn't pull on her emotional strings any longer – that she finally saw him for what he truly was.

'Tell me about the hands,' she said.

'I did not kill my Linda, and I did not kill Tom Whittington, and so I know nothing about—'

'Not those hands!' Paniatowski interrupted contemptuously. 'The other hands. The ones you cut off in the prisoner-of-war camp!'

For the first time in the interrogation, Szymborska looked as if he'd been knocked off balance.

'How did you . . . who told you . . .?'

'Doesn't matter, does it?' Paniatowski asked. 'I *do* know. All I'm missing is the details. So why don't you fill me in on them?'

'No,' Szymborska said firmly.

'Why not?' Paniatowski asked, in a hectoring voice. 'Because you're ashamed of what you did? Because that's one of the things that you think you deserve to go to prison for?'

'Because if I tell you, you will only use it as a prop to shore up your suspicions about me.'

'I don't *need* any prop to shore up my suspicions,' Paniatowski told him. 'Why should I? I already *know* you're guilty as sin. So why not come clean! Why not be a man about it!'

'All right, I will tell you,' Stan said, suddenly weary. 'But not because of your bullying and your pathetic mind games.'

'No?'

'No! I will tell you because it will show you, for good or bad – and only you can decide which it is – what kind of man I *really* am.'

It surprised Paniatowski to discover that her heart had begun to beat a little faster, and that the room was suddenly stuffier.

Stan was right, she thought. She *had* tried to bully him into telling her this story – but now that he was about to tell it to her, she was no longer sure she wanted to hear it!

'Come on, then, let's have it, Mr Szymborska,' she said. 'I haven't got all day!'

'You were wrong when you talked about *hands* earlier,' Szymborska said. 'The truth is that there was only one.'

He told Paniatowski about the prisoners' growing suspicion that there was a spy in their midst, and how they had searched Tadeujz's belongings and found the chocolate bar. And then he told her about the hatchet that Stefan had produced from the hiding place in the wall.

'And you thought it was a jolly good idea, did you?' Paniatowski asked, still hectoring.

'No,' Szymborska said seriously. 'Not at first.'

Stan looks down at the hatchet, glinting in the pale light of the oil lamp.

'But you're not going to . . .' he says.

'If thy right hand offends thee, cut it off,' Stefan quotes, almost in a whisper. 'In this place, we are all each other's right hands.'

'But you can't . . .'

'This vermin has caused the death of two good men,' Stefan says. 'But I will not inflict his righteous punishment on him unless everyone agrees.' He raises the hatchet high in the air, so that all the other prisoners – with the exception of Tadeujz – can see it. 'Do you all agree?' he asks.

Everyone except Stan says they do.

'Well?' Stefan asks.

'What if I say no?'

'If we do this, we will probably be shot for it,' Stefan says. 'And that means that if you agree to it, you are almost certainly choosing to die. And none of you – my comrades – should be forced to make such a decision. So if you do not give your consent, Stanislaw, it will not happen.' Stefan puts his hand on Stan's shoulder. 'If you say no, none of us will hold it against you. I can promise you that.'

Stan believes him. If he says that Tadeujz should be spared, Tadeujz will be spared. And none of the others will blame the man who saved the traitor – because they will respect his right to choose life for himself.

Then Stan thinks of Józef, who was training to be a doctor before the war. And of fat, jovial Piotr, who was one of the kindest men he ever met.

'It is the right thing to do,' he says. 'It is just. Betrayal must be punished. Give me the hatchet, Stefan.'

'So, in a heartbeat, you went from not wanting it done *at all* to wanting to do it *yourself*?' Paniatowski asked sceptically.

'Yes.'

'Why?'

'What better way can a man convince himself that he has made the right decision than by making himself responsible for carrying out that decision?'

So far, Tadeujz has only heard the words, and though he knows that something bad is about to happen to him, he has no idea what. Now Stanislaw steps in front of him, and he can see the hatchet. His eyes widen with fear. He struggles harder, but it is useless. He tries to scream, but the gag will not allow him.

Stan brings down the hatchet with tremendous force, severing the hand at the wrist. Blood spurts everywhere.

The two men holding Tadeujz release their grip. He falls to the floor, blood bubbling from his severed limb like water from a fountain.

'What happens now?' Stan asks.

Stefan shrugs. 'He has no friends here – no one who wishes to help him. If he can make it to the wire, perhaps his new *friends, the guards, will save his life. If he cannot . . .'*

He cannot. He bleeds to death on the floor, without ever regaining consciousness.

She was starting to like Stan again, Paniatowski thought. She was starting to *admire* him again!

And that was bad!

'It's a cracking story, I'll give you that,' she said. 'But, you see, it just doesn't add up.'

'Doesn't it?' Szymborska asked.

'No, it certainly doesn't. If it was true, you'd have been shot the following morning, wouldn't you? Yet here you are, sitting in this room, still alive and telling me the tale.'

'When Stefan said that we would be shot, he was forgetting one important thing,' Stan told her.

'And what was that?'

'Just how much the camp commandant – the man with the power of life and death over us – despised Poles. *All* Poles!'

When morning comes, and the body is discovered during a routine check of the hut, the prisoners are all marched into the yard, where they are addressed by the commandant.

'Whoever killed this man will be punished,' he says. 'The killer should give himself up now to spare the others.'

None of the Poles moves.

'If one of you does not admit to the crime, I will consider you all guilty – and have you all shot,' the commander says.

He nods to the guards, who raise their sub-machine guns and point them directly at the prisoners.

And still the Poles say nothing.

The commandant turns to go away.

'Should we shoot them now, sir?' one the guards asked.

The commandant thinks it over for a second, and then shakes his head. 'The dead man was only a Pole,' he says. 'Why should we waste our good German bullets to avenge his death?'

'Does the story add up now?' Stan asked.

'Yes, it does,' Paniatowski admitted. 'And yes, you were right when you said it would point even more convincingly to your guilt. Tadeujz betrayed you, didn't he, and you cut his hand off.'

'Yes.'

'And when Linda betrayed you, exactly the same thing happened to her.'

'Linda did not betray me,' Stan said.

'Oh, come on now!'

'Not in the way that Tadeujz did.'

'You're surely not going to start denying she had an affair with Tom, are you?'

'It was a moment of weakness,' Stan said. 'In my mind – in my heart – I had already forgiven her, even as I stood watching her drive away, the night that she was killed.'

'Why *did* she drive away?'

'Because we'd had an argument.'

'Over the affair?'

'Yes.'

'You confronted her about it?'

'I did.'

'And what did she say?'

'She denied it.'

'And you left it at that? Why? Couldn't you just have said you didn't believe her, but that it didn't matter, because you forgave her anyway?'

'Yes, I could have – but she wasn't ready for my forgiveness. She needed time alone. Time to come to terms with what she'd done – to conquer her shame.'

'Conquer her shame!' Paniatowski repeated. 'That's really a very good line. I really must remember it. But tell me, how do you know she had any shame *to* conquer? How do you know she hadn't fallen in love with Tom, and no longer gave a damn about you?'

'If she'd had no shame, then what would have stopped her from admitting the truth?'

'You see, that's where the cosy picture that you've been trying to paint of your marriage breaks down,' Paniatowski said. 'You say that you loved her and that you trusted her . . .'

'I did.'

'Yet when she tells you there was nothing going on between her and Tom Whittington, you refuse to believe her. How much trust does *that* show? And how much does it reveal of a jealous nature which had probably been eating away at you for years?'

'She *was* having an affair with him,' Szymborska said. 'You know that yourself.'

'Yes, *I* know it, because I've got witness statements to prove it. But you had no proof at all, did you? And you didn't need any! Because for a jealous man like you, even the hint – even the merest suspicion – that she'd been unfaithful to you was enough to drive you into a rage.'

'I *had* proof,' Stan Szymborska said firmly.

'And what proof might that have been?'

'Someone – I don't know who it was – sent me a photograph of them together.'

'Oh, well that's it, then,' Paniatowski said scornfully. 'Imagine – a photograph of them together! And I've got a photograph of me and my inspector. Does that mean *we're* having an affair? Of course not. But for someone with your nature, even the most inconsequential trifle is proof enough.'

'They were kissing,' Stan Szymborska said.

'Ah, I see where you're going now,' Paniatowski said.

'Do you?'

'Yes. You've finally given up hope of getting away with murder, and now you've begun the process of justifying yourself. I can almost hear what your brief will be saying in court. "My client is guilty of a terrible crime, ladies and gentlemen of the jury, but he is not accountable for his own actions. Imagine, if you will, how he must have felt when he saw this photograph. He temporarily lost control of himself. And who among us could say, with absolute certainty, that he would not have done the same?" Something along those lines, do you think?'

'You don't understand me at all,' Szymborska said.

'Did you show this photograph to your wife?'

'No.'

'Why not?'

'Because in the face of such damning proof she would have been forced to confess.'

'And you didn't *want* her to?'

'Not then. I wanted her to confess when she truly believed that it was the *right* thing to do.'

'Where's this photograph now?' Paniatowski asked. 'Do you still have it?'

'No.'

'Now isn't *that* convenient!'

'*You* have it,' Szymborska said. 'It was in my wallet, which your officers took away from me.'

Colin Beresford was reading a copy of the Whitebridge *Evening Chronicle* when Monika Paniatowski finally entered the public bar of the Drum and Monkey, but the moment he noticed her coming towards him, he rapidly folded it up and slipped it on to his knee.

Paniatowski sat down, and held her hand out across the table. 'Let's have the paper, Colin,' she said.

'You don't want to spoil a victory piss-up by reading what's written in that rag, boss,' Beresford said, uncomfortably.

'Ah, but you see, I do,' Paniatowski replied. 'A good battering from the newspaper is just what I need to round off the day.'

'Really, boss . . .' Beresford remonstrated.

'Hand it over,' Paniatowski told him firmly.

The headline said it all, but Paniatowski forced herself to read the rest of the article anyway.

Do we have the police we deserve?
By Mike Traynor
An arrest in the Linda Szymborska and Tom
Whittington murder case is good news for the
citizens of Whitebridge, who will be able to sleep
more peacefully in their beds tonight.

But why was it so long coming, sources in police
circles have been asking. Why was the obvious
suspect – the only man with a real *motive* in the
killings – allowed to remain at liberty for so long?
Indeed, this reporter put exactly that question to
DCI Paniatowski during her press conference.

And it is not merely a matter of justice postponed.
A man who has killed twice may kill again, and who
is to say whether it is more a case of luck than
judgement that he did not strike for a third time?

This newspaper has always crusaded for the
advancement of women in all walks of life, including
the Police Force. And it will continue to do so. It is
only proper that some senior police posts should be
held by women. But the question we must ask
ourselves here is not whether it is right that women
should be chief inspectors, but whether the one who
is a chief inspector is the *right* woman for the job.

'He was well out of order writing that – and he knows it,'
Beresford said. 'It wouldn't surprise me if he's already written
the apology that will appear in tomorrow night's edition.'

It wouldn't surprise me, either, Paniatowski thought. But
the damage is already done.

'Well, after all, tomorrow is another day,' Beresford said,
trying to sound philosophical.

'No it isn't,' Paniatowski countered. 'Not for me – because
this case isn't over yet.'

'Not over?' Beresford repeated. 'How can it not be over?
We've got the killer behind bars and . . .'

'I want the man who *pushed* Stan Szymborska into killing
his wife behind bars as well.'

'Sorry, boss?' Beresford said.

Paniatowski took a black-and-white photograph out of her
bag, and handed it to her inspector.

In the background was the Old Oak Tree Inn. In the foreground, a man and a woman were kissing. The woman had long, dark, wavy hair, and was giving the kiss her all. The man – judging by his stance – seemed far less comfortable with this public act of affection.

'Bloody hell!' Beresford said.

'It was this photograph – sent anonymously through the post – which tipped poor Stan over the edge,' Paniatowski said. 'If he'd never received it, Linda and Tom might still be alive today – and I'm holding *the man* who sent it partly responsible for their deaths.'

'How can you do that, when you don't even know who he is?' Beresford wondered.

'Because I can make a pretty fair *guess* at his name,' Paniatowski told him. 'And so can you.'

'I'm not sure I can,' Beresford confessed.

'Think about it!' Paniatowski urged him. 'Who would reap the benefit from causing discord at the bakery?'

'*Another* bakery!' Beresford exclaimed. 'Warren Tompkins!'

Paniatowski nodded. 'Tompkins wasn't directly involved in the murders, as poor deluded Jenny so firmly believes, but he has been responsible for a number of dirty tricks aimed at hurting Brunskill's, and I think this one of them.'

'Even if that's true, Tompkins couldn't have *known* Stan would go so berserk when he saw the photograph,' Beresford pointed out.

'That may be your opinion, but a judge and jury might think differently,' Paniatowski said.

'You're . . . you're actually going to *arrest* him?' Beresford asked, incredulously.

'I am,' Paniatowski confirmed.

For some moments, Beresford was silent, then he said, 'You're on a hiding to nowhere with this one, boss. Even if you can get Tompkins to admit to sending the photograph, you'll never be able to make the charges stick.'

'You're probably right,' Paniatowski agreed. 'But I'm still going to give it my best shot.'

TWENTY-EIGHT

It would have been something of an understatement to describe the managing director's office at Tompkins' Bakery as large. The room ate up almost half of the second floor, with the result that most of the other offices were the size of broom cupboards. Even so, the way that Warren Tompkins had chosen to furnish it – with a huge desk, two big sofas, a conference table, a full-sized snooker table and a rowing machine – made it seem almost cramped.

The term 'large' would have been a charitable way to describe the man himself, Paniatowski decided. But she was feeling very low on charity that morning, and what *she* saw was a fat man who, though dressed in a sober suit, still reminded her of a dodgy used-car salesman.

'It's a pleasure to meet you, Chief Inspector,' Tompkins said, standing up and reaching across his desk to shake her hand. 'May I introduce my associate, Mr Cutler?'

Paniatowski turned towards Cutler, noting his bullet-shaped head and the scar on his cheek. He was a nasty piece of work if ever she'd seen one, she thought, and if she were to learn that he had a criminal record – especially one that involved crimes of violence – she would not be the least surprised.

Cutler did not follow his boss's lead by standing up to shake her hand. Instead, he gave the briefest of nods, which did no more than acknowledge her presence.

'I take it that you're not exactly a big fan of the police, Mr Cutler,' Paniatowski said.

Cutler shrugged. 'If they promise to leave me alone, I promise to leave them alone.'

Tompkins laughed, as if all three of them were doing no more than sharing a good joke.

'As you've probably already worked out for yourself, Chief Inspector, Mr Cutler works in our maintenance section, *not* our public-relations department,' he said. He waved a flabby hand in the direction of one of the expensive leather chairs facing his desk. 'Do take a seat.'

Paniatowski sat.

'Before we get down to any other business, let me just ask you this,' Tompkins said. 'Are you completely happy with the company which supplies your police canteen? Because if you're *not* happy with it, you should certainly consider coming to us. I think you'll find we can offer you a very good deal – a very competitive deal.' He paused, but only for a second. 'Not that I'd like you to think that we're touting for business, of course?'

'No?'

'Certainly not. We've no need to tout. Business is thriving as it is.' He pointed his thumb over his shoulder, at a large – and brightly coloured – chart on the wall behind him. 'See that?'

'It's so bloody ostentatious that I could hardly miss it, could I?' Paniatowski asked.

'Well, there you are, then,' Tompkins said. 'The figures more than speak for themselves, don't they? Bread sales are up over thirty per cent in twelve months, our new lines in confectionary are selling like hot cakes – that's just a little bakery humour! – and a deal is already on the cards to supply one of the biggest supermarket chains in the country with our muffins. Yes, things are certainly going very well indeed. Onwards and upwards, that's my motto.'

'By any means necessary?' Paniatowski asked.

'Pardon?'

'You said "Onwards and upwards" was your motto, and I asked, "By any means necessary?" '

'By any *legitimate* means, certainly.' Tompkins paused again. 'What was it you wanted to see me about?'

'Ah, I was wondering when you would remember that I wasn't here just to listen to you tell me how brilliant you are,' Paniatowski said.

'I could take offence at that,' Tompkins told her, though the expression on his round face said that he'd already decided to treat what was clearly a barb as if it was just another joke.

'Yes, you certainly could take offence,' Paniatowski agreed, deadpan. 'And most people I can think of probably would.' She reached into her bag, took out a tape recorder and placed it on the desk. 'You don't mind if I tape this conversation, do you?'

'Why would you want to do that?'

'So that we'll all be perfectly clear about exactly what was said in this meeting.'

Tompkins was beginning to look a little uneasy. 'Do I need to have a lawyer present?' he asked.

'That depends,' Paniatowski replied. 'If you're guilty of something, it would certainly be advisable to have one here. And even if you're not, I think I'd still recommend it.'

'Why?'

'Because you'll probably feel much more confident if you have a mouthpiece to do your talking for you.'

Tompkins banished the worried look from his face, and replaced it with a salesman's assurance.

'A lack of confidence has never been one of my failings, Chief Inspector,' he said.

'So I *can* tape the conversation?'

'I suppose so.'

That was Phase One completed, Paniatowski told herself. But then, with an overblown, self-important man like Warren Tompkins, Phase One was *always* going to be easy.

It was Phase Two – getting him to say something which could provide the basis for criminal charges – which was going to be complicated.

She pressed the record button on the tape recorder, stated the date, time and those present, and then said, 'We've received complaints that you've been involved in unfair trade practices, Mr Tompkins.'

'Complaints from whom?'

'I'm afraid I'm not at liberty to say.'

'Isn't that sort of complaint a rather minor matter for a chief inspector to be investigating?' Tompkins wondered.

'Ah, but that's one of the perks of my job, you see,' Paniatowski lied. 'I can investigate whatever I want to.'

'That may be the case, but I still fail to see *why* you would want this particular investigation,' Tompkins said.

'I expect that will become clear to you later,' Paniatowski said offhandedly. 'Are you *quite* sure, given what I've just said, that you don't want a lawyer here to hide behind?'

Tompkins hesitated. 'No, no, I'm perfectly happy with things as they are,' he said finally.

But the way in which he folded his chubby arms across his chest showed that wasn't quite the case.

For perhaps a full minute, they sat staring at each other, and then Tompkins said, 'I don't wish to appear to be rude in any way, Chief Inspector, but my time is valuable, you know.'

'I'm sure it is,' Paniatowski replied.

'Then you'll understand why I . . .'

'And so is mine. In fact, since I'm charged with upholding the system of justice in this country – rather than merely baking *bread* – it could be argued that my time is even *more* valuable than yours.'

Another minute ticked away before Tompkins finally said, 'All right, so what am I supposed to have done wrong?'

'For starters, you've been bribing a number of small shop-keepers to take your bread, rather than Brunskill's bread.'

'Have I, indeed?' Tompkins asked. 'And do you have any proof for this ridiculous assertion?'

'Yes,' Paniatowski said, lying again. 'We have photographs of your delivery men handing over the money.'

Tompkins looked rocked, but only for a second, then he turned to his 'associate' and said, 'Is that true, Mr Cutler? Have we been paying shopkeepers to take our bread, rather than Brunskill's?'

She'd got the measure of him now, Paniatowski thought. He was the kind of man who didn't mind what was being done in his name, as long as it couldn't be traced back to him.

But however slippery he turned out to be, she promised herself that she'd have the bastard.

'Well, Mr Cutler, have you been paying bribes?' she asked the bullet-headed man.

'Might have been,' Cutler snarled.

'Bribery's the wrong word,' said Tompkins, now fully back in control of himself. 'What I imagine my people have *actually* been doing is paying out what we in the business call a "loyalty bonus". If it would make you any happier, think of it as a sort of discount.'

'A discount which results in the shopkeepers not only ending up with their shelves stacked with your bread, but also with more money in their pockets than when they started out?'

'That can happen,' Tompkins said, waving his hands expansively in front of him. 'And sometimes it does – in certain trading circumstances. It all depends how the particular deal, on the particular occasion, is structured. And there's nothing illegal about it.'

No, there probably isn't, Paniatowski agreed silently.

'Let's cut the crap, Mr Tompkins,' she said aloud. 'We both know you were trying to drive Brunskill's out of business, don't we?'

'No, we most certainly do not,' Tompkins countered. 'The last thing I wanted was for Brunskill's Bakery to close down.'

'Right,' Paniatowski agreed, sardonically.

'It *is* right,' Tompkins said. 'What I *actually* wanted was for it to still be a going concern when I took control – but a going concern with a much less healthy turnover than it had had formerly.'

'You were planning to *take control* of it?'

'I still am, if I can make Jenny Brunskill see sense. I need more capacity for my expansion programme, you see – and Brunskill's Bakery could provide that for me. Plus, I'll freely admit, I would also be acquiring a certain amount of goodwill.'

'I can see the logic of acquiring it from your point of view,' Paniatowski said. 'But whatever made you think they'd *sell* it to you?'

'Linda did,' Tompkins said, disarmingly.

'What?'

'We were in the middle of a complex negotiation when she was murdered. And just between you, me, Mr Cutler and the tape recorder,' Tompkins smiled, in what he probably liked to believe was a winning way, 'that's what our bread incentive scheme was all about. You see, if we could bring the argument to the table that they were less successful now, than they'd been in the past, we'd have got the bakery at a better price.'

'Let me just get this straight,' Paniatowski said. 'Linda was prepared to *sell* you the bakery.'

'She was.'

'And you were doing everything that you could possibly think of to make the value of her business fall, in the belief that would make her willing to accept a lower price?'

'That's absolutely correct. It was a pretty smart move on my part, don't you think?'

He was convinced he'd weathered the storm, Paniatowski told herself. More than that, he was now under the foolish impression that he could take anything she threw at him and deflect it with ease.

Now was time to spring the trap.

'And part of this *pretty smart plan* was to send the photograph to Stan, wasn't it?' she asked.

Tompkins gave her a puzzled look, as if he had no idea what she was talking about.

'What photograph?' he asked.

Paniatowski took the picture out of her bag, and slid it across the polished surface of the desk.

'This one,' she said.

Tompkins gaped at the picture.

'Bloody hell, but that's Linda and that head baker of hers . . . Tom What's-'is-name.'

'Tom Whittington,' Paniatowski supplied. 'Was it you who took that picture, Mr Cutler?'

'No,' Cutler said, though he was addressing Tompkins, rather than Paniatowski. 'I swear on my mother's life that it wasn't me, boss. I'm as surprised as you are.'

'Ah, but you see, Mr Cutler, Mr Tompkins isn't surprised at all,' Paniatowski said. 'Isn't that right, Warren?'

'I . . . I . . .' Tompkins said.

'Let me see if I can trace the way your nasty little mind must have worked,' Paniatowski suggested. 'You knew that Linda and Stan each owned a third of the bakery, didn't you?'

'Yes, but . . .'

'And together – as a happily married couple, which they undoubtedly were – they made a formidable negotiating team. But what if you could find some way to set them at each other's throats? you asked yourself.'

'You're talking nonsense,' Tompkins protested.

'If you could set them at each other's throats, they wouldn't be a team any longer, would they?' Paniatowski pressed on. 'In fact, they'd be so keen to see the back of each other that they'd probably sell you the bakery for a song.'

'I swear to you I didn't . . .'

'But the problem was, as it turned out, that Stan didn't just *get angry* with Linda, he *killed* her. And I think you should have foreseen that. In fact, I think you *did* foresee it – at least as a *possibility* – and you just didn't care! Which brings us to the real point of this meeting.'

'The . . . the real point?'

'That's what I said. I'm here to charge you with soliciting murder under Section 4 of the Offences Against the Person Act.'

'You can't . . .' gasped Tompkins.

'Oh, but I can,' Paniatowski countered. ' "Whosoever shall solicit, encourage, persuade or endeavour to persuade, or shall propose to any person, to murder any other person, shall be guilty of a misdemeanour." And that fits you to T, wouldn't you say?'

'But I'm innocent,' Tompkins whined.

'Of course you are,' Paniatowski agreed, mockingly.

'I didn't send Stan the photograph. I swear I didn't. I didn't even know Linda and Tom were having an affair.'

'Oh, come on!' Paniatowski said contemptuously. 'From the look on his face, I'm perfectly prepared to accept that Mr Cutler – for all that he's as bent as a corkscrew – knew nothing about this *particular* nasty trick. But that only means that you used someone else to do your dirty work for you. Who was it?'

'I . . . I didn't use anybody. I had nothing to do with it.'

'I'd guess it was a private detective who specializes in divorce work,' Paniatowski said, treating the denial with the contempt she thought it deserved. 'And just how long do you think it will take me to find the man, Mr Tompkins – whoever he is? And when I *do* find him, how long will it be before he admits that it was *you* who sent him to the Old Oak Tree Inn, a week last Wednesday?'

'I've never hired a private detective in my life. I promise you, the idea would never have occurred to . . .'

'Would you stand up, please, Mr Tompkins?' Paniatowski asked.

'Why?'

'Because it's hard enough to handcuff a thin man when he's sitting down – and it would be almost impossible with a fat bastard like you.'

'Do something, Mr Cutler,' Tompkins gasped.

Cutler rose to his feet, his hands already bunched up into fists.

'If I was you, I wouldn't even think about it, Mr Cutler,' Paniatowski advised him.

An unpleasant smirk spread across Cutler's face. 'Wouldn't you?' he asked. 'Why not?'

'Two reasons,' Paniatowski said. 'The first is that any man should think twice before assaulting a police officer.'

'I could say you completely lost your rag, and I was only defending Mr Tompkins from your attack,' Cutler said. He paused, thoughtfully. 'What was your second reason?' he wondered.

'Oh, that!' Paniatowski replied. 'Well, you look to me like the kind of man who might be very dangerous if you've got a weapon in your hands or the element of surprise on your side – but neither of those apply here.'

'So what?'

'So I'm a fifth dan in judo – and in any *fair* contest, I'll spatter you all over the walls.'

Cutler's fixed smile stayed firmly in place, but his eyes were busy assessing the situation.

'Do you know something,' he said finally, 'I think you might be right about that.'

'You'd better believe it,' Paniatowski told him.

'And if that's the case, then I think the best thing for me to do would be to just sit down again.'

'Good plan,' Paniatowski agreed.

She turned her attention back to Tompkins. The bakery owner seemed to be frozen to his chair, and with his mouth he was doing a more than competent impression of a landed fish.

'For the second time of asking, would you please stand up, Mr Tompkins?' she said.

'Did you . . . did you say this photograph was taken a week last Wednesday?' Tompkins asked.

'Yes?'

'And you're sure of that?'

'I am.'

'But . . . but that was when the Leeds Catering Convention was on. I know that for a fact, because I was there myself.'

'That's no alibi,' Paniatowski pointed out. 'Whether or not you actually took the photograph *yourself* is irrelevant.'

'No, no, you don't understand,' Tompkins said, almost babbling now.

'*What* don't I understand?'

'I wasn't the *only* one at the convention. Linda was there, as well.'

'She was certainly *supposed* to be there,' Paniatowski agreed.

'And she *was*! She definitely was.'

'You're lying,' Paniatowski said.

'No!'

'Then you're merely mistaken. Possibly you caught a glimpse of a woman across a crowded room, and just *assumed* it was Linda.'

'She was there,' Tompkins insisted. 'We had *dinner* together – in a crowded restaurant where dozens of people will have seen us. And after that, we went to the bar, where we spent *another* two hours talking about our deal.'

TWENTY-NINE

J enny Brunskill seemed in much better shape than she had the previous day, Paniatowski thought, examining her from across the desk. She looked tidier, her hands were still and – most significantly of all – the half-crazed look had completely disappeared from her eyes.

'Before we go any further, Chief Inspector, I want to apologize for the way I behaved the last time we met,' Jenny said. 'I know it's no excuse, but I'd been under a lot of strain and . . .'

'Forget it,' Paniatowski said. 'The important thing is that you're all right now. You are all right, aren't you?'

Jenny nodded. 'Yes, I am.'

Paniatowski gave her a gentle smile, full of understanding and sympathy. 'So you no longer believe that it was Warren Tompkins who was behind your sister's murder?'

'Of course not. The man would do almost anything to ruin us, but even he has his limits.'

'And you accept that Stan killed both Linda and Tom Whittington in a fit of jealous rage?'

'I still don't want to – but I think I must.'

'Which means you now also accept that Tom and Linda were having an affair?'

'In some ways, that's the hardest thing of all to come to terms with,' Jenny said. 'You didn't know Linda, but if you had, *you'd* have found it very hard to believe, too.' She sighed. 'But if you say you have proof . . .'

'I do,' Paniatowski said, placing a copy of the works outing photograph on the desk. 'Look at the four of you, standing on the front row – you next to Stan, Stan next to Linda and Linda next to Tom.'

Jenny Brunskill sniffed. 'It was a different world,' she said. 'A much happier world. And now it's gone for ever.'

'It was this picture which led us to find out about the affair in the first place,' Paniatowski explained. 'One of my smart young detective constables showed it to the receptionist at the

Old Oak Tree Inn, and she picked out Linda and Tom Whittington immediately.'

'How could they have been so careless about it?' Jenny wondered. 'If only they'd been more discreet, they might both still be alive today.'

'Do you know, I don't think it's anything like as simple as that,' Paniatowski said.

'What do you mean?'

'Anyway,' Paniatowski continued, ignoring the question, 'since the detective constable *was* so young – and the young, in their enthusiasm, *can* make mistakes – I thought I'd better make sure he'd got it right, so I went to the Oak Tree myself. In fact, I've just got back.'

'Oh?' Jenny said, noncommittally.

'I showed the receptionist the photograph, and again, she picked out Linda immediately. I asked her if she was sure – I was being thorough, you see – and she said yes, she was.'

'So it looks as if there's no doubt at all.'

'And then I did this,' Paniatowski said, picking up a pen, and quickly sketching in long wavy hair on the Jenny in the photograph. 'And *after* I'd done that, she wasn't sure at all.'

'Linda was my sister,' Jenny said. 'It's only natural that some people will confuse us.'

'Linda wasn't at the Oak Tree Inn at all that day,' Paniatowski said. 'She was in Leeds – just as she was supposed to be – and I can produce a dozen witnesses to confirm it.'

Jenny started to cry.

'I should have told you that it was me, not Linda, who was having an affair with Tom,' she said. 'But then I thought of what Father would have said, and I was so ashamed that I just couldn't.'

'So *you* were the one at the Oak Tree Inn?'

'Yes, isn't that obvious?'

'But you were driving Linda's Jag?'

'She was going to Leeds by train, so she said I could borrow it if I wanted to. And I said I'd like that. I've always been the mousy one, you see, but I felt so glamorous that day, driving a Jag and having an affair. If only I'd known then what it would lead to.'

'What it would lead to?' Paniatowski repeated, sounding puzzled. 'What it would lead to? Oh, I think I see what you mean! You must be partly blaming yourself for Linda's death.'

'I am,' Jenny agreed. 'Because if *I* hadn't had an affair with Tom, Stan would have had no grounds at all for suspecting that *Linda* had.'

'But you did have the affair, and then Stan saw the photograph,' Paniatowski said.

'What photograph?'

'The one of you and Tom, kissing in front of the Oak Tree Inn. Who took it, by the way?'

'I don't know.'

'And who sent it to Stan?'

'I don't know that, either.'

'What a lot of things you seem not to know,' Paniatowski said reflectively. 'Well, let me ask you something you *do* know the answer to. Why were you wearing a wig?'

'I don't . . .'

'You *must* know that!'

'I do – inside me – but I can't really explain it in words.'

'Try!' Paniatowski said.

'I suppose it just felt *right*. Perhaps, subconsciously, I felt the need for a disguise.'

'A disguise?'

'That's right. I knew that what I was doing was wrong, you see, and perhaps I thought that by wearing a disguise, it would be as if it wasn't really *me* who was doing it at all.'

'Yes, that makes sense,' Paniatowski agreed. 'If I'd been brought up in the kind of home you were brought up in, I might have felt the need to do that, too.' She paused for a second. 'But what I still don't understand is why you chose a wig which was an exact copy of your sister's *real* hair.'

'I . . .'

'And that kiss is another thing that's got me puzzled. So passionate! And in such a public place! What made you do it? Tom was clearly uncomfortable with the whole idea. You can tell that by the way he's standing.'

'I couldn't help myself. I was in love with him.'

Paniatowski shook her head. 'No, you weren't. And that wasn't why you did it.'

'What do you mean?'

'You *do* look a lot like your sister, but even with the wig on, you wouldn't fool anyone who knew you really well – not unless you were partially hiding your face.'

'I never wanted to pretend—'

'Of course you did,' Paniatowski interrupted. 'When did you first learn that Stan and Linda were planning to sell the bakery?'

'I never learned it, because that's a *lie!*'

Paniatowski shrugged. 'Have it your own way. Let's say it was three months ago. You must have hated the fact that they were going to abandon Daddy's little kingdom . . .'

'Don't you dare call him that!' Jenny hissed angrily. 'He wasn't Daddy at all – he was Father.'

'All right, that they were going to abandon your *father*'s little kingdom. But they held two-thirds of the voting shares between them, and so there was nothing you could do to stop them. Unless, of course, they died.'

'What a horrible thing to say!'

'I imagine you thought of killing both of them at first, but since you would have been the main beneficiary of their deaths, suspicion would be bound to fall on you. And there was no point in killing just one of them, was there, because the other would simply inherit the shares. But say it could be made to seem as if Stan killed Linda. He couldn't inherit her shares, because you can't profit from a criminal act, so they would have gone to you.'

'It's not true,' Jenny said, sobbing. 'None of it's true.'

'I have to give you full marks for both planning and foresight,' Paniatowski said, unmoved. 'When you sent the photograph to Stan, you knew exactly what would happen, didn't you? You knew that Stan and Jenny would have a blazing row, and that Jenny – distraught at being falsely accused of having an affair – would run straight to her beloved sister for comfort. Because that's exactly what she did, isn't it – drove straight from her house to yours?'

'I never saw her that night,' Jenny said stubbornly.

'I'm guessing that when she arrived at your door, the first thing you did was to pour her a drink with a knock-out drop in it,' Paniatowski continued. 'Then, once she was unconscious, you bundled her into her own car and drove to the old bakery. I'm also guessing that she was still unconscious when you tied her to the baking table. But she wasn't unconscious when you cut her hand off, was she?'

'I didn't do that. It was *Stan*! *He* cut off her hand, just like he'd cut off someone's hand before.'

'Now how did you know about that?' Paniatowski wondered.

'I . . .'

'Stan told Linda that story – and possibly she was the only one he *ever* told it to – because he loved and trusted her. And she told you, because you were her sister, and sisters share things. And you used that knowledge to help build up the case against Stan.'

'I couldn't have cut off her hand. I *loved* her,' Jenny protested.

'You might have done once,' Paniatowski said, 'but when she tried to destroy your father's monument, that love quickly turned to hatred.'

'That's not true!'

'Of course it is. You've proved that by what you did to her. You could have cut off the hand once you'd killed her, but you hated her *so much* that you did it while she was still alive.'

'You're wrong!' Jenny said.

'I'm right,' Paniatowski replied firmly. 'And then there was Tom. Poor hopeless lonely Tom. A man without friends. A man who didn't even know how to *make* friends. It must have been so easy for you to seduce him. And for only the second time in his entire life, he was really happy. The *first* time he was happy, he stole a car in order to hold on to that happiness. And what did he do to hold on to it the *second* time? Did you force him to help you kill Linda?'

'I'm not playing your mad game,' Jenny said.

'No, on reflection, I don't think you did,' Paniatowski said. 'That was a pleasure you wouldn't have wanted to share with anybody. But you did get him to dump Linda's hand down on the river bank. And you did get him to ring up the press to announce the fact. And it *had to be* a man who made those calls, didn't it? Because, in the careful plot you'd spun, the murderer *was* a man. But that was the *last* thing poor Tom did for you. After that, he was of no more use. In fact, it would have been dangerous to let him live, because he was the weak link in the chain. And besides, how much more convincing it would make the case against Stan look if he appeared to have killed not only his wife, but also her lover.'

'Stan *did* kill them both,' Jenny said fiercely. 'Why won't you . . . why won't you believe me?'

'But at least you didn't make Tom suffer,' Paniatowski said. 'So perhaps you did care about him *a little*, after all. You poisoned him, and strangled him, and cut off his hand. And then you left the hand outside the newspaper office. But this time, you *couldn't* let Mike Traynor know by phone – if he'd heard a woman's voice, the whole structure you'd so carefully built up would have collapsed – so you sent him an anonymous note instead. Is there anything I've missed out?'

Jenny Brunskill said nothing.

'Ah yes, the other clues. After you cleaned Tom Whittington's flat thoroughly – to make sure there was no trace of you there – you planted one of Linda's scarves for me to find. And you also took a pair of Stan's shoes, which you'd dipped into his wife's blood, and hid them at the back of his wardrobe after the first time my men searched his house. I think that's about all. Is there anything *you*'d like to say?'

'You'll never prove any of this,' Jenny told her.

'Of course I will. The process has already started. You had an important meeting on the morning that Linda's hand was found, and I've sent one of my men to find out if you turned up for it. And, of course, he'll discover that you didn't – even though it *was* so important – because you were too busy killing Tom and leaving his hand outside the *Chronicle* offices.'

'I . . . I was too nervous to go to that meeting on my own, so I just walked around town.'

'I'm having your home searched even as we speak. We'll find traces of glue there – the same kind of glue as was used to stick the words to the anonymous letter that Mike Traynor received. We may even find the magazines you used to cut out the words. And we'll find the chemist's shop where you had the picture of you and Tom developed. I could go on, but there's really no need to.'

'No, there probably isn't,' Jenny agreed, her head slumping forward. Then she raised it again, and when she did, there was fire in her eyes. 'I'm not ashamed of what I did, you know,' she continued. 'I did it all for Father – and he approved.'

'Your father's dead,' Paniatowski said.

'But he still talks to me. And *I* still talk to *him*. Where else do you think the plan came from?'

'The plan?'

'Making it seem as if Linda was having an affair! Blaming the murders on Stan! Cutting off the hands! You didn't think that came from me, did you? Poor stupid me! Of course not! It was all *Father*'s idea!'

EPILOGUE

It was the morning after Jenny Brunskill's arrest, and as Monika Paniatowski drove her red MGA past one of the old cast-iron milestones that the council had somehow never got around to replacing, she felt as if she was passing a significant milestone in her life, too.

Today would be the day she tied up the final loose ends of her first case as a chief inspector. But it would also be the day that Charlie Woodend left England on the first stage of his journey to his new life in Spain.

She was experiencing a double sense of loneliness – the loneliness that Charlie's departure was already causing her, and the loneliness that command brought with it. Well, she couldn't do anything about the former, and the latter had been her own choice, she reminded herself, so she'd better learn to live with it and – maybe – start to bloody well enjoy it.

She arrived at her destination – Brunskill's Bakery – at just after nine o'clock, and when she entered the managing director's office, she found Stan Szymborska staring thoughtfully up at the oil painting of Seth Brunskill.

'The first time I came into this office and saw that picture, I thought Linda was as obsessed with her father as Jenny was,' she told Szymborska.

'And so she had been,' Stan replied. 'As I told you, even after his death, it took her some time to come out of the box, but though she died horribly, she at least died *free of him* – and that is some little consolation.'

'If she was as free of him as you say, then why didn't she take the portrait down?'

'She tried to, once, and her sister wouldn't have it. Even the *thought* of removing it made Jenny hysterical. She said this was the managing director's office, and he was the managing director. She often talked about him like that – as if he was still alive.'

'When Jenny accused Tompkins of being responsible for

the murders, I really did think she was doing it in a desperate attempt to save *you*,' Paniatowski said. 'But saving you was the last thing in the world she wanted.'

'Then why *did* she make the accusations?'

'Partly it was designed to make me think she actually *was* the loving sister-in-law she pretended to be. Partly, I believe, she was hoping that I'd take her accusations just seriously enough to close down Tompkins' for a few damaging days, while I conducted an investigation.'

'She would have to have been crazy to think that,' Stan said.

'Yes, she would, wouldn't she?' Paniatowski agreed. 'And maybe, by that point, she'd convinced herself that Tompkins really was responsible for Linda's death – because if he hadn't wanted to buy Brunskill's Bakery, none of this would have happened.'

'Do you think she'll ever be tried for the murders?'

'I don't know,' Paniatowski admitted. 'It all depends on what the head-shrinkers say – on whether they think she's competent to stand trial.'

'And do you think she is?'

'No,' Paniatowski said. 'To be held responsible for your actions, you have to be able to distinguish between right and wrong in their widest possible sense – and all Jenny ever really knew was what was right for *Seth Brunskill*.'

Szymborska sighed. 'We had a plan, my Linda and I,' he said. 'We were going to sell the bakery to Warren Tompkins and use the money to buy a boat. We'd sail around the world, and keep *on* sailing, until the money ran out. And only then would we worry about what we'd do next.'

'It sounds wonderful,' Paniatowski said wistfully.

'It *would have been* wonderful,' Stan Szymborska agreed. 'But there'll be no boat now. Now, when I sell the bakery, I'm going to give most of the money away to charity.'

'I'm afraid you can't sell the bakery *at all*,' Paniatowski told him.

'Why not?'

'Because, under the law as it stands, you're not allowed to profit from your own crimes.'

'I don't understand,' Stan Szymborska said. '*Jenny* murdered Linda. You *know* that!'

'Indeed I do,' Paniatowski agreed. 'But that's not the crime that I'm talking about.'

It was a beautiful summer's day, and the English Channel was as calm as the proverbial mill pond.

Charlie and Joan Woodend stood on the upper deck of the ferry which would take them to France. Charlie was reading the *Daily Globe*, and Joan – perhaps just a *little* regretfully – was taking a last look at the White Cliffs of Dover.

'I've just been readin' this article by Mike Traynor,' Woodend said. 'You remember him, don't you?'

'Isn't he a reporter on the Lancashire *Evening Chronicle*?'

'That's the man, right enough – reporter on the *Chronicle*, an' a world-class dickhead.'

'Language, Charlie!' Joan said.

'Sorry,' Woodend replied. 'Anyway, yesterday Traynor had a go at Monika, an' today he's been forced to eat his own words. An' I mean *forced*. Readin' the article, you can almost see the editor standin' over him, with a whip in his hands. Listen to this. "I was wrong about DCI Paniatowski, and I'll be the first to admit it. Her handling of the Linda Szymborska murder has been little less than brilliant." *Little less than brilliant!* The bastard never said anythin' that complimentary about me.' He paused. 'Sorry! Again! I promise that now I'll be spendin' more time with you, I'll try to get out of the habit of usin' bad language.'

'You'd better do more than just *try*,' Joan warned him, though they both knew – after all the years they had been married – that she was not being serious.

The hooter on the funnel blew loudly, and the ferry began to slowly pull away from the dock.

A small, almost secretive, smile came to Joan's face. 'She never *did* ring you, did she?' she asked.

'Who?' Woodend asked innocently.

'Don't start playin' that kind of game with me, Charlie Woodend,' Joan said sharply.

'Oh, you mean Monika?' Woodend asked. 'No, she didn't.'

'An' how do you feel about that?' Joan wondered. 'Are you pleased? Or are you disappointed?'

'A bit of both,' Woodend admitted. 'But mostly, I feel very *proud* of her.'

*   *   *

They faced each other across the interview table in Whitebridge Police Headquarters – two Poles who had each, in their own way, known both triumph and despair.

'It was Len Monkton, the bakery nightwatchman, who first put the idea in my head,' Paniatowski explained. 'Now what was it he said, exactly? Seth Brunskill was "hardly ever out of the bakery. Didn't believe in holidays. Never took a day off. And in the end, I suppose, that's what killed him." And he was right, in a way, wasn't he?'

'In a way, he was,' Stan Szymborska agreed.

'Because if he *had* been able to stay away from the bakery – if he *had* been able to give his daughters a little of the freedom that any woman has the right to expect – he might still be alive today.'

'Yes, he might.'

'As I said, it was Len who first put the idea in my head, but it was my own desperation with the way the case was going which *really* pushed me to ask for the exhumation of Seth's body,' Paniatowski continued. 'I was *hoping* to find evidence of foul play, so that I could use it to put pressure on Linda's murderer – who, at the time, I thought was you. But, if I'm honest with myself about it, I never really *expected* to find that evidence.'

'But you did?'

'Yes – or rather, the estimable Dr Shastri did. Seth died of heart failure, right enough, but it wasn't a *natural* heart attack. It was induced by a high concentration of potassium chloride. How did you get him to take it?'

'He was destroying my Linda,' Szymborska said, ignoring the question. 'Every day that passed, there was less of her, and I knew that if he lived much longer, she would *never* be able to find her real self.'

Paniatowski reached across to the tape recorder. 'Interview suspended at eleven-oh-three,' she said, pressing the off-switch.

'Why have you done that?' Stan Szymborska asked.

'You still haven't explicitly admitted killing Seth Brunskill,' Paniatowski said.

'I know.'

'And without a confession, it's going to be very hard – after all this time – for us to actually *prove* you did it.'

Stan Szymborska smiled. 'But you will *try* to prove it, won't you, Chief Inspector?' he asked.

'Oh, I will *try*,' Paniatowski assured. 'I'll give the investigation all I've got, because that's my job. But I'll tell you honestly, Stanislaw, I don't hold out much hope of success.'

'Turn the machine on again, please,' Szymborska said.

Paniatowski pressed the record button. 'Interview resumed at eleven-oh-four.'

'Seth Brunskill died of potassium-chloride poisoning, which I administered to him, knowing exactly what its effect would be,' Szymborska said.

Paniatowski glanced at the tape recorder, and then back at Stan Szymborska.

'*Why admit it?*' she mouthed silently. '*Why?*'

'In my mind, the only possible justification for the murder was that it would give my Linda a new life,' Stan Szymborska said. 'But now she has no life at all – and neither have I.'

CPSIA information can be obtained
at www.ICGtesting.com
Printed in the USA
LVHW111400300620
659385LV00002B/391

9 781847 511706